GW00457005

ORCHIDS

&

ROSES

You can overcome challenges, remain true to yourself and thrive!

S. P. SCOTT

To my children

Ruel

&

Jayda

In life; you will face challenges, and will have to take some tough decisions but, before you do, may you find that inner strength to embrace sound guidance, and take the time to seek clarity.

I wish you will always be surrounded by people you can trust, who mean you well and may your life be filled with love and joy.

Lots of love

S. P. Scott

Set in the post-feminist era, Orchids and Roses draws your attention to Elizabeth Savannah Dawes, a young lawyer who lost everything when she encountered a series of challenges, that led to some personal setbacks. It took some time and some hard truths, embracing friendship and revisiting her core values, to find herself and ultimately, true happiness.

Orchids and Roses brings to the fore the value of true friendship and community, hope, and their amazing ability to add depth to the human strength. It inspires the reader to be resilient in their pursuit to find themselves and their purpose, to have the courage to take a step back to reassess where you are at, and like Elizabeth, you too can fulfil your goals … and thrive.

CHAPTER ONE

When you meet someone, there is no way of knowing the impact that person will have on you or your life. These two met as two people met, by chance. Little did they know what the outcome of their unlikely encounter would be. It has been over a decade since the incident, and now, as the car turned into the main entrance, those old feelings washed over her again. She adjusted her Chanel sunglasses, not wanting to miss the sheer grandeur of the building towering immediately above her. Had it been another day, she would have been far less tolerant of the combination of the sun's golden glow bouncing off the vast expanse of glass and the three imposing columns, determined to obstruct her view. The last time they were here, was a special day for her. However, this time around, Mathew had not been forthcoming with the details, which left Elizabeth wondering, just how this evening would end.

"Something tells me, for the first time in your life, you are actually on time!" Mathew applauded, wide eyed. "And all dressed up as well. What's the occasion?"

Faking her best grin, she berates herself for being too busy looking around to have heard him approach. "Court." She whispered, but after only just about managing to adjust her vision to the person who asked, who was responsible for her being there. At that moment, Elizabeth was happy it was only a monosyllabic word. On days like these, the mere utterance of the word, made her extremely exasperated. Determined to relax and be completely present, she managed to loosen the few pins holding her chignon in place. This allowed her hair to fall effortless down; first past the thin single strand fresh water pearl necklace, a gift from her mum, to rest against her olive skin at the nape of her neck. With each step, it quickly made its way further down to rest comfortably in the region of her scapula, against the olive-green dress, her most recent on-line sale find.

"I often forget, you do have a very important job, which makes me wonder what makes you do this kind of work?" He shook his head. He too was proud of her but had always felt she would have been better suited being a counsellor or join him in business. Anything that did not require the apparent unavoidable emotional investment, or the brutal hours that comes with being an Attorney.

"Days like today, I guess." Just then, she smiled at him, knowing full well her intent, to have him mystified by the irony of it all.

"But it does seem to take so much out of you. Well, maybe not physically but emotionally. Which, hats off to you…"

"I couldn't do what you do." They said in unison, as their eyes met and held. He had been saying that for most of the three years since she took the job, with her being the one always to hazard a poker-face as she chimed in, this time being the only exception. She was left totally drained from her experience earlier that day. Mathew knew her well, and she him. He could tell it was an arduous one. They have been friends long enough and have been through a lot together.

"Come here. I like your hair black, you know that, but I must say, autumnal hue is pretty cool too." Her friends at work have often complimented her on the highlights she claimed to have had herself talked into by the stylist, on her recent trip to the hairdresser's. Instinctively, they shared their customary warm embrace, and with impeccable timing, the waiter appeared.

Hugs now out the way, he ushered them to the table Mathew had booked earlier that month. He was always the first to give a hug, and especially today, he could tell she needed one.

"We've been here before, haven't we?" By now she had a firm grip on her companion's left hand, as she pretended not to be curiously looking around in amazement. Anyone who can afford to have an evening at The Fairmont, speaks of its grandeur. The beautiful floral mosaic patterns which contrast perfectly with the gorgeous marble textures, came into focus and for a moment, she found herself gazing fully at its opulence. "Wow," she whispered, but only loudly enough for Mathew to hear. On que, he pulled her hand up to encircle his elbow as he patted it gently like an old soul consoling an old friend. She could not help but wonder how much of *that*, is factored into the price of the actual meal, and chuckled sarcastically at the thought. "Tell me, was the food any good?" She whispered, wondering why their first visit had not left a lasting impression.

"Somehow, *that* has escaped me." Mathew confessed. "Guess we will soon find out."

"Hmm, oh dear." She murmured. "I guess it's fingers and toes crossed for a good evening then, huh?"

Entering the dining room, he paused, and then muttered. "Ah, let's see, I can vaguely recall some birthdays ago, there was a certain bill on my bank statement, which was not at all within my budget." He sighed as he firmly placed his hand over hers and proceeded into the depths of its beauty, to sit at their designated table far enough away from where the live pianist is stationed.

"So, why are we here again?" She feigned a smile. "And, I must say you don't look too bad yourself. Love your blazer!" She noticed he was wearing a new one; a single-breasted check blazer in brown, which he told her is from Brunello Cuccinelli's Spring collection.

"It's a bit fancy here, isn't it? It's not your birthday or mine, so ...?"

Overtaken by the luxurious softness of the dark-red velvet bucket chair, by which she was now enveloped, she paused briefly, made herself comfortable before looking him squarely in the eye, as she teased with a wink.

"Tell me, have you met *the* girl of your dreams and she's expected to walk through those doors any minute?"

"If you are asking, am I here to make a 'good' first impression, it is a no. I did that a while back; after all, we are still friends aren't we? So quite the opposite."

She rolled her eyes. "Aww, I'm disappointed." She muttered tersely, knowing full well he was already spoken for.

He was not sure if she was serious or making fun of him and very slowly, he told her, "I have met the girl, but it's not likely she will be walking through those doors." Not long after he hastened to correct himself. "Well, I thought I had met the girl, guess I thought wrong." He inhaled deeply, through closed teeth as he busied himself with the menu folder.

Leaning slightly forward, she pressed. "What's that supposed to mean? Has something happened between you and Cara?"

Politely interrupted by the waiter, they thoughtfully made their menu choice, as per request. The intruder was not long out of earshot when Mathew replied.

"I have made a purchase which I think is worth celebrating." He said, pensively.

Eagerly she demanded, "Let's hear it!" She was never afraid to be herself with Mathew, which is one of the things about their friendship she cherished the most and he did too.

"You are looking at the proud owner of three office units on the exclusive Further Fell road, each just under nine thousand square feet."

She thought he looked pleased when he alighted from his Porsche earlier to greet her at the main entrance where her Uber had left her standing for the last five

3

minutes, but she was not expecting this. Straightaway, she told him how pleased she was for him and with a wide grin, she pulled him in for a kiss on both cheeks. "I'm happy for you, Mathew." Not long after, when it occurred to her. Her office is moving to the largest of the three offices that were for sale on that road, and immediately, her mouth fell wide open. Patting his right hand rested on the table, she exclaimed. "O.M.G! You own my office block now?"

The block of offices had not been on the market exceptionally long when the email alert popped-up on his desktop. He had wanted to diversify his lettings portfolio for some time, and this seemed like the perfect opportunity.

"That's - just brilliant!" She has always known he was less risk averse than she or his sister but didn't know he was interested in that sort of venture." Genuinely surprised, she rambled on and this time she opted for a prolonged hug instead, this she felt was more fitting.

"Serious expansion this year, Lizzy. You know what they say, never put all your eggs into one basket."

"Diversification, that's the word, right?"

"Right."

"What a way to start the year, huh?" All along she wondered why he appeared so pensive and not as celebratory as she would have expected, given the magnitude of his purchase. How far he has come really touched her, and her heart went out to him. She wondered if he were wishing his dad could have been here or was it his humility, afraid to let his newfound financial freedom change him. Hoping to lighten the mood she conceded. "At least I've learnt something from you, to keep in the bag if ever I decide to give up practicing law." She gave a miniature applause accompanied by a wry smile as she made her way back to the comfort of her assigned seat. "You'd never know, we could be business partners, one day."

He raised an eyebrow then. "You know *we* would make the best team."

For a minute there she entertained the thought, then, shook her head almost immediately. Not only did she not want anything to get in the way of their almost two decades of friendship; deep inside she knew that, what she was doing now, the children and the people she was able to help, meant more to her than lying awake worrying about her profit margin.

Both of her parents had made sure she would be financially comfortable, at least for a while, by which time they had hoped she would have been married and settled with children. Besides, she was happy with the career path she had chosen and now, she is still stunned that she has managed to get a job working for a company she has always wanted to. With her signature half smile, she told him to dream on. There was a thought she could not shake though, the nagging question of what it is he is not saying. It is not like him to hide anything from her. Momentarily, she scolded herself for questioning the depth and openness of their friendship. Not one to give up easily, very quickly she vowed to get to the bottom of it.

Had he noticed her perplexity, he made nothing of it. "Okay, dream I shall then." With an incredibly determined look he made his statement or more like, a quiet resolve, as he met her gaze full on. Anyone could understand him wanting to be successful; after all, he did what his father told him to do; get good grades, finish university, be a good man and now he insists he owes it to himself to reap the fruit of his labour.

At twenty-seven, Elizabeth knew it was only just the beginning and like a sister to her brother, she was proud of him. As if timed, she reached for the drink menu, in unison with his confession. One she did not see coming, which she described later to her mum as, 'the bombshell'.

"Cara and I have decided it is best not to prolong the inevitable. We have parted ways. Separated. Broken up." He stated, matter-of-factly.

It threw her, just how 'blaze' that came across. Like one of those things a person does daily. Sort of like, 'well, I'll have a medium tea then; nah, I've decided, I'll have a large black coffee instead. Hmm never mind, make it a latte'.

The last time she saw them together, she was convinced he was getting ready to propose. She had always thought they looked so beautiful together. A typical handsome couple. Marriage to her seemed the next logical step. Often, she had said to Susie; 'he will propose soon'. She could never accuse him of being vain, quite the opposite but who would not want to date beauty and brains - with the intention to marry that is. Her 'frog' encounters had been few; and although content with being single, she has hopes to one day meet her prince, and until now, was certain Mathew had met his queen. Cara was the shortest among the three girls, and although two years younger than both Elizabeth and Mathew, the young woman is a very smart, witty, and intelligent senior Marketing Executive, who knows how to make the right connections. She has her eyes set firmly on the top job. She has what Elizabeth calls, 'the entrepreneurial gene'. With big plans to set-up her own marketing and public relations company, which she insisted would rival them all. Everyone knew she was not joking about that. Cara was widely hailed as being the most assertive of the girls, a point on which Susan begged to differ; but did agree however, that she was always well made up. This, sometimes left Elizabeth feeling slightly under attired in her presence.

"What, are you serious?" Not wanting to overreact, but the menu folder fell from her hand, and he watched as she scrambled to regain composure.

"Shh! Be quiet, woman." He scolded.

And she wanted to, if only to not disturb the nearby patrons, but concealing her surprise, was proving to be much more difficult.

In the past he had accused her of 'mothering him', when there is only eight-months separating them, with him being the older of the two. And now, once again that nurturing instinct, seemed to have overtaken her. They paused abruptly, as their appetizer arrived in what Elizabeth thought was record time, which contrasted Mathew's opinion of it not arriving soon enough. Not long, and they both admitted to being happy with their choice. Being the seafood lover as he is known, he opted for grilled lobster tails with lemon, garlic, and parsley butter while; Elizabeth, inclined to follow suit, ordered charred asparagus with smoked salmon nestled beneath shrimp in rye crumb. He omitted his usual routine, of taking some of whatever it is she is having, which was not lost on her, an action which pushed her to ask about what he had mentioned earlier.

"I'm not ready for that sort of commitment, Lizzy I'm truly not. That is what happened … and no, I do not want to talk about it. Please. I am here to celebrate. Remember?" He begged. He knew her well and secretly he hoped tonight was not one he would live to regret. Ignoring his plea, she continued, nonetheless.

It was his only known meaningful relationship and like his other friends, she too thought Cara was for keeps. But now, his tired look confirmed his confession, that it went on for much longer than either of them should have let it.

"Maybe, that's because there is something *special* about her?" Elizabeth stressed, cautiously.

"Lizzy, please. Cara is a lovely girl…"

"…and, beautiful too!" She interrupted. That, he did not deny.

Not long after, when finally, he confirmed what his sister, Susan, suspected long ago, to be a mismatch in their values. "Unfortunately, we do not share the same passion for philanthropy." He looked up at her, then paused. "Amongst other things, of course … but that aside, she wants what I cannot give right now and that's that."

Without him saying it, Elizabeth thought she knew exactly what Cara wanted, what every woman in a committed relationship wanted.

In time he would divulge; but for now, he wanted to celebrate his first acquisition for the new year. Besides, he was not ready to tell her what he had already told his business partner. He stiffened now, thinking of the run-in he had with her parents at her birthday party, when they made their expectations clear, which hastened the decision for him. It was pretty clear they had high hopes for their daughter, in her own right, they wanted her to have the power and fame they all have as known socialites. He grimaced thinking how they weren't in the least covert about it.

"You know what they say about values being like a magnet attracting like values, guess we are different." He murmured.

"Yea, and it also repels." She quipped.

They spoke about his choice not to form a partnership with her or involving her in any of his business ventures. He was adamant, he had no intention of being a 'power couple' with her or with anyone, but he did not want to talk about that now. Her parents had reminded him they had a reputation to protect and he respected their honesty. It took him a while, but eventually, he accepted her future would not include him. Cara's apparent 'personal brand' was at stake. He had only to remember his father and knew that they are from two different worlds. While silently he assured himself, that life was not for him; openly, he admitted the advertising business was not his passion. He wanted to do something that makes a difference to the everyday people around him. If they could manage friendship, he would be somewhat happy with that, but he did not see a life with her, and he was not keen on doing business with her either. He had seen how ruthless and self-centred she could be, and he did not want to be tied into anything of a contractual nature with her, particularly, as he long since acknowledged he did not want to marry her. After all his father had been through, it was important to him that he lived up to his ideals, and stringing anyone along, would belie his upbringing.

Time and again he had replayed how livid Cara was at the time. She told him he didn't have to starve himself to prove he is a good person and just then he shook his head as if to shut out the shouts and taunts as she screamed at him - "Whimp!" Her version of who he is was made noticeably clear to him. In her opinion, he was yet another one of those whimps who is afraid of a strong and assertive woman. It took him a while to no longer question himself, and after the longest twenty-four hours he had ever lived through, he knew he had to be honest and not prolong his unhappiness. He was afraid of doing what his mum did. Afraid his life would end up like his parents'. Afraid he would die a lonely old man.

"Mathew?" Jolting him from his impromptu reverie, she pleaded again and laying down his pair of cutleries, he took a big gulp of his red wine.

"Will you just swallow that thing, please?" Somehow, the words managed to make their way through her tightly clenched teeth and unmistakably closed eyes. Mathew, without hesitation, did one of the things he knew Elizabeth hated most. Loudly, the liquid was pushed from his mouth, down into his oesophagus. Instantly, she knew he did that spitefully.

"Don't you look at me like that, Woman. I did say I do not want to talk about it! Not now, Okay!"

"Well, if it bothers you so much, why are *you* walking away?" She shot back once again, and this time without a second thought.

He could tell she was a bit annoyed. He could see too that she was bent on coming after him, but wasn't sure if it was due to his most recent misdemeanour at the table or, the curious case of him and Cara's break up. She heard her name in full and thought better then to prolong the conversation. It was clear he was in no mood for whatever she was up to. They have been friends long enough for her to see that. Surrendering, she whispered, "Okay," and raised both hands to confirm. "This is shaping up to be a very interesting evening." She whispered and, very skilfully proceeded to do as is customary.

They discussed an edited version of her most recent challenging case. This time, it involved a set of twin girls, who had to be taken into care. Their mother had a mental breakdown following their father's sudden remarriage.

"The neighbours informed social services when two weeks ago, the younger of the twins ran out in the garden crying and shouting hysterically." She sighed, then continued. "They thought the mum was going to kill her." She recounted physical and emotional abuse leading to both being removed adding, "God only knows how their lives will turn out. We can only hope for the best." She sighed again, this time deeply and he could tell, from the sound of her voice, that this is the part of the job she liked the least.

"Didn't anyone tell the mum, that when someone can walk away from you, you should let them. Just let them walk." She grimaced at his tone, and thinking of his mother then, she wondered if he had tried to be the first to walk away from his and Cara's relationship.

"Mathew! Are you being frivolous when this is something profoundly serious?" She scolded thinking it could otherwise be a profound statement, but now just did not seem to require it. Not when the only two people she could think about are two vulnerable nine-year-old girls.

"Okay, ma'am! Why, what happened to the dad?" This time when he spoke, he looked genuinely concerned. She always knew he has a special place in his heart for children and would sometimes call him a 'big softie'. He never misses an opportunity to interact with any of the small people, "the younger the better", he would say, to which both his sister and Elizabeth would concede, 'he has issues'. They would always laugh, while he took no notice of either of them. He did not seem to care very much about what they thought.

"He is not a fit parent. Thank goodness he stayed clear of getting any more children. There's no way we could allow him anything other than supervised visits." She hissed. One could easily hazard a guess as to what her eye-roll just then implied.

"What's 'not fit'?"

"Previous allegations of neglect, physical and emotional abuse, and that's that. He is just a selfish man. Anyway, do not ask, I'll say no more."

"Sounds like someone I know." He retorted. As always, she reached out to him and just then, she touched his hand. At that precise moment, the one thing they both agreed on, was that the future of two nine-year-old girls, was quite likely changed irrevocably.

She did not like it when she had to assist with cases like these. The ones involving children. This is her third of its kind. For many reasons, they have always left her emotionally spent. One day, she hoped to have children of her own and has alluded to adoption after having her planned two, but only when the time was right. When she met the right person. Someone like her dad, she often said, calm and good natured. He was known by the whole community, the opposite of her mum who was more reserved, but pleasant, nonetheless. She wished for a stable home like what she grew up in. Coming home to her mum's cooking and dad's warm hugs, whenever he was off duty, that is. Her childhood home was simple and straightforward, stable, predictable and except for it being a little less regimented, she refused to have it any other way.

"You know, they are as rewarding as well as, they can be the most painful of experiences. Every case is different." She was always mindful to maintain confidentiality, and he understood better than to push any further for details.

"Yes, I'd imagine, each has its own challenges." He concurs, with another deep sigh in tow. They chatted on and off throughout the evening. He mentioned other investment opportunities he was considering which involved the acquisition of office spaces in prime locations in Dubai with the aim being to let; but first, he was after investors, those with the capital. There are still a few important clients he was trying to 'land', whom he is certain he can give a worthwhile return. His primary goal was to diversify his lettings portfolio, and he went full throttle in confiding in his best friend. Neither was ever afraid to share their plans, his hopes, or her dreams. They were both focussed young people; she on opening her own legal practice by thirty and him, on residential lettings until recently. He has hopes of having similar or better luck with commercial properties and she was confident he had enough money to do that. He had been working on his property portfolio since the day he received his first paycheque from his old employer, The Investment Bank in the city. She had watched him scrimp and saved every penny for a couple of years, and when finally, he bought the first flat with a little help from his sister, Susan, they all celebrated at Paul, his brother-in-law's expense.

He knew better than anyone, of her long-term goal. They spoke of it every chance she got. To eventually have her own legal practice, was her heart's desire; but in the meantime, she knows she must amass more experience, and of course, enough money to be able to fund it until enough clients came in to keep it afloat. They were incredibly supportive of each another, including Susan and Paul too. All of them shared a bond. There was never any competition amongst the four. She was acutely aware of his willingness to take care of all her overheads until the client-numbers increased enough for her to take a salary. As usual, and much to his dismay, she reiterated, "I know, Matt; but right now, I need the experience." She did not say it often, but he knew that with her Mum now living in the care home, that will be something she would have to put on hold for a while. Possibly a long time even; and his heart goes out to her now, as it does each time, he thinks about what she must be going through.

"Later, I can think about the finances. Right, Mr. Businessman, Mr. Investor?" She refused to be phased and she rolled her eyes at him, which she noticed was another thing he chose to ignore on this occasion.

For now, whatever the reason he and Cara had taken the decision to separate, she could tell it was different this time. Both her and Mathew have been friends for a long time and often refer to each other as siblings. He means a lot to her; they both mean the world to each other, and she knew him well enough to know, he did not arrive at this decision easily and for a second, she scolded herself for thinking so in the beginning.

"Come on, don't you like your choice of dessert?" She noticed he barely touched the Berry Eton Mess, he ordered. She hesitated then added. "Under normal circumstances, you would have already totally devoured that." And voicing her observations would, at another time, be nothing to think twice about!

"What do you mean, 'normal circumstances' - *It is* 'normal circumstances' is it not?" His sarcasm was evident, and to her, made him appear defensive. She knew she was not seeking to start a fight, but she felt he was not being totally honest with her about his feelings for Cara, or what caused him to arrive at this decision. Still, she decided, now is not the time to speak her mind about the goings-on in his private life.

Unusually, they sat in silence for a while, giving her the opportunity to peer out the dining room window unto what must be the garden she spotted earlier as they entered, while the sun was still desperately trying to hold the spotlight. She reflected on how many of these Friday evening meet-ups they have had over the years, since leaving sixth form, and recalled how they made a pact over their high school graduation celebratory dinner, not to let the pressures of University separate them. Somehow, until now, they have managed to honour that. Momentarily, she felt sad for the pain, which is now so evident in his eyes, and wished there were something she could do to help him. She has always attributed his 'issues', to his absentee mother and now was no different. She felt certain Claire was to be blamed; and, once again she was appreciative of her own mum and the sacrifices, she had made for her and her late dad. She knew her mum was the quintessential wife, mother, who looked after the home and ensured husband and child were happy, as she took work hours around her family. And somehow, she knew she could never be that architype. She has always considered herself a modern sort of girl; while, still holding dear to some traditional views. She wants the family of course, and the career too; neither should be sacrificed. She wants the big church wedding and the 'till-death-do-us-part-marriage', but she also wants to be able to travel, to see the world, experience other cultures, enjoy nature and have a long and successful career. Never does she want to feel she is merely existing but that she is living - thriving! She thought then about her best friend's mother, Lynette, who is only a few years younger than her own mum, Hazel, and how different to her, Lynette is. Sadly, Lynette did not manage to keep her marriage although she has managed to have a remarkably close relationship with both her girls while enjoying a very lucrative, fulfilling career. Which again led Elizabeth to wonder, why could not Claire have done the same with Mathew and Susan.

Susan, Mathew's older sibling has always appeared to be more understanding of their mum's actions, stating she was 'just wired differently'. That is her conclusion. For the most part, she appears unscathed by Claire's absence from the age of five. At first, and for a long time, her friend's disposition surprised Elizabeth. She thought about how she would feel about not having any memories of a mother brushing her hair or scolding her to tidy her room or bringing back something for her from her travels or having those talks before bath time or bedtime. All the things her mum did. How could she not have been affected by not having that? Surely, it must hurt when others share their experiences. She knew their father never remarried and thought maybe he never did for fear wife number two would also do a runner. She exhaled and glanced at Mathew as she recognised how in his own way, his father did his best job as mother and father to him and his older sibling, which compliments to him, it's everyone's opinion that he did a very good job.

Again, she vowed, she had to get it right. But again, that sense of foreboding persisted. That sinister thought which refused to leave her be - *what if all the dots are connected and tees crossed, but fate happens. Like what if my dad had died when I was much younger, what then? Guess that would be different from having a parent alive who has chosen to walk away, she argued inwardly. Well, either way, how do I become both parents to a child, on my own, and at the same time, try to have it all? I have seen the effects on Mathew and maybe on Susan too, I do not think she is left unscathed, after all. Maybe she's found her way of dealing with it – her 'I am a strong independent woman way', while Mathew does it the only way he knows how. By becoming a total 'commitment-phobe' who is focussed on acquiring more – things. No child should have to go through that because of an adult's selfish choice.* None. The ramblings, the mash-up of thought ended abruptly, as just then she had an idea.

"What do you say, we could both visit, a group, like … a group for people who have lost, you know, like I have lost my dad and technically you've kind of lost, your mum?" Conscious of being someone rather far removed from the supposedly intelligent Lawyer she is known to be, she rattled on almost unintelligibly.

"I wondered what was going on in that mind of yours." He said, as she managed a hopeful smile. "Elizabeth, it's called a 'Support Group!' Seriously? If you feel the need to be a part of some 'group' of any sort, please, I am happy to accompany you, should it fit in with my busy schedule, of course. No commitments here, though. But, for the record, I am actually okay." He reached across the table for both her hands.

She thought if she pressed, he would give in. She has always had a little sister effect on him, she was sure of it. "It would be nice if we could, you know, if we could go together. I can't bring myself to remember anything from my dad's funeral and …" She stuttered, employing every effort to remain calm and composed while all the time desperately wanting to shout, "You are not okay!"

"Never mind, I can remember everything from *her funeral*. Meaning, that is a no! N.O!"

"Okay, okay. We can talk about it some other time." She sighed.

"You think I am some sort of commitment-phobe for not having a mother around, so I can't have a meaningful relationship, isn't it? And that, my dearie that, right there, is stereotyping which doesn't become you."

She wondered if he had a drink before their meet-up as just now she was certain he was nothing short of inebriated, well intoxicated somewhat, she concluded as she brought her thoughts in alignment with reality.

"Not everyone, my friend, has the same needs. In other words, it is complicated. No, I will rephrase that. What is happening with me, in my case, it is complicated. See Liz, I know what and who I want I just haven't, well never mind..." He ended abruptly. She knew then he was just pretending, trying to throw her off.

"I've said too much already." He concluded.

His phone rang and insisting it is from one of his Saudi Arabian partners, suddenly he appeared sober as he excused himself to take the call. She watched as he hastily made his way from the almost full dining room. Almost like he was doing the Cha-Cha-Cha, he made every effort to avoid colliding with the elegant furniture or any of the waiters who are all attired in black suits and crisp white shirts with neatly done up red bow ties which she would have admired earlier, had she not become so preoccupied with Mathew's dilemma. Very slowly, she took one of her more therapeutic 'deep inhale then slowly exhales' routines and watched as he danced himself out of view.

CHAPTER TWO

Being married has not separated Susan and Mathew. Over the years, they have remained inseparable. Almost like this unspoken, 'it's just the two of us' bond. Being two years older, she was already entering her third year at University by the time Elizabeth and Mathew started, and as often as she could, would join them on their once per month Friday evening meetups. The trio partnership was strengthened particularly during her fourth year, after she decided to listen to their Father and stay on to complete her Master's in Education. Not long after that when Thomas said the same thing to his only son. They all agreed that as they were already there, in study-mode, they would all just get it done. Neither has regretted it.

"Besides, no one is bothered about a degree anymore, they're a dime a dozen. Get your masters in your economics, whatever it is you are studying and later you can try for a PhD." Their dad had looked at each of them pointedly, and they both knew how serious he was. They have always had immense respect for their father. Mathew knew his dad was right. Some of his friends with whom he had played rugby during his time in sixth form, had also given him similar advice.

Susan was always hailed the 'Mother' of the pack and was quick to enquire about the cost of the tuition, but Thomas had reassured them that, that was never to be any of their concern. And throughout university, they never had to worry about anything other than getting good grades; to which, Susan always teased how much better she did than her younger sibling. They have continued to meet with Elizabeth as a trio, one Friday of each month and while the venue sometimes varied; they had kept to either the last Friday or the first. However, in recent months, Susan, has been unable to attend. She bemoans her added responsibility as Deputy Head of school and contributes her lack of attendance to workload and timing. Both Elizabeth and Mathew were acutely aware of her two miscarriages. The more recent occurred at fourteen weeks and has continued to be a huge assault on her friend's psychological health, and strongly implicated as the reason she was not yet ready to 'hang-out'. In fact, Elizabeth was aware that it is now approaching four months since their loss and her friend has not showed any sign of returning to work. According to her husband, Paul, her mental state is of some concern to him too. They all feared she was bordering on depression and prayed she would seek help.

"Hello?" Only then she noticed Mathew had returned to the table and was waving his hand, trying to get her attention.

"You were deep in thought there, Ms Dawes. Again. Pray tell or dare I ask?" He took a deep breath then.

"And here I was thinking you are the one with the problem, huh?" She mused.

His pointed stare confirmed what she suspected he knew to be another one of her valiant attempts to bring the subject of his and Cara's separation, back to the fore.

"Don't worry, it just occurred to me, how far back we go with this our 'monthly-Friday-evening' meet up ritual and…"

"I always look forward to seeing you, Lizzy, and Sue too, of course. You both keep me grounded. Keep me sane." He interrupted, and for a moment she was taken aback by how serious he appeared as he spoke, in comparison to when he made his confession earlier.

"Yeah, me too." She hurriedly interjected and then hastened on.

"I love hanging out with you guys. I still cannot believe we've managed to keep this up for what, nine years … soon to be ten?" Her softer tone bellied her concern for his psychological health, but she knew self-control was important now.

"That's insane!" He was grinning as he spoke, which made her happy. Looking at his big broad boyish grin; reminded her of old times, almost like he was back to his old self again. With happy thoughts, they made their way to the bar, where they stopped only briefly. What seemed like a good idea at the time; in the end, neither felt much like drinking, and unanimously, they decided to head to their respective places of abode. Arms around each other, they made their way to the main entrance when she reminded him, "You do know, Sue and I are looking forward to little nieces and nephews sometime soon, right?" She teased, straight faced.

"Sounds like your turn and Susan's to dream on, madame et mademoiselle!"

"D'accord, Monsieur!"

They giggled like school children, as they waited for his car to be brought around, and suddenly neither was in a rush to go anywhere.

They drove along slowly, reminiscing on their gap year working at the Hope Gardens Zoo in Jamaica, before moving on to the French Caribbean Islands of Martinique and Guadalupe and for the final three months, headed to Zambia. She was about to re-describe her favourite spot in Lusaka when he firmly pulled her to him.

"Come, I've got to show you something." He said excitedly, with one hand now on the steering wheel.

"Better be good. Remember I'll be at Mum's all weekend."

Slowing down just enough to attack the deep bend on his impromptu detour, then continuing below the speed limit as he drove farther along, he reassured her, it would be.

"Oh, wow! Can we even get in?" She whispered wide eyed, as he stopped just outside the gates. The size and beauty of the houses before her, in the distance, were astounding.

"I know. That's me a few weeks ago when I gave one of my soon to be partners a lift *home* after our flight." He grinned and waited on the camera for confirmed licence plate recognition.

At that moment, her pupils dilated. As the limited light flood in, so did the sheer size of each of the admittedly beautiful detached edifice in her field of vision. She muttered, "Now, these are insane!"

He made his way slowly through the now fully opened gates, when randomly her mind wondered back to their earlier conversation and she enquired if he had shared the news of the break up with the other one third of the 'triplet', otherwise known as his older sister.

"Not yet." He turned to her with furrowed brow.

"Sue has her own issues to worry about, with the recent miscarriage." He paused, then looked away. "Anyway, I am seeing her this weekend; we are having dinner at hers on Sunday afternoon, I'll tell her then. Now, are you going to spend the rest of our evening worrying about Cara and me, or what?"

She noted this time he looked less pained as he spoke and reminded herself again, to let it go, at least for the rest of the evening. They drove around in admiration while all the time she was convinced the inhabitants were and never would be her social equal, as silently she vowed to knock on his friend's door should anyone finds them suspicious.

"It's official – we, are crazy!" She shook her head in disbelief, then continued, "But, these people are even more crazy. Who would want to live in houses like these, houses one could easily lose their children in, and the poor pets!"

"Dogs bark, don't they?" He smirked, while she giggled. "Come on Elizabeth, wouldn't you love to live in this neighbourhood?"

She could tell he was surprised at her reaction. "No, Mathew! Knockholt is simply fine. That is home. This is - these are show houses, not homes." Then she remembered what her mum did some years ago and bolting upright in her seat she asked, "You haven't bought one of them have you?"

He grinned.

"Come on, you didn't!" Firmly gripping one of his hands as she enquired, wondering if history was repeating itself.

"You're thinking this is like the impromptu Sunday evening trip your mum brought you on those many years ago then to end up with a new home in Knockholt? No, I didn't." He grinned. "I don't have that kind of money. Not yet anyway. But let us call it, 'an aspirational family home.' Those nieces and nephews you mentioned earlier, they will need to live somewhere. You do know that, right?"

"You'd need at least a dozen to fill these rooms, surely!" She giggled more at the thought of him being totally bothered and surrounded by two let alone all of twelve children and wondered if he will be any better at fatherhood than he is at cooking. No thanks to Claire, she concluded, but as his father was such a good example, she was convinced he would be.

"Well then, a dozen it shall be." He was totally straight faced now.

Not long and they were sharing silly stories and in a fit of laughter, while all the time she acknowledged that lingering thought of what, if anything, could one day fill that absentee mother void; that emptiness created by emotional neglect. She has seen it so many times in her work. Shaking her head, she once again fully immersed herself in the moment. They teased each other, all the hour-long-drive back to Knockholt, just like old times, and when they finally turned into her driveway, she insisted he stay the night.

"How silly to drive the hour back to your place, when I will be here alone." She told him, as she deposited her keys and bag on the entrance table.

"The guest room may be a little bit dusty, but you know where to find whatever it is you need, don't you?" At first, she thought he was ignoring her rhetorical question, and smiled when his infamous 'grumpy-self' re-emerged and from somewhere deep he muttered, "I know I should have gone home."

She rolled her eyes as she made her way up the stairs and smiled playfully when eventually she saw him smile back. He was asleep when her scheduled Uber announced its presence early the next morning; when, suddenly she found herself struggling to get the left pair of brown flats on, and with her Never-Full tote containing the latest teddy bear for her mum firmly tucked away under her arm, quickly, she scribbled a note to him.

"We love you, sort your head out."

CHAPTER THREE

The driver must have downloaded all of Tchaikovsky's Swan Lake. She wondered, but as beautiful as it sounded, Elizabeth felt it was extremely intrusive and quickly inserted her Ear Pods. In no time she was back to practicing her deep inhale then exhale routine which is fast becoming her go-to form of 'exercise'. With her head firmly placed against the headrest, she smiled as she replayed the time she met Mathew at her then new school, the day after her best friend, Isabelle managed to send the pictures she had promised a few days ago, just before she boarded her flight to Los Angeles, California. The day she moved away to live with her mum.

She remembered being so relieved as she bounded up the stairs, full of excitement. Isabelle had sent the pictures, she promised faithfully she would have. Excitedly, Elizabeth had only just sent the love heart in reply when his accusatory tone managed to wipe the smile off her face. "It would be nice of you to say sorry; you know."

Elizabeth had only just turned right, along the corridor, away from her earlier class on law, when he approached her. Apologising, she stepped back so she could look him squarely in the eyes. He was much taller than her, and for a moment she found him a bit intimidating.

"You hit, no *knocked* my phone out of my hand as you practically ran up the stairs."

"I didn't run and if I did, *knock* your phone out of your hands, I'm sorry." She circumvented him and continued in the original direction to the library.

"And don't you want to know if you broke it?" He looked puzzled and continued after her.

"Sure." Maintaining her pace, she replied sarcastically.

"Sure?"

"Well, did I break it or not? You are going to say, aren't you?"

"Are you new here?"

"As a matter fact, yes, I am new. So, did I break your phone, or will you just follow me around? I haven't got the time for an inquisition."

"Hmm. Welcome to Campion College." He extended a hand which she rudely ignored.

She could tell he was determined not to leave her alone just yet, and she was now quite irritated.

"I've been here since year seven and can't say I have met anyone as *polite* as you." He quipped.

"Thank you." She was not about to enquire any further about the condition of his phone but fake pleasantries, she was certain she could do that.

As they both approached the library, she paused abruptly. "Now, I need to get to the library, to conclude my philosophy and ethics assignment, if you don't mind."

"Sure; sure, me too." He stammered.

Elizabeth was puzzled by his response and sought clarification.

"You are doing philosophy and ethics? I've never seen you in my class."

"No. I am not, but I *am* going to the library. Isn't that where you said you are heading?"

"Okay." And she rolled her eyes in annoyance.

"Okay?"

Hurriedly, she entered the library determined in her attempt to leave him in tow. Elizabeth had made every effort not to acknowledge his presence; and finding it a challenge to concentrate, she decided to give her search for the journal she intended to find, a miss, and instead, pretended to be on a telephone call as she glided stealthily out of the building, thankful not to have her Ear Pods in place at that time as she held her makeshift face shield tightly in place. Without looking back, she swiftly made her way to the gate and exhaled only when she saw no sign of the young man in her peripheral visual field.

It was a week later that they came face to face again for the second time and Elizabeth decidedly looked towards the desert table away from her preferred cold salad section when suddenly there was an altercation between two juniors. The two dutiful sixth formers immediately intervened; de-escalated what they knew was a potentially flammable scenario, and as they escorted both students in the direction of the vice-principal's office, they exchanged names. Then, together, they alerted the students about the possible trouble they were in while; the younger of the two boys accosted, insisting he was not the one responsible for hitting the female student's bum. All three students safely deposited outside the head of year's office instead, and after what seemed like forever, Elizabeth was surprised how easy it was to 'work' with him. She felt like he was someone she had known for a long time, and not just for that one-time run-in at the library a week ago.

Mathew was first to confess to being famished. And without notice, he exclaimed. "Oh, hell no! Sorry for my bad language but the lunch hall is now closed!" He was not happy.

"Oh yeah, I forgot. Aww, I am kind of hungry too, actually." Startled at first, she muttered, nonchalantly. "Hey what time do you finish today?" She remembered him going with her all the way to the library and wondered if he was in a habit of following ladies around, 'surely he has some friends he would much rather be with', she said to herself.

"I have one more session and then I can go. I have a mild headache as well though. Guess I'll do my Literature assignment at home, or tomorrow."

"Oh, ok." She thought he looked disappointed and wondered what he had planned.

"I was thinking we could stop at the small pizza restaurant on the corner of Manor Park and Angel's afterwards, and my sister could come too, if you don't mind. My dad isn't in 'till late, and my sister who is home on break from University, cannot be trusted in the kitchen and well, to be honest with you, I am hopeless in that respect as well, so what do you say?"

She was laughing by now as he feigned innocence.

"Okay. A pizza sounds good. That should heal me."

A few hours later and they were on their way to the little family-owned Italian pizza restaurant located a twenty-five-minute walk down the high street. Elisabeth confessed she had no knowledge of a pizza restaurant nearby.

"That's because you have your mum to cook for you. Susan and I don't." He mused.

"Guess you are right. Yes, I must say Mum loves to put her classic Range Master to its full use." She rolled her eyes and he smiled as he admitted being unapologetic about not having a clue as to what make or model their stove was.

They chatted like old friends as they walked along to their desired eatery, and that was when he told her about his mother.

"She left us to go and live in the South of France. She's a freelance Political Journalist." He told her, and without saying it, Lizzy could tell he missed not having her around, and she was happy now she had obliged. Later they ate pizza and drank diet coke. He passed on desert while after a rather painstaking moment trying to decide what to have, she eventually settled on two scoops of lemon sorbet. They made no further mention of his mum or of Susan's refusal to come out with them, stating only that she already made other plans with Paul whom she had been very close to prior to going off to University. Before dark, he waited for her to board her bus.

Later that night, she decided to follow him on Instagram and Facebook, using the links he texted her as they exchanged numbers over pizza. They carried on meeting for lunch whenever they could, and at other times, they would meet in the library. They learnt a lot about each other and before long both parents met, and with rules firmly in place, the teenagers arranged evening hangouts and weekend visits at their convenience. Very soon, everyone at school was certain they were a 'couple'; which, while she neither confirmed nor denied in some circles, Mathew proudly declared it, indubitably so.

They were happy to have found each other. For her, he was the sibling she had longed for and for him she was the friend he never had. She admired his sense of focus but appreciated his loyalty even more. They made a point to study together even though they took completely different subjects. Pretty soon Elizabeth was convinced she could sit his business and economics exams and thought he could give her law papers, a rather good try too.

Not long, and with September firmly behind them, it was fast approaching their first of two Christmases at Campion College. Now, settled into her new home, Elizabeth was determined to enjoy her time there. Like her mum, she was happy for the fresh start and was beginning to embrace all the changes that were occurring and very much wanted to put all the sadness of losing her dad and long-distance best friend, behind her.

Weeks before, Mathew had confirmed receiving his ticket for the school's upper school Christmas party and Elizabeth had ordered hers only that evening as soon as she sat on the bus on the way home. This time, they were both happy that Susan came out with them. As they drove home after the disco, the older girl confessed to being summoned by her little brother to be their chauffeur, and together with Mathew, 'the inseparable-threesome' was born. And, late that night when her friends' father's car pulled up outside her side entrance, Elizabeth could not wait to get home and share the evening's entire occurrence with her long-time best friend, Isabelle.

It was a little while ago that the Uber driver announced her destination, but with her favourite Mary Mary blaring through the Ear Pods and completely lost in thought, she heard none of it. For a while she stood at the entrance of the Care Home and watched pointlessly as the car pulled away. Adjusting the Teddy Bear under her right arm, she made a valiant attempt to bring herself back to her goal of the day. Then, ever so swiftly she pivoted and made her way to the main entrance and along the wide glass-lined corridor which all year round, brings the beautifully manicured lawn with its beautifully arranged alternate vegetable and flower patches side by side in sharp view. But all the while, quietly she hoped Mathew would be able to fight his demons and that it would be sooner rather than later.

CHAPTER FOUR

Hazel loved the Teddy Bear Elizabeth brought for her. It was meant to be her valentine's gift. For a long time, she sat holding it close to her stomach, as she rocked herself rhythmically in the smaller of the two chairs opposite each other in her room. Back when Hazel was well, she loved spending time with her daughter and made use of every opportunity presented to bond. Today, Elizabeth was hoping to play a board game, just like they used to each Sunday evening after dinner, back in the old house. Or even in Knockholt, when they would watch one of their favourite comedy dramas from any of the streaming platforms Mathew had installed as a birthday gift when Hazel became more unwell. sometime before last Christmas, just before the Care Home became her new home. Desperately, she held on to the memories of her and her mum and was finding it increasingly difficult not to say, 'remember when', to Hazel. She knew from the short weekly lessons delivered by the education team at the home, that while it may be tempting to try to jog the memory of somebody living with the disease, it can be a painful experience for both parties and could lead to frustration.

It's been two months, but Elizabeth's heart breaks every time she visits. Not simply for visiting but for being unable to care for her at their home, in the house she knew Hazel loved and had bought for them both, which she intended to be Elizabeth's one day. And now, her heart aches each time she contemplates selling it to fund her care. With Dementia, one never knows. Early on Hazel's consultant had told her it was a rare form of the disease and, overtime she suspected soon, she would become even more unwell. Hazel's Dementia was an aggressive rare type, and she was rapidly deteriorating. Elizabeth knew she was left no choice but to move her there, where she could be safe, and although she has not seen the usual bruises she had regularly come home to in the earlier days, she has continued to live with the guilt ever since. Without thinking, she had made it a point to tell everyone, that moving her to the care home, was the last thing she wanted to do and often prayed that her dad would sympathise too.

Over the past two years as Hazel's Dementia worsened, she found it more and more difficult to care for her on her own. Even with a live-in carer, her dependence increased with such rapidity, it made keeping her safe at home impossible. What was left of her parents' savings had been depleted and she has resigned herself to selling the first house to fund her care. She was determined to do her best by her mum and told Mathew that she would sell her house if she had to or even take on additional jobs. But Mathew had insisted he would help if it came to that and told her pointedly, he will not take no for an answer. Ss close as they were, family almost, she knew she could never put such pressure on him. They both heard the words of the consultant, but neither knew exactly when the end would come, and she would never want him to be broke because of her. She could not bring herself to put him through that.

Her only focus now is to be the daughter her mother can be proud of. As she brought out the snakes and ladders, she attempted conversations in short sentences. Hazel attempted to reach for the dice, to deliver her first throw but it simply landed on the floor. Elizabeth kissed her on the cheeks and stroked her hair. It is all white now – fully grey. After her father's plane went down, she had long suspected her mother's fragile mental state, and at times, was fearful she may fall apart. Elizabeth had very quickly adopted the obedient teenager persona and was quick to do as she was told. She made sure there was no complaints from her teachers about homework or any misdemeanours and was confident her mum was pleased with her. Both mother and daughter were happy when her high school exams were completed and were optimistic for exceptionally good grades. Neither had any reason to believe otherwise and when they set out that Sunday evening, ten years ago on what was to the younger of the two, a rather mysterious journey... although dying inside, the curious teenager thought better than to question her mum and so quietly she obliged. But sensing her apprehension not long into the journey, Hazel confessed how hard the past year had been for her and that staying in the house she had shared with her dad, for almost twenty years, was becoming increasingly difficult. It became apparent Hazel had relocating to another house in a totally new neighbourhood, on her mind.

"Lizzy, it has been tough." Hazel's tone softened as she kept her eyes steadfast on the road ahead, as if afraid to blink.

"I know mum. It's okay." Recognising the sacrifice her mum had made over the years, Elizabeth's mind was racing, and she desperately wanted to text her long-time friend Isabelle to share with her feeling of apprehension but, she would not dare. Not now.

As an only child, Elizabeth could not be accused of being spoilt. If anything, her regimented-like household made her a disciplined thoughtful girl who was always respectful and respected by her peers and teachers alike. Her parents were

25

immensely proud of her and she wanted them to be. Self-control was her dad's mantra and she harnessed that now as she did her best to show no sign of her increasing anxiety.

"I didn't want to disturb your studies, so I did what I could to hang on; but I have to…" Her voice trailed off and Elizabeth could hear the pain in it. She knew then, the purpose of the trip. She only hoped it would be somewhere as nice as, or even better than where they were, where she has been her whole life with her friends, and although her dad wasn't around as much as her mum was, she knew when he would be home, his current rota was always pasted on the notice board in the utility room and the one time he didn't, they both knew something had happened, although neither was prepared for the news the burly policeman brought on that windy cold Thursday evening. The evening she has ever since tried so desperately to forget.

"I saw - somewhere in Knockholt, it's one less bedroom but we should be happy with three bedrooms, shouldn't we? There is still room for sleep overs, a big sitting room for your friends to hang out and it even has a large conservatory for games, parties, whatever you like, Orchid." It has been a while since her mum called her 'Orchid', and she could tell she really hoped she would at least like what appeared to be a house she had already found.

"It's okay, mum. I suspect I am going to be busy with A 'levels and, not long after, I am off to UNI anyway. So, not much time for sleep overs."

"You are right." Her mum sighed then hastened on. "Time goes by so quickly doesn't it, Lizzy?" Her parents very rarely called her Elizabeth. She had long since become accustomed to being Orchid or Lizzy to her mum, and to her dad she was Lizzy or flower, and on the odd occasions when she was Elizabeth, she knew she was in big trouble. Like the time when she was accused of talking back to her science teacher, of being argumentative.

"Before you start worrying, yes, they are all ensuites." Again, Hazel stole a glance at her only child.

"Okay." Elizabeth replied, cautiously.

"I know you like having your own bathroom," her mum smiled, and Elizabeth reciprocated warmly.

"In fact, it's even bigger than what you have at the old house; and there is also a walk-in closet in each bedroom. Oh- and some reputable secondary schools too. I have seen a few Grammars and Independent ones as well, so if you like the house and want us to, we can get it. I'll let you decide where you go for your 'A-levels'." Her mum smiled again. She knew Elizabeth would make a 'sensible' choice.

"That sounds pretty cool, Mum!" The teenager could only but moderately remain self-composed as her anxiety dissipated and her excitement began to build.

Hazel continued her description of the house as Elizabeth nodded, letting go of her trepidation and as they approached the exit, off the motor way, she was bursting with excitement. Very easily they chatted about all the good times they had at the old house and laughed out loud when Elizabeth reminded her mum of the sight of her dad in the onesie she had bought him the Christmas before the accident.

"Which was *a-bit* short"

"But he insisted on keeping it anyway. We know he would do anything to make you happy."

"I know, Mum"

"In the end; he had to cut the foot of it off!"

"Which was cringe." Elizabeth rolled her eyes, and they both laughed out loud.

"I miss him so much."

"Me too Orchid, me too."

All of two hours later, her mum stopped outside an elegant detached late Georgian double fronted three-bedroom house. Both mother and daughter really liked the period checkered entrance, and the three wide steps which led to what Elizabeth thought was an enormous front door, painted dark grey.

"Mum, no garage?" She enquired with only a hint of disappointment.

"There is sweetheart, at the side entrance. Come, let us walk this way; and it's a double, so enough room to store your artwork."

Hand in hand they walked to the right of the property which was when Elisabeth noticed the estate agent's car. Not long after, she turned to face a very heavy-set shiny black electric wrought iron gate which opened to the garage and is adjacent to what she thought to be a cute little pedestrian entrance with the same decorative tiles similar to what led up the front steps.

"Oh, no back gate?" Elizabeth noted.

"No, Orchid. This is it." She could hear her mum's tender voice from just ahead.

"Wow; Mum the garden is beautiful, and big. How big is this place?" Her mum, seemingly familiar with the layout, made her way in and through the already opened folding garden doors which let them both into a big well-lit kitchen-diner. Elizabeth had never seen anything like it before. She looked fully up unto the huge sunroof which she noticed covered almost half of the ceiling, then allowed her eyes to follow the light down to two big double windows. One of which overlooked a beautiful but sparsely decorated conservatory.

"Are those remote operated blinds?"

"Yes, and they are temperature regulating too." Elizabeth was not expecting a response from anyone but her mum, when a voice intercepted, and with a very upbeat, "Hello, Mrs. Dawes, how are you?" The hidden figure then appeared in full view as she stepped up to the raised area which housed the sink and forms a large enough area accommodating the six-stool island. She appeared to come out of nowhere although the young girl had noticed the estate agent's car earlier, she had been so taken with the sleek clean feature of the house, that she was totally startled.

"Oh, Hello Eileen, I wondered where you were hiding?" The very petite middle-aged looking woman with well-groomed hair and a tattooed left calf, fully extended her right hand for a very firm handshake. Then she turned fully to face Elizabeth as Hazel introduced her daughter.

"What are your thoughts so far, Elizabeth?" Eileen wasted no time in seeking the girl's opinion, as if she were aware the sale depended on it.

"Ahm, it's okay." Elizabeth said pleasantly.

"Let me show you around, if that's okay?" The eager estate agent turned around so effortlessly on what Elizabeth thought looked more like ten-inch Louboutin's; as opposed to maybe, six, to lead the way.

"Certainly." All three ladies laughed as Elizabeth and her mum consented in unison.

The property had been recently renovated to what her mum pointed out as an incredibly high standard, creating a perfect blend of period and highly specified contemporary finishes; most of which, to the teenager's surprise, she liked a lot.

"I love the high ceilings, Mum, and the fireplace, that's huge. Those chandeliers have to go, though. They look like something out of Horrible Histories!" They all laughed. She could tell her mother was pleased she liked it.

Elizabeth was happy for the nicely raised and decked patio area just off the conservatory and mentioned how it would be easier for them to maintain. Her father had confided that their childhood house was bought with the plan to have three children but after several attempts to conceive they were lucky when at forty-two and following a difficult pregnancy Elizabeth came along. Her dad was fifty-one then, and fearful of losing his wife as the doctor had warned, they concluded it was too late to contemplate or risk having another child.

"I was looking forward to an early retirement," He joked at the time.

They went upstairs where she was pleased to see the size of the rooms and again her mum was quick to point out the En-suite, as if it was a well-documented deal breaker. The continuation of the high ceilings also impressed Elizabeth; and later, when they met by the staircase window; without thinking, they hugged each other and cried. Hazel was first to compose herself and as she sat on the padded window bench, she reassured her daughter, 'everything will be okay'.

"We will be okay." She had said, to which Elizabeth nodded in agreement.

"Mum, how can we even afford this?" She felt compelled to ask. The last thing she wanted was any additional strain on her mum. She could not decide whether she had bought or was planning to buy what looked like an awfully expensive property. They had always lived well, with her dad being a pilot and her mum a part time clinical coding specialist, still she never suspected they would be able to afford anything like this.

Smiling through her tears, Hazel reassured her. "Your dad took care of it, Orchid. Both his savings and life insurance have given us enough to be comfortable for a long time."

Elizabeth nodded. "That explains it," she mumbled in acknowledgement of her new-found information. It really didn't matter to her where they lived as long as they were together, and she wondered if her mum knew that. But as the thought entered her mind, her mum clarified.

"Besides, by getting this now, you never have to worry about your future or getting on the so-called infamous property ladder because, this can be a wonderful family home for you, for a long time. You know, someday." Hazel smiled and hugged her daughter again.

That explained the emphasis on the En-suite and walk in closets. This was meant to be her home for as long as she wanted it to be. They spoke about how they would both make new friends and Hazel confessed to researching local charitable organisations she could volunteer at now that she had retired. She smiled when she mentioned the Church of England building, the one they saw about a mile away as they drove in. Elizabeth knew her mother was looking for a new beginning and, although she had never voiced it, she needed one too but nothing on this scale had entered her mind. The girl did not know how to ask about the old family house. She wondered what her mum had planned to do with it but figured she would find out soon enough.

She was aware her dad had some savings, she heard when the lawyer visited the house after the funeral; but could not remember how much it was. It was still a bit of a blur hearing the news of the plane's disappearance, the wait to hear if any of the one hundred and thirty-six passengers on board one of the smaller aircrafts had managed to survive. Then it was reported to have been found; and later having to live through the funeral and of course life without her beloved father had not been the same ever since. John was a devoted father and husband and was a technology enthusiast who would always bring her something back from his travels. She did not think they could afford to have both properties and although her mum noticed her ever so slightly furrowed brow, she was satisfied that at the very least, she liked this house.

"As you can see, it is a safe neighbourhood," Eileen reminded them. "A nicely established community in a suburban area with many large green spaces and excellent schools. Incredibly attractive to families. The Town centre is only a ten-minute drive away with lots of places to eat and a wide variety of shops." Not knowing Elizabeth saw shopping as her least favourite past-time, and that art was far more appealing. Eileen glanced at her, then smiled as she hastened on.

"There is a picture gallery and a theatre there too and a five-screen cinema. So, lots to do, Elizabeth." Eileen continued her estate agent's charm. Elisabeth was pleased with what she saw and heard; and later, they spent as much time as possible, driving around the neighbourhood. She listened and was impressed when she heard how her mother had managed to make the acquisition without disturbing her exam preparation. Eventually, they parked in a cul-de-sac, and proceeded to walk a few yards until a narrow river came into view. In the distance, they could see acres of farmlands, but Elizabeth was more drawn to the beautiful sight right in front of her. There were little children splashing about in the shallow water. She laughed and pointed her mum in the direction of a little boy running determinedly after his white and black cocker spaniel as his wellies collected water along its path. They walked farther along then sat on one of the benches lining the grassy river bank while the sound of chirping birds filled the air. As their eyes travelled further along, bearing right, the beautiful array of colours from people meandering across a narrow bridge came into focus. Some paused as they enjoyed their escaping ice cream, there were couples holding hands and many people pushing children in push chairs. Some Elizabeth correctly guessed to be proud grandparents on duty.

"There must be a tennis club around here somewhere!" Elizabeth was happy to note as she pointed discreetly to the group of people walking not too far away, laughing, and chatting amiably with rackets in hand but looking rather tired in their soiled full white tennis attire. As they approached, she could hear their celebratory wins and conceded loses with noted high fives and nods. She smiled at the thought of joining them one day and her mum was happy to hear of her plan. It did not take much convincing by the older woman and soon both were holding their own smoothie from the nearby juice bar as they continued to enjoy the scenery. Both were thankful it was a tropical day and were convinced it was a nice neighbourhood. However, it was with mixed feelings, that Elizabeth looked forward to moving into their new house.

Later that evening, on the way back, she wondered out loud why there was no 'for sale' sign on their soon-to-be old house and was quietly relieved to learn that that's because it's not for sale. Hazel could not bring herself to sell it just yet and planned to keep it for Elizabeth. It would be put up for rent until she decided what she wanted to do with it.

"That way you do not have to work immediately after University, you know – you could give yourself a break – some time to figure out what you want to do. You do not have to rush into anything. You won't have a mortgage and you will have rent coming in." Hazel smiled as she looked tenderly at her only child. Her pride and joy.

They discussed how it, along with what was left over from the money her dad left for them, could also help her with university, which was a relief to Elizabeth. Somehow, a part of her was not ready to let it go just yet. Suddenly, she felt like so many things were happening, and so quickly too. One minute she was happy in high school, then, without warning her dad died; and with all her focus on her exams, there was no time to grieve. And now this; they were moving to a new house, a totally new community, and leaving all that was familiar behind and another move would be coming her way later that year as she was certain she would be accepted for one of her three choices for sixth form. She cried again just as she allowed herself to fully relax in her bed later that night, and again when she forced herself to get up in the morning. The wet pillow caused the events of the evening before to all come flooding in.

Soon it was graduation, and as neither of her parents was from a large family there was only a small gathering of friends and family over for a celebratory dinner. Just over a month later, most of those same people were there to help with packing. Afterward, they all ate homemade sandwiches and kissed goodbye, the removal truck arrived.

Elizabeth sighed deeply now as she was unable to tell who was winning this game of snakes and ladders, thinking how much their lives had changed. How her life now revolved around work, chatting with Izzy on FaceTime in the evenings when either could find the time or with her siblings: Mathew and Susan, as they had now come to call themselves. But, most important of all to her is her weekends with her mum. She would not let anything prevent her from being there and everyone who knew her, knew that. On Sunday, Elizabeth arrived earlier than she did the day before. She wanted to be with her mum when they went for their usual swimming lesson in the indoor pool to the rear of the property, but shortly after, Hazel became restless and her session was aborted. But later, after intermittent short walks around the grounds, they settled in as Elizabeth read the Bible to her. Not long in and both were exhausted. Hazel was sound asleep when Elizabeth accepted defeat and left for home.

CHAPTER FIVE

She had long come to accept that visits to her mum would always led to no social life and late nights on the weekends trying to complete work needed for the coming week. All of which was piled high on her desk now as she looked out over the city from her office window, drenched in the rain. It was pouring down outside, and as usual, she was woefully ill-prepared for the weather, which was somewhat deliberate on her part. Always doubting it would really rain as heavily as it always did and again, she was caught out. She raised her feet up to the radiator as she reached for her emergency blow dryer. Normally, she would be refreshing her make up now, getting ready to face her clients, but the discomfort of wet feet took priority.

Mathew called and they chatted briefly about his prospective tenants for the yet to be rented third office space, but he was adamant and in no rush. He too was contemplating its use as a place for himself.

"Wouldn't that be way too big for you?" He was asked, but when he explained he had planned to move all his business activities under one roof, she understood his aim. Her first client of the day was a young couple with what they term at the firm, a 'soft case' involving a party wall for an extension which took more time than she expected it to as the wrong documents were submitted by the team's assistant and by evening, her whole schedule was thrown. As usual she called the home to check in on her mother and satisfied that all was at least as she had left it on the weekend, she headed home.

Speaking to Susan was on her list of things to do but with the time difference, Isabelle took priority. Both girls chatted for most of the night while each did what work they could, given the nature of the conversation. Mathew and Cara's break up dominated their catch-up and Elizabeth was taken-a-back to see that Izzy was nowhere as surprised as she had been.

"But why?"

"Why? Lizzy, come on. You know Mathew better than anyone." Isabelle chuckled.

"Well, I thought I did"

"You do. Come on. He would never want that life, her world. He is his father's child."

"I guess. You are right. I just thought with the passing of time he had changed and well, you know, with money and all."

They chatted until Elizabeth was convinced of her friend's take on the matter and when they hung up, it was too late to call Susan. They were looking forward to seeing each other over the summer. Falling asleep she thought of Izzy's last visit, last summer and how much fun all four of them had. The late-night chats and house parties, she could not wait to see her again and had planned her annual leave around her visit.

By middle of the week, there was enough going on at work to keep her busy. She had an adoption case to settle between a Caucasian family and a toddler from a mixed Caribbean-Caucasian background. By Friday, she was exhausted but looking forward to her time with her mother. There was a concert by the local church, her favourite Mary Mary would be performing or ministering as indicated on the poster and there was no way she was going to miss it. Mathew would have come but he told her he had already made plans with a friend, which made her wonder if he had a date. She figured she would hear more about that on Saturday evening when they met. The sun was out after the down poor at the start of the week, but the air was crisp. Her brisk walk covered the journey in just over twenty minutes and she was relieved when the building of the local community church came into view; but couldn't help but growl as the long queue came into focus, even from a distance. As she came closer still, the sound of instruments getting tuned in time for the show became audible. That for her was, part of the allure of Knockholt, its tranquillity on evenings other than this one. It is a place where everyone knows everyone, or so it seems.

On summer evenings, she'd stroll along the river nearby or take the thirty minutes' drive to the sea, which; although not much to the short strip of sand, had its own peaceful charm and had become her favourite place for a walk to clear her head. She could not imagine herself living any place else.

"Elizabeth, so lovely to see you." It was Pastor Lammy, her mother's Pastor and Pastor of the church. He was always inviting her out and she could tell as he embraced her, he was genuinely happy she came. They talked about her mother's failing health and she was surprised how knowledgeable he was about Hazel's current condition. She knew he visited sometimes but now it appeared he went by more often than she thought. It made her happy to hear him speak of her mother so highly. Pastor Lammy was truly a remarkable man, so patient, he made time for everyone and she was beginning to think that something about him reminded her of her late dad.

"Come, there's someone I would like you to meet." He always did that. Pastor Lammy was the old school clergy man who believes in community and relational evangelism and was always looking for ways to make visitors feel like they belonged. He was always the consummate host. On the way to be introduced, he told her about a young man who had not long returned from working for a year at the renowned John Hopkins Hospital in Baltimore. She had no idea what that was supposed to mean but figured it must be important for him to have mentioned it. Pastor Lammy was very animated, one of the things she loved about him when presenting his sermons and he was just as excited now. She could not help but smile as he hastened her along.

"Ahh, Richard, Son, this is Elizabeth - she's the daughter of a dear friend and member of this church. Elizabeth this is Richard, the son of a dear friend, a member of the clergy."

Elizabeth was all too happy to have beaten the queue that she was prepared to sit with a member of the clergy anytime. They chatted easily about Mary Mary and Richard made it clear it was not his thing but as he had promised to take his sister's children, his niece and nephew, he could not possibly have reneged.

"She is expecting her third and her husband is away. He's also a doctor." He explained. "He's into bones, I focus on the head."

"Oh." She nodded and smiled as she feigned interest. Thanks to Pastor Lammy she got one of the best seats and was as noisy as a teenager when the show got going. Although she wanted to leave early, she could not help but stay until the very end. Pastor Lammy had made his way over to where she stood with Richard as he waited for his niece and nephew to return with the juices they went to purchase. He was happy they enjoyed the concert and invited them to Harvest the following weekend, but tempting as it was for Elizabeth, she knew she wouldn't miss a visit to her mum's any weekend. Not even for the lovely Pastor Lammy's charitable cause, but she made a note to make a donation online. He then mentioned going by to serve communion and to pray with her mum in the coming week. His gesture really touched her and after a warm embrace thanking him for his support, she attempted a hasty escape, but Richard was quick to offer her a lift. She gladly accepted. She accepted she could not be certain her feet would have held up to make the whole journey back home.

Susan had called during the concert. Her voice message was to cancel her friend's visit on Sunday evening and alluded to being under the weather. Elizabeth

35

suspected another one of her avoidance tactics and when she asked if she could make it the following weekend instead, she knew she had to be forceful. They both knew that had the shoe been on the other foot, her friend would never leave her alone and she was not prepared to leave her either. After a well-deserved warm bath and with her visit to Susan's firmly on her mind, she set her alarm and retired to bed.

CHAPTER SIX

Her job at Stevens and Stephenson's had come at a price. It is a longer commute than had she stayed local, but she needed the experience and now, she needed the money. She needed the peace of mind that she could meet the monthly payments for her mum's care. On the way in that morning, she had lofty plans of getting the sale on the old house arranged. Until that call from Lynette. And now the ringtone she had assigned to Mathew, alerted her to his call, but she was too devastated to speak, even to him. Instead he texted her, 'call me ASAP', with an accompanying smiley face emoji. She wanted to, desperately; but just not then. She had her shared office assistant clear her appointments for the rest of the day and hurriedly, she made her way to the Care Home. She could not think of anything else now. Or anywhere else for that matter. It seemed like an unusually long time for the train to come and just as she opted for an uber, it seemed to appear. The perfect seat was to the rear, just after the toilets where she was completely alone in a carriage.

Finally, she was able to settle and was obviously less fidgety as before she boarded the train, the way she had been all that afternoon. In its place now, was all the memories of her and Isabelle's friendship. It all came flooding in and she was completely overwhelmed with sadness. Raw grief. She could remember it all, just like it was yesterday. It was almost a week ago when they last had their facetime meet-up. Both always looked forward to their time together. Being fully cognisant of the eight-hour time difference, they always made the time for each other. Very rarely did they have to check in first to see if either of them was free. They knew well that Elizabeth's wake up time was Isabelle's settle-into-bed, time.

How or when it happened, was a blur now, but both conceded that they gradually grew on each other and throughout high school, were inseparable. They celebrated birthdays and exam results together and cried together when Issy's parents separated. And later, when the divorce was finalised and Isabelle's Mum, Lynette was head-hunted by Google and moved to Silicon Valley, they both cried on the phone until daybreak. Although Lynette thought it would be a great opportunity for both Isabelle and her younger sister, Sarah, to come, she did not want to force either of them. Sarah had wanted to go from the outset, but not Isabelle, she wanted to finish high school and was not ready to leave her dad or the large extended family she had all her life. She had come to rely on all of them, and of course, her amazing social life and best friend who her mother and sister knew were important to her too. Isabelle had insisted on a sleepover at Elizabeth's when her father's plane went down. Both girls were well known to each other's parents and got on well with them. Soon after graduation, Isabelle confided in her best friend that she wasn't fond of her step-siblings, and said she respected her step-mother but would much rather be with her mum. Sadly, she was looking forward to sunny California.

"Beaches, beaches, beaches." She sang to Elizabeth when her ticket arrived, the day before the removals truck Hazel had booked, came.

"Okay, stop showing off," her friend teased.

"You've got to pop over as soon as you can, anyway." Isabelle had said firmly.

"Oh, definitely!" Elizabeth was confident her mum would let her and felt her heart race at the thought even as her eyes welled up.

Both girls met several times prior to Lizzy's house move and as planned, they had made sure to spend plenty of time together and were together at her new house in Knockholt the weekend before Isabelle's scheduled travel to the United States.

"Well, at least now you will, if anything, be even closer to Harvard," Elizabeth teased, as her mum chauffeured them on the one-hour journey to the airport, in the middle of the week.

"Yeah, geographically at least. Yeah right." They both laughed. Both were intent on reading law and Isabelle was really hoping she could get into Harvard.

"That's if a certain girl with long skinny legs is not distracted by the 'fit' young men she meets in California." Elizabeth teased. She knew her friend's favourite adjective as it pertains to the opposite sex was, 'fit'.

"No! No way. Mum would not be impressed." Again, they were in hysterics and as if to pretend that this was a normal occurrence, they found any reason to laugh and poke fun at each other. At London Heathrow, Hazel made herself scarce, which at first, Lizzy didn't think was necessary but found useful in the end when during their breakfast together, they allowed themselves to reminisce on the past nearly four years that they had been best friends. Many selfies and long lingering hugs ushered in the inevitable, and before they knew it, they were blowing kisses across security check lines and giving assurances. Both very hopeful of their future.

"Remember, you must send me a WhatsApp pic as soon as you land!" Elizabeth warned as they bade each other goodbye.

"Come on, Lizzy. She's out of sight." Hazel urged her daughter on gently. "Think of the many skype chats you two will have after she has recovered from that, what, an eleven-and-a-half-hour flight?"

Elizabeth and her mum drove back in silence, as if Hazel knew her daughter wanted to be left alone with her thoughts and was still reeling from her father's impromptu disappearance. Elizabeth wondered if she would indeed still have her best friend around that same time the following year. She was relieved and completely beside herself when Isabelle visited for her summer break. And now, not even the rambling sound of the moving train could keep out the forceful memories of times passed. Suddenly, she could remember her dad not coming home from his flight. She recalled too, closing her eyes on the way home from the airport as she pretended to be resting. Shy almost to let her mum see her cry then. That day, other more melancholy times made their way into her thoughts too; but she had managed to think of happier times like, when she won the mathematics competition and became the friendly geek all the boys tried at first to stay away from; and Isabelle's many attempts to get her a boyfriend in time for their prom. She remembered too, switching her phone off as she entered her bedroom the night her friend left, thinking, just in case Izzy tried to talk to her from the plane, she didn't want to have an unfinished conversation when it got to time to put her phone on aeroplane mode. Somehow, she thought she would miss her even more, if at all that was even possible.

Now, hurriedly, she dried her tears, as the voice boomed over the intercom to announce her stop. The usual eight-minute journey from the train station to the Care Home was covered in what appeared to be half the time and without her mannerly salutations, she hastily made her way past the receptionist and headed in the direction of her intended destination. All her thoughts now on her mum. She did not care whether she recognised her or not. To be near her, with her, was all that mattered. Maybe, if she was lucky, she may even get a hug from her. Even in her sorrow she hoped for a good evening with her and when she arrived, Hazel was taking a nap.

Feeling a little dazed herself, she plunked herself down in the single seater recliner couch and brought her hands to cover her face. Immediately, she felt the tears pushing through her fingers as they make their way into her palm, down her cheeks and finally overflowed like a river totally disregarding some make-shift obstructive sand bags, and down to cover the entire front of her grey Reiss jacket. Once again, she could not hold back the flood. She did not want to.

The thirty-minute train journey was long enough. She had not thought about what to say or do should her mum awake and was disorientated. In fact, she had not thought at all about anything but simply being there, in the room, with her. When finally, she spoke, it was only a mere saliva filled whisper.

"Mum, Mum Izzy is gone." She whispered; initiating a conversation with her mother, whose only sign of life was the synchronised rising and falling of her chest.

"She had a brain haemorrhage, Mum." She sobbed. Almost childlike, was her expression of grief. "How, how can someone have a brain bleed at twenty-seven years old? It is so unfair, Mum, so unfair." She cried herself to sleep and only stirred hours later when the nurses entered the room to check on her mum. Unbeknown to her, Hazel had awakened and was now standing by the window with that affect Elizabeth recognised immediately.

"Hello Elizabeth. Hello, Hazel are you ready to have your supper?" The nurse walked further in the room and was slowly making her way to where Hazel was standing by the window. All the staff knew how much she loved to look out at the garden, particularly the beautiful rose garden situated just below her window. Elizabeth remembered then that she needed to put water in the orchid plant in her mum's En-suite, as well as the other by her little coffee table in the beautiful white and flowery plastic vase she had bought for her, not long after she moved in.

The nurses confirmed what her mum's affect suggested, and what Elizabeth suspected. It was one of the days when Hazel totally forgot who her only child was. Like everyone, Elizabeth understood and thought it better for the nurses to assist her with her meal. Totally unaware of the time, Elizabeth promised to take her for a walk around the grounds later that evening, as Hazel left for the dining room to have a light supper, with the nursing aids.

Not long after, Elizabeth could feel the vibration from her phone. It was a while past her working hours and both Mathew and Susan were concerned about her inexplicable lack of communication. Very quickly, she sent them each a text intent on being brief, not thinking that the brevity was sure to arouse their concern. Quickly she typed, 'Izzy died this morning,' and tried to reassure them that she was fine. 'I'm with Mum.' She didn't want to talk, just to be left alone with Hazel's company being the only solace she could think of, and without waiting for a response, she turned her phone off. Switched the light off too, leaving only the last of the faint golden sunset's glow streaming into one corner of the room. Putting everything and everyone out of her mind, she climbed into her mum's bed, where she cried again and as she drifted into unconsciousness, out too went all memory of her promise to take her mum for another one of their tour of the grounds.

The sun had long gone when she awoke to the sound of noise coming from the adjacent bathroom, and curiously, she climbed out of her mum's bed, only to find two members of the night team helping Hazel with getting ready for bed.

"Mum?" She approached cautiously, making her usual attempt not to startle her. She asked if her mum was okay; but one of the nurses, very apologetically explained that she needed a little more help than usual. Hazel had forgotten even more of her routine that day. Elizabeth then apologised profusely for not taking her for a walk as promised and when she offered to help, they smiled and told her there was nothing left to do.

"I've only got to moisturise her face and hands and get her into bed, Ms Dawes, we are fine, thanks."

"I am so sorry; I lost my best friend today and …" Elizabeth attempted to speak but found it difficult to continue.

"It's okay, Ms Dawes; I understand. I am so sorry to hear." The younger nurse patted her shoulder sympathetically.

"Your driver is here for you. He's in the waiting area." The older of the two announced.

"I didn't book a cab, did I? I can't recall anything these days." Feeling flustered and frustrated, she scolded herself for her poor memory, and immediately reached for her phone to check, when the nurse explained.

"No, Ms Dawes, it's not a cab/. It's the gentleman who was with you on the day your mum moved here, you know, the one who visits sometimes. Sorry, I have forgotten his name."

Elizabeth noticed then that she had a kind smile too. "Aww, It's Mathew. Why did he come all this way? He must've been waiting there a long time." Mumbling, she moved as quickly as she could to the bathroom where she splashed a few hands full of water on her face. Convinced he must have seen her tear-stained face earlier, she shook her head to sort the many thoughts going through her mind. Just then, she recalled the nurse's report of him being in the room while she was asleep, at which time he had decided not to wake her.

"He said he would wait until you were awake." They told her, almost in a chorus.

She knew she had no choice but to go out to him, when the last thing she wanted was for anyone, including her unofficial adopted sibling, to see her so distraught. She knew he… they meant well. Their love for her was evident. Like blood family, they had always been there for her, especially when she was left with no choice and had to place her mum in a safe place. They knew how devasted she was. They both helped her in her search for the most suitable Residential Care Home, where Hazel could be properly supervised, medicated, fed on time, and fully assisted according to her various health needs. Elizabeth had told them in her brief, it would be nice if it was easy to get to, but her safety and quality of care were her primary concern. She was even prepared to relocate if she needed to and commute to work. The decision and the ensuing home search totally tore her apart. They could see that too. For a long time, it had made her incredibly sad. Luckily, Pastor Lammy told her about Hillview and now she took comfort that it was not too far from work or from the house. It was a bonus that as a private accommodation, she could visit anytime. She was delighted when they pointed out the flexibility for next of kin. Both Susan and Mathew helped her pack all her mum's belongings and would sometimes accompany her to the Home whenever they were able to.

From where he sat, the full length of the long wide corridor was in full view, and as if on look-out duty, he saw as she descended the last few flights of the stairs to the ground floor. Even in the distance, he could sense her despair and instinctively he hurried to meet her. Coming along, she did tell herself that she was strong and straightened her tear-stained jacket as she made her way to main reception. Somewhat self-composed and with no intention to, she fell in his arms. As if under a spell she felt the last ounce of strength leave her and so too, all sense of composure. He caught her and held back a smile as she blamed the walk down to meet him for her total lack of energy. "It totally sapped what little I had left."

He could tell she was crying again. Very quickly he whispered to her how sorry he was. He held onto her and reminded her that both him and Susan would always be there for her. He promised to take her home whenever she was ready. "We are a family; do I need to remind you of that?" He ushered her outside to not disturb anyone and to prevent unwanted attention from the visitors in the waiting room or the staff and residents randomly passing by.

"I know. Thanks. Is Susan alright? I will call her tomorrow." She was blowing her nose now while valiantly she wiped away the flood of tears that refuse to recede.

"It's okay; she said she will see you tomorrow. She is fine. Let us talk about Sue later." They found a dark brown memorial bench on which they sat together in the semi-dark gardens and there he held her for a long time.

"There are some things we just can't comprehend, or even begin to explain." Mathew told her, sadly.

They both had been down this road before with the loss of each of their fathers and having each other now, in some ways lighten the burden of the memory. But nothing, Elizabeth thought, could compensate for the cruelty of life taking her sweet young friend. Worse of all, not giving her time to say goodbye. She wondered if her mum had even fully grieved the death of her dad and somewhere deep inside, she knew that was something Hazel had not and may not fully come to terms with. It was much later when Mathew's warm body could no longer shield her from the onslaught of the fresh wind, that she started shivering.

"Goodness, you're cold and look at the time." He had left his blazer on a chair in main reception as he rushed to meet her.

"You go, I'll be fine." She could not look at him. She could not look at anyone. She held her face to the ground; but she was happy he was there, and she dreaded going home to the empty house. It occurred to her to ask him to stay, and knew he would not mind, but she did not want to impose. As if he read her mind, he told her, "I am taking you home, Lizzy. Besides, as flexible as they are here, you know you cannot stay the night, unless your mum is dying, which she is not. Of course not! Oh, so sorry, I should not have said it like that. Come on, let us get you inside before you catch a cold."

On the way to hers, he mentioned that she could stay with him at his place, but she refused. She knew he had been in and out of a few relationships since Cara, but she was not sure if there was anyone living with him at present and she insisted on not imposing.

Later that night, she left the care home only when she knew her mother had settled in and was sound asleep. It had been one of those days when she wished she could talk to her, but Hazel still had not recognised her. Mathew had once again asked her to come and spend a few days with him but again she had refused a room at his penthouse, stating that it would make it difficult for her to get to work even though he offered to call in for her as sick or to drive her in later in the day if she felt up to it.

"Why are you being so obstinate? Okay, I am staying here and before you say a word in protest, I am not leaving. So, throw me out. Call the police!" He sounded completely exasperated. She rolled her eyes and gave him a quick hug. "You were there every step of the way when my dad died. Susan and I were never alone, you would not leave. So now, it is payback time. Tit for tat." He smirked in triumph. She could tell he was not leaving and secretly, she was happy he was not going to.

At some other time, she would have at least smiled but now she was too broken to even remember how to. She made her way to the kitchen where she poured herself some water and turned to offer him a glass which was when she noticed he was not behind her as she had thought. And when she called out to him, he told her he was locking up.

"Do you know it's after midnight?" He called back.

"Thanks, Matt. I love you too." They smiled at each other as he made his way towards her and she made her way to the first sofa in her line of vision.

He rerouted to join her, and they sat in silence until he admitted he was famished and that he would make himself an omelette. "How about you, Lizzy? I could make you one as well."

She declined. She figured he must be starving because she knew him well enough to know that cooking was his least favourite pastime. He insisted and although she accepted, when he brought the tray, she could tell it is his famous mushroom and egg white omelette and attempted a small piece.

They talked way into the night but only briefly about the call she received from Isabelle's mum a week before to say she had what the doctor told her was a cardiovascular accident. Lynette explained that it was also called a stroke and that her daughter had a bleed in the brain which blocked the oxygen from getting to the brain cells.

"I am so sorry, Lizzy." Deep down she knew he was. They all knew Isabelle from her many visits from California to see her best friend, and they all had been out on occasions during the visits. They have also had few hellos at the times when she video-called and Elizabeth was with them.

"We were all very optimistic, Matt. Lynette and I spoke everyday as she monitored her progress; or, what we thought was progress." She could only toss the omelette backwards and forwards on the plate as once again, she felt she would be sick from the lump forming in her stomach and feeling totally defeated she decided against putting another piece into her mouth.

"It's okay, Lizzy. When we spoke last, I could hear the optimism in your voice, and I was hopeful too." He went to sit with her in the double seater and she unfolded her feet to make room.

"I thought she was getting better, Matt. She was trying to get better. I know she was." Suddenly her father's tragic death, her move to Knockholt and her mum's illness all became too much. Elizabeth was inconsolable. She had never felt so much grief before and wondered if she had ever truly grieved for her dad. Did she even allow herself to? At some point, hours later, she felt the warmth from the sun on her exposed feet and a voice in the distance. At first, she sore afraid. The thought of an intruder filled her with dread, and she bolted upright in the couch knocking over the vase with the single white orchid her mum had kept on the medium nest of table beside that sofa.

Mathew was then alerted to her altered state of consciousness and called out to her. As he made his entrance into the large open plan kitchen from the conservatory where he was working on his laptop, one could say their startled expression mirrored each other's, although for completely different reasons.

"What are you doing here, how did you get in here?" Confused, but happy it was him; she breathed a sigh of relief.

"You are awake. You have been sleeping for ..." He paused. "Let's see, for the better part of, a day?"

Isabella's death came back to her now and she shook her head.

He placed her hand on her chest as he spoke, reminding her of carrying Izzy in her heart. He too had all but forgotten all the memorabilia he knew she had from her dad's time in the Air Force before becoming a commercial pilot as well as the many little gifts from Isabelle. Just then, it did not occur to him to remind her of them.

"You have all the amazing memories of your time together right here, Lizzy. Where no one can steal them from you."

"Oh, sorry! Work, did they call?" She ignored him and quickly chimed in.

"Nope, I called. They understand. You can deal with the time owed when you get in. Or so your manager or boss or, '*I still don't know why you insist on working for someone else,*' her name was that I spoke to."

Again, she totally ignored him. The entrepreneur in him had always been impatient for her to start her own practice; but the timing wasn't right. As miserable as she was working on cases that most often were in the best interest of some of her client's selfish greed, as she longed to help real people whom the firm normally didn't have time for, she continued nonetheless. She did not tell him the details of her financial needs and how much she needed the money. Most of the money from her father had gone into buying that house and already what was left had been severely dented from the monthly payments to the care home. Her great aunt was seeing to the sale of the old house while she needed to put away more and more of her salary to meet future payments to the Care Home.

"I spoke to Lynette, too. She called while you were asleep. She said they will be sending ... Izzy - home. In her view, she would have wanted to be here. This is where she has always called home. Oh, and Susan is on her way over with Paul. They should be here in just under thirty minutes."

She noticed his voice adopted a gentler tone now, and very slowly she brought her eyes up to meet his gaze. She had never been happier for Mathew's support and now more than ever, she was happy he refused to leave her on her own. She hated the loneliness since her mum went to the home and coming home to an empty house was new to her. Not to mention, no fun at all. Knockholt was as safe as Eileen had said. Except for the intermittent flow of tourists, it was an otherwise quiet place to live. But she longed for someone to talk to when she got in from work, or to have dinner with, or have them take care of her sometimes. She missed her mother every day for so many reasons. She had often thought of renting a one bedroom flat in the city, close to her office where she could stay and come home at weekends; but she needed to save as much as she could, if at all she was to meet her mum's monthly payments or start her own practice. Both of which were particularly important to her. She knew that more than ever she had to keep her goal in focus, but she also knew how much she needed to be careful with her finances.

CHAPTER SEVEN

Elizabeth had taken the rest of the week off. On Friday, the trio went out for dinner as was customary, only this time Susan's husband, Paul, made an effort to be with them. Usually, he liked to give them time alone but said it was in the spirit of the past Valentine's weekend that he was making his appearance. The 'siblings' all laughed; they were happy he came. And, although other than Issy, they didn't talk about much, none of them would have missed their meet-up for anything. Elizabeth was happy to be out with them, she knew too, that they wanted to support her. It was what they did. What they had always done. Their support meant the world to her. And, on the weekend, she made her usual visit to spend the entire two days with her mum. She was so happy when Hazel recognised her on Saturday as soon as she walked into the communal dining room. After breakfast, she had remained seated, nearest the window. And again, on Sunday.

It crossed her mind to take her outside of the grounds, but she dismissed it. She was not sure how long Hazel would be lucid for, and she knew she would not be able to cope should her mood swing, and she become agitated, anxious or even unmanageable. Elizabeth settled with walking the large gardens and helping her mother tend the smaller flower-patch just below one of her windows, the one with the different variety of roses. She often remembered her mum telling her that not all roses have thorns, although most do. While there are some of the thorny variety, there are still some that have fewer thorns than others but to Elizabeth, once stuck that was enough not to like any variety. But her mum insisted it was always good to keep roses around.

"Just to remind you how beautiful but prickly life can be, my Orchid." Hazel had reminded her many times and again this time, as she stroked her hair, totally oblivious to the fact that she had retained some of the wet earth on her hands as they tended to the rose garden earlier.

"I know mum...and the Orchids, why do you love them so much?"

"You mean … besides … the … exotic look … and feel of the plant?" She stuttered but brought her words out eventually. Hazel paused, and for a while Elizabeth thought she had forgotten what else to say or how to say it. She knew her mum sometimes said the wrong things in her sentences which could make it difficult to understand what she was trying to communicate which led to her becoming frustrated and upset and even angry at herself. She did not press her and sometime later, long after even Elizabeth had forgotten their conversation, Hazel attempted to write to her.

"The orchids, they, they remind me not to worry or get stressed about anything, really. You know, when I get pricked by life's roses because I have misjudged something and may have become beguiled by its beauty, the orchids tell me it's okay. That I am still strong and special and loved by your dad." Tears filled Elizabeth's eyes as she read the scribbled note which was damp and stained with tea. Happily, Hazel told her, "I have a wonderful daughter who is even more beautiful than my precious orchid. You will see her later, sometime. You will see."

Elizabeth was not sure what to make of her mum's explanation on the damp crimpled note, but she was impressed that she was able to even make more than a mere sentence.

"She attempted a paragraph." Careful to keep her hope in check, she told Mathew, later that evening when he called to check-in on her.

After another one of her daytime naps, they had such fun with muddy hands and hugged each other until they collapsed on the grass still wet from the dew. They were laughing and even crying together. Elizabeth had not felt happier to be with her mum and as many times as she wanted to tell her of Izzy's passing, she thought it better not to. She was so hopeful each morning as she alighted from the Uber, hopeful that she would at least be able to talk to her or sit with her, although very cautious not to expect too much from her. She was just to be happy she was alive, and for most of the days, Elizabeth learnt so much more about her mother. Some things she had not remembered for most of her life or wondered if indeed they happened, some of which she suspected but never asked. From now on, she promised herself, to just be grateful for her mum's and her life and for Mathew and Susan. And as she meandered along the wide corridor away from her mother's room on the ground floor towards her waiting cab, she made one of her rare Facebook posts, '#grateful!'

For most of the ride home late that Sunday evening, Elizabeth smiled as she reminisced on happier times, like the time with her dad. What her mum said about how they met and how they enjoyed doing long walks together when he was off duty from his pilot job, was somewhat amusing. Curiously, she had asked her mum if there was anything, she regretted but she shook her head always reminding Elizabeth how loved she was by her, and by her dad who Elizabeth remembered to think of in the past and to remind her mum he was still watching over her. Hazel had made several incoherent refences to Pastor Lammy's church which reminded Elizabeth to visit the community Church of England just down the road from her, sometime soon. It had been hers and her mum's church ever since they moved to Knockholt and she liked going there. Although she has not been able to visit in a while, due to her time between work and the Care Home, Elizabeth promised she would visit a few more times other than at Easter and Christmas time.

It was midweek, in the evening when she was called to say her mum had a temperature, but when she visited it broke and the community doctor was visiting. It was a very windy evening and Hazel wanted to spend most of the time in the large conservatory. Elizabeth did not think it was warm enough. Together with the nurses they convinced Hazel to return to her room where they knitted a gift for Mathew. She told Elizabeth she missed him, that she missed seeing them together and although she didn't speak clearly, Elizabeth understood that she wanted to know if he would come to see her again soon and promised to tell him. But she knew she did not want to burden him and was certain he would come by when he had the time. Elizabeth sat in silence as she watched her mum's attempt to knit a cardigan for her but when she put her red and white non-skid socks on, she was once again very warm and immediately she called for the nurse who gave her the evening medications. It was not long after that she fell asleep leaving all her artwork in a bundled heap on the floor. Still, Elizabeth refused to leave. She stayed the night and became concerned when she saw how restless her mum was. As morning broke, she insisted they take her to the hospital where she was told she had a chest infection.

For the entire week, she worked from the hospital and only went home to change. Between Mathew and Susan, she was never alone. At the beginning of the next week, Hazel was discharged back to the care home. By Wednesday she was happy as her mum volunteered to water all the indoor plants and when Hazel was finished, she asked Elizabeth to read some of her favourite Bible stories by handing her a book and pointing at it. "David, "King, David!" She muttered repeatedly. Elizabeth recognized the request to read about David becoming King and knew it was a story from the Bible she too had always liked. It was after a brief google search that she settled on something short and simple, which she did her best to paraphrase.

The weeks that followed, Elizabeth was in a spin. By the second week after the news, Sarah and Lynette had returned to London and had visited Hazel once in the hospital. Although she desperately wanted to see more of them, her mum was her priority. She had to know her mum was well, which she knew her late friend's mother and sister understood very well.

By the end of the third week, she knew she had to see them. Not fazed by the long journey in the direction of her old neighbourhood, she knew it was one she had to make. Isabelle meant the world to her and she wanted to show her family that she did. Mathew was busy and Susan had a few more gynaecological assessments. It was hard for her, but friendship meant the world to her. She was relieved that she was able to see them and unsurprised to see how happy they were that she came. For the ensuing weeks they were only able to talk on the phone, but Elizabeth always made time to talk to Lynette or to Sarah. They always had something to talk about, Izzy, what she would like and what they had to include in the service. What was optional. They made her an integral part of the planning process and she was happy they did. After all, Isabelle was like her sister. Her twin, she thought sometimes. She knew that she would miss her forever.

By March, she noticed Hazel's gait was becoming more unsteady and that each week she seemed to be requiring increased assistance and this time she made a note to discuss obtaining a wheelchair for her.

"I think we have to think about getting you a wheelchair, Mum. You are a big girl." Unsure whether or not she heard her, she carried on talking to her in childlike tones. Once she settled in another one of the bright padded coloured chairs, she filed and painted her nails and brushed her hair and applied moisturiser to her skin. Elizabeth had inherited her mother's Olive complexion but her father's features and thick black hair, and twice during the visit Hazel told her so. Elizabeth was happy and knew her mum was happy too, to always have her 'family', her 'sisters' around. When Elizabeth returned from pouring her some water, she told her to get the house built and painted and to bring wood and that Robert would help her because he was so proud of her. He really was.

"We love you so much." Sometimes Elizabeth finds it hard to hold back the tears from her mum and this time she only smiled. As jumbled as it all was, she knew the words were coming from the kindest most caring place. Whenever Hazel made her rare form of enquiry, Elizabeth was always quick to say everyone was well. Today she told her that Mathew was doing very well with his business and that Susan was still trying to have a baby and although it hadn't happened yet, she was certain it would be soon.

"Baby shim me. To." Hazel insisted before falling asleep. Elizabeth wondered if her mum had misheard and thought that Susan had already had a baby. She shook her head as once again she dismissed the thought saying it was best not to burden her with the details or even the sadness of Isabelle's death. She was happy they could be as normal as was permitted under the circumstances, if only for just that little time. She did not want her mum worrying about her to cause her to forget about her again. She found the memory lapses most challenging. For that time, she was happy, she felt like mummy's little girl again, and when her mum became tearful and anxious about not getting her a birthday or a Christmas present, she knew she was possibly tired and needed some rest. Together with a Carer, they helped her to her room as her feet appeared to have forgotten what to do. She left only at the time when Hazel began to snore.

CHAPTER EIGHT

The sale of the old house had gone smoothly. It needed updating which Elizabeth could not afford to do, so she was happy when it closed at just below the asking price. With contracts exchanged and certain it had completed, she was a little less anxious about meeting the monthly payments as well as all her other financial commitments and was hoping the upcoming annual administrative increase along with her mum's increased care needs, would be met and that she would still have enough money to pay the care home for at least another year. Myrna, her shared secretary, had cleared her diary for that Friday afternoon. she had planned to scour the neighbourhood in search of a studio or a one bedroom flat. She wanted to know how much she could save by renting a flat close by and putting her house up as an Airbnb. Her job paid well but not well enough as she was not one of the partners. Besides, she did not yet have enough experience. It would be difficult for her to manage, but she was determined to do so somehow. She had made an appointment with one of the local estate agents for early afternoon. Very quickly she made her way down the lift. As it grounded to the lower ground, almost desperate, she positioned herself to step out quickly. She wanted to get there before the office closed. The lift opened and they almost toppled over each. It was Mathew, he was on his way up to pay her a surprise visit.

"What are you doing here?" He laughed as he caught her.

"I work here, remember. What are you doing here?"

"Let's see, I happen to own the three offices on this block including the one you supposedly work in." He looked as smart as usual and she was happy to see him while all the time she wondered how to lose him so she could accomplish her mission without his intrusion.

"Supposedly?" She hissed.

"Okay. You work here and I had a meeting here and was about to have dinner but I thought of you labouring away and thought I'd save you this once. So, no is not an option."

She had the meeting with the estate agent all planned and the last person she wanted to know about it, was Mathew. She knew his thoughts on the matter, but she was determined not to be deterred. She had to do right by the mother who would have done everything for her. And, as much as she valued his and Susan's opinion, loyalty, and kindness, she knew this was something she needed to do on her own for her mother. She wondered how to get out of it and admitted she would have to reschedule the meeting for another day.

They stayed in the city that evening, and for the first time, Mathew joined her in having roast beef tenderloin with wine sauce. He was known to be incredibly careful about what he ate and with taking care of his health. He very often encouraged her to do the same for herself, but this was her first decent meal in almost a month and although it wasn't time for their usual meet-up, she was happy to have someone to talk to and have an evening meal with. She admitted to having thoroughly enjoyed it too. She was full and together, they skipped desert. On the way home, he reiterated pretty much what they talked about at dinner, Isabelle.

"And she is, Lizzy, she was so proud to have had you as her friend and said so many times. You both had an exceptionally close friendship, a bond. Hope ours is just as special." He quipped.

Mathew always seemed to know the right words to say and she needed that reassurance. Sometimes she felt helpless, not sure of the right words to say to Lynette or to Sarah and wished she had Mathews wit. In recent times, very often Elizabeth wondered how her own mother must have felt during the preparation of her father's funeral and recalled how she felt completely closed out by her mum at the time. She could vividly remember not being included except to be told where to sit, and which scripture to read at the service. She concluded it must've been her mother's way of preventing her becoming overtaken with the loss so much so it could have had an adverse effect on her exams. Almost like a way of shielding her as much as she could from worry. She knew how much her getting a good education meant to her parents. She closed her eyes then wondering what her mum had done that day and smiled as she looked forward to their time together again that weekend.

It was the day of Isabelle's funeral and Elizabeth was up early that morning. Lynette had opted for a Friday service and celebration of her daughter's life; which Elizabeth was grateful for. This way she could still have a full weekend with her mother. She did not have to neglect one for the other. Today, she was adamant she wanted to be on time, and was pleased to see the young almost playful sunshine had decided to grace the day with its presence.

"How lovely," she said with a smile, and throwing the shutters to her bathroom window open she pleaded. "Please, please stick around for the whole day, please." She thought about how much like the beautiful golden sun her friend was and how a gloomy day would not be the most fitting way to say goodbye. She was thankful it was the middle of March with the bitter winter months behind her now and not yet time for the summer mugginess. It shouldn't be too bad being out and about between the church service and the short ride to the grave side. With a determination not to cry, she thought about the beautiful outdoors and how much of its beauty reflected her late friend and she so wanted to be strong, for Lynette and for Sarah.

Matthew and Susan knew how much she meant to Elizabeth and were always respectful of their friendship. He offered to accompany her to the service only and she was happy she would at least have his company to that point. They arrived at the church in good time and although she hesitated, she went with Mathew to view the body privately with the rest of Isabelle's family. They all hugged afterwards. Lynette insisted that she sat with the family. Mathew sat immediately behind her Although she was his friend too, he did not feel he belonged there. Unlike her late friend Izzy, Elizabeth spent her whole life visiting churches and when she was younger, she would always help her mum with various church projects from harvest celebrations, to feeding the homeless. However, now that she was working, she had not been able to visit as often as she would like to. Still, on many occasions, she would give to charitable causes. She enjoyed doing so and she had never been afraid to stand up and read the Bible on her mother's or her mother's church friends' request. Today however, she was shaking. She looked around the large grade-two listed majestic looking edifice, as if showing off its grandeur with its beautiful stained windows and period features complete with the most melodious sound coming from the built-in organ. For fear of looking around at anyone specifically, quickly she confessed to Matthew via text that she had never been in a church building this big.

"It's so majestic, isn't it?" He could tell what she was thinking. "You will be simply fine, promise. You will make Isabelle smile." There was a silly grin on the face of the emoji he sent which made her smile too.

She told him on the way to the church that she had just about managed to prepare the reflection Lynette had insisted she do, stating that Isabelle would be smiling as she reads it. They both knew she wanted to work in the background, and that she had no desire to stand in front of any crowd larger than the fifty or so she has to face in court or at her local community church in her little village of Knockholt.

During the service, she was drawn to the beautiful stained-glass windows up ahead and the magnificent painting of Christ and his disciples; at the last supper, she concluded. She wondered if He could still the butterflies in her stomach or hold back the unwelcomed tears which like Lynette's wished, insisted on forcing their way through her impeccably applied mascara and curled lashes. She remembered some of the Bible stories her mum shared with her many times before, particularly about God separating the waters of the Red Sea to allow the children of Israel to get away from their enemies, the Egyptians.

"Please" She whispered. "I need your strength right now, please." She begged. "Surely a few tears are not hard for you to hold back now, are they?"

Startled by what felt like a gentle but forceful nudge from behind, Mathew jerked her from her reverie. It is then she realised it was time for her to give her reflection. She envisioned herself approaching the bench to plea her case before the judge and hoping to appear confident, she made her way to the podium. And when she finished speaking, she knew God had answered her prayer, he had held back the tears. Isabelle's family were really pleased with, "those were such beautiful words, Elizabeth," as Lynette told her afterwards.

Which Sarah reiterated. "Those were absolutely beautiful words, Elizabeth. They so aptly reflect my sister and her beautiful spirit. Thank you. You are a wonderful friend and always part of our family."

Mathew texted her. "Without a doubt, Izzy is smiling too." There was a big grin on the face of the current emoji, and she wondered if he had designed that one. And smiled as he put her phone away to focus on the message from Pastor Daniel.

"No power in the sky above or in the earth below, nothing – indeed – nothing can separate us from the love of God that is in Christ Jesus our Lord." The Minister ended his almost ten-minute sermon with words of hope, and although Elizabeth didn't feel very hopeful of ever getting over her friend's passing anytime now or anytime soon, as they formed the queue to exit, she confessed to Sarah that she felt stronger than when she entered the building.

Outside in the church yard, Mathew told her how brave she was and how proud he is of her. She whispered to him about the prayer she prayed just before he nudged her, and they agreed God had answered her prayer. She knew he was religious, and that like her parents, his dad ensured they had a Christian upbringing. Although these days he admits to being too busy to make church, like her he did make his charitable contributions and today he promised to go by more often too, if only to honour his dad. They smiled. Not long and they had to bid each other goodbye. She recalled that he mentioned a late flight that evening to Dubai and she told him how grateful she was that he was there for her and to call when he returned next week.

On the way to the burial, she spoke to Susan and arranged to go over to hers after the funeral. She then rang the home to see how her mum was and the nurse told her she was fine. "She is out in the garden, Ms Dawes."

"Tell her I called, please, Sophie?"

"Will do, as soon as I put the phone down."

She did not want to know her state of mind. It always hurt whenever her memory went on hold or when she became withdrawn. In the last week during the visit to the specialist to enquire about her mobility, she warned that she was in the moderate to advanced stages and that things would get progressively worse. There was nothing they could do as there was still no cure. Elizabeth had made a mental note to visit more than only weekends and to get her a wheelchair just in case she needed it, which she suspected she would soon.

Back at the reception hall, she stayed close to Sarah, Isabella's younger sister and on occasions they had to comfort each other. As she reached for her phone to check on Mathew, someone approached.

"Hi, that was a beautiful reflection; one can tell you two were very close." The tall gentleman extended his pale, long, slender hand to her, as he introduced himself as Richard Browne, a family friend.

"Thanks. I am Elizabeth. Izzy was one of my best friends. I miss her terribly." Sarah, who had now returned from getting drinks for them both, she hugged Richard as she handed Elizabeth a glass.

The two chatted about what happened with Izzy and as Elizabeth listened, she suspected he was either a vet or a doctor and then she recalled why his face looked familiar. Later, when all three spoke about Izzy, each relayed their version of the Izzy they knew and how she loved her messy buns and her contagious laughter which often caused the most straight faced to at least smile.

"She was so much fun." Sarah moaned. Elizabeth hugged her. Then she told them how she had the biggest heart. Just then, Mathew's call interrupted her. He wanted her to know he had boarded the flight and asked how she was doing. They chatted briefly and then she told him she would be leaving shortly and that she would be staying at Susan's before going to her mum's that weekend.

"That's great! That way Susan or Paul can accompany you there." He was always so thoughtful and protective of her and she loved those things about him. She knew he would make a great husband to someone someday, if ever he was able to get past Claire.

56

"I will be fine. I know they are busy people. Let us see what happens after I see her this evening."

"Okay, then. Bye. Miss you." He would have insisted, but he knew she had already made up her mind.

"And you too, Matt." For some strange inexplicable reason, she found herself looking at the phone a while after he had already hung up and shook her head in time to hear Richard's voice.

"I am guessing you are Pastor Lammy's daughter's friend he introduced me to at the concert I was forced to attend out of not wanting to break my promise to two little brats."

She smiled at his choice of words and confessed to being the person he recalled.

"Are you leaving? I am going as well. Which way are you heading?" Richard insisted.

"If I didn't know better, I'd think you were listening in on my conversation."

"No, I am sorry. In fact, I overheard only that part of it, and thought we could get to know each other a little on the way to our respective places of abode." He was as straight faced as a headmaster, she thought.

"I misplaced your number after the concert."

"Really? Hmm, somehow I can't recall giving it."

"Okay. My error. I thought I had asked or at least given mine. Silly me."

"That's ok. A friend of Pastor Lammy's is, I suppose – O.K., I would like to think." She hazarded a smile as she said it.

Nonplussed, she reached in her purse to retrieve her phone once again where she wrote 'note to self, check with Lynette before leaving. Need to know who on earth this man is.' and saved to notes. With another forced smile, she met his gaze.

"I can give you a ride home, if you like?" He offered again, but she was in no hurry and wanted to clarify his meaning of 'family friend'. She decided, from Sarah's relationship with him, the older woman would be the best person to fill her in.

Susan was standing just outside her door as Elizabeth arrived. She thanked Richard for giving her 'sister' a ride home and quickly, escorted Elizabeth inside. "Paul is away and won't be back before next week," Susan volunteered. "He's in Sweden at a conference." She sighed.

"So, Paul talks Cyber security and we have tonight to talk babies. Perfect!" Elizabeth was hopeful for her friend and wanted to sound a bit more upbeat than she felt.

"I have another round of IVF booked during the half term break – so, I should have news for you soon, mademoiselle." They were all hopeful. It was already five years since they set out on this journey and it had been one disappointment after another. Elizabeth was happy her friend had sought help, was back at work as deputy head teacher and appeared to be doing well. But they both knew that having a baby was important to the couple. Much of their money had already been paid into investigations and they had explored adoption as well. Paul would have been happy to do so now but Susan had insisted on trying for a baby on her own; Paul could only oblige. Elizabeth had always admired the way they loved each other and could only hope that one day she too would find what they had or even what her parents had. But for now, she planned on enjoying their friendship and what time she had with her mum.

Susan spoke at length about how important it was for her to keep her weight controlled and eating well. She had stolen one of Mathew's green smoothie books and they laughed as she twirled to demonstrate the magic of the greens.

"Oh, wow Sue, that's great. You look amazing." Again, Elizabeth tried to evoke her more lively self. She could not say exactly what it was but something the minister said earlier or was it the way he said it, made her hopeful. She had opted to stay at Susan's to catch up with her friend, and to get her mind off the day's events. And they were both happy she did. They had not seen each other in almost a month and after a big hug and apologies for not being able to attend the funeral, Susan poured them both a glass of her latest green smoothie and they made their way to the guest room. Both girls were happy to have each other. Time to talk was becoming more of a rarity than they had imagined, and they had begun to relish these moments.

CHAPTER NINE

March ended and Elizabeth was in good spirits. She had closed an ongoing sexual harassment dispute between a young apprentice and a biomedical scientist at the local District General Hospital. The same week of Isabelle's passing one of the senior partner's had thrown the folder on her desk and told her to 'take care of it'. She did not mind but thought the timing was off. Both her and her assistant were at first dubious any of the witnesses would come forward but Elizabeth remembered her case at her local high school when she stood up for Isabelle after the science teacher sent her out the class to go and 'wrap' her hair. Isabelle had long curly brown hair and that day she decided to wear it loose and it flowed below her shoulder, which according to the teacher, was a way of drawing attention to herself. Elizabeth's parents were happy she had stood up to this form of social injustice but felt a meeting with the teacher and parents would have been better than what they heard was an all-out brawl. Elizabeth had apologised to her mum but refused to apologise to the teacher. She felt apologising to the teacher would be apologising for standing up for her friend and insisted it was not her fault that other students got involved and staged a whole day sit out until the following day when Isabelle was allowed back in class with her hair down just like other kids with hair that long or longer. At home, she was grounded for a week, and had not been in trouble again since. Throughout school, she became known as a scholar and a leader and overtime, most of her teachers admired her and often referred to her as, 'sensible'. Throughout the investigation leading up to the trial, she hoped too that in the end people would feel empowered to speak up and was happy and tearful when they did. She was sad he had to be dismissed, but she knew everyone including the brightest among us was not above the law and had to take responsibility for the hurt evoked. She knew Claire had to and wondered in what way she would get her comeuppance; but not wanting to fuel Mathew's fire, she would not dream of saying any such thing to him. She would only hope he would access the counselling she suggested and get the help he needed to be the amazing husband to someone she knew when he stopped running, he would be.

She had just returned to the office after sharing the good news of the outcome of the case with her senior and bravely she sat with her feet up on the desk. She knew the outcome would in no way heal the hurt. In her mind the young lady would look back and sometimes feel as she described in court, 'feeling dirty', and that she may for a long time especially as she was bound to experience the usual flashbacks but, she was happy she had helped to stop another perpetrator in his tracks. She still hoped others would come forward. She had a feeling the three were not the only ones, but she would wait. And when they came, she would be better prepared and happy to help. She was thinking of a pay raise when her phone reminded her to return Richard's call. He had called her earlier while she was with her secretary dictating the terms of a draft agreement for the resolution of an out-of-court dispute, just before she went in to announce the good news of the sexual harassment outcome to the senior partners. She was only too happy when both parties had reached this agreement after an initially fierce battle, and she wanted the process expedited before either party reneged. Elizabeth knew that for her client, a new pensioner, this would be a faster and cheaper and a more comfortable way forward for her, for everyone. She had mentioned this during their meeting the day before.

His phone rang and was answered in record time and when they just about got passed salutations, he wasted no time in asking her out on a date. She wondered if that was the Minister's idea of hope and thought. Well, why not. She already knew from Lynette and Pastor Lammy that he was a Doctor, and although she could not remember his speciality, she clearly stated that they were neighbours albeit a long time ago. She could vaguely remember her referring to him as her 'adopted nephew', and from the ride to Susan's a month ago, Elizabeth learnt that he was thirty-eight years old, with no children and currently unattached.

"That would be lovely but unfortunately, I am unable to have dinner with you this Friday." She had not yet heard from Mathew or Susan but knew that apart from sickness, they would not miss their monthly meet-up for anything, or anyone.

"How about Saturday, are you free then?"

"I can't, I'm afraid." She did not want to tell him about her mum, that for the last year, she had reserved her weekends for time with her.

"How about next week?" He was persistent, she could tell.

"Ahh, next Friday looks … Okay." She checked her Google calendar. "Yes, why not."

"Shall I call you midweek and we can finalise our plan, at that time?"

"That would be fine. Take care."

"Lovely to talk to you, Elizabeth. Speak to you soon."

"Bye, Richard." She was at work and did not wish to prolong the conversation and suspected the same for him too.

Elizabeth sat at her desk for a moment, then it occurred to call Susan and Mathew. Susan had promised to meet-up even if her brother was unavailable, but when she rang, her friend was unavailable. It occurred to her to ring in and check up on her mum then, but thought it better to wait until after work, she already had plenty of work to catch up on. The rest of the day was a blur and when she rang to find out how her mum was, she was happy to know she had asked for her that day, which made Elizabeth sad to have delayed because now, she is asleep.

Their time out on Friday was the first time since Isabelle's funeral, and they were all in good spirits except that Susan confessed to have deliberately missed her In Vitro Fertilisation appointment. Paul had gone urgently to Chicago for one of his high-level international Cyber Security meetings and she could not do it without him. She had said that the last cycle left her feeling rather rough.

"You know, the hyper stimulation of the ovaries. It was awful. I didn't want to go through that alone." Both her little brother and friend told her, they understood and reminded her that they were all in it together.

"I know; but hey, come on time to eat!" The eldest of the three perked up.

"Time to eat, it is." Elizabeth echoed. She felt her friend did not want her problem to be at the centre of their time together, again.

"I'm starving." Mathew made a face.

"Mathew, you are always hungry." His sister scolded.

"And he's still so skinny." Elizabeth chimed in as she poked his stomach.

"Got to be prepared to be up at five a.m., three times per week with your personal trainer, if you want this body." Mathew retorted sternly, giving them both the stare.

"No one wants your body." Each girl echoed the other, and both were now in hysterics. They knew what he meant.

"I knew you *heard* me. What do you say we make this a lobster night, on me?" They all knew how much he loved his sea food and neither wanted to deprive him of his treat.

"I'll order a bottle of prosecco or two and some starters?" Susan raised her hand to signal the waiter.

"And, whatever for dessert, that's my treat." The youngest of the three was acutely aware of her financial constraints but refused to be left out of paying her share.

While they waited for their order to arrive, Susan suggested Mauritius as their annual summer week away.

"Just think, in just under six months, for a whole week we could be enjoying its flour-like sand and year-round soothing sun." She told them about a work colleague who had not long returned from the island and that the pictures were amazing.

"I must confess, that does strike an irresistible chord, but you know it would have to be a five-day trip. That is, we or shall I say, I would have to leave on Sunday evening and return late on Friday or early Saturday morning."

"Lizzy, you would be drained – it is a 12Hr flight you know." Susan was quick to point out.

"It's o.k. I want to go with you guys. It will just have to a be a shortened week for me, that's all."

Susan touched her friend's hand then. "But one weekend, Liz-beth, would not cause any harm. Ms Hazel will be simply fine. You know that."

"…and I do, but I would never forgive myself if …" She lowered her head as her voice trailed off.

"I know. I know. A rain check on Mauritius then. There will be other times to go that far. We can stay a bit closer this time around, how about that?"

They knew Elizabeth would not want to miss time with her mum and they all agreed to make other arrangements around her visit to see Hazel. Mathew was quiet. He gave his sister room to poke and if he thought she was going too far he would step in. He did not have to as Susan recognised the pain in their friend's eyes and took it as seriously as it appeared.

After that slight snag, they went on to enjoy a pleasant evening out. It had rained earlier in the day and luckily for them it stopped in time for them to venture out. Elizabeth did not mind the rain, but in small doses only. She hated having to skip puddles and knew that if it rained long enough her mother would not be taken outside. She knew the outdoors was an especially important part of her psychological and physical health and quality of life. After dinner she would check the weather for the weekend. If possible, she wanted to plan what they would do outdoors.

During desert, which Mathew decided to miss, Elizabeth noticed his change in countenance each time he looked at his phone and asked what was wrong, but he told her he was fine. Susan who knew her brother very well, was quick to push.

"Is everything okay, Matt?" The girls could tell he was worried about something and were relieved when he relented.

"It's Claire, she said; let us see … she will be in town next week and asked for us to meet her at yours on Saturday." He looked directly at Susan then poured what was left of the wine.

Susan looked from her brother to her friend, as Mathew emptied the glass. They both knew how he felt about their mother. She left them years ago to pursue her career. Their dad thought she was only going through a phase and would come to her senses later but on his death bed, he knew they should never have married let alone had children. He loved her dearly, but realised later he was only the helping hand she needed to get her career started. He had friends, connections and she used him. Susan didn't speak about her with such venom as Mathew did and one would think she had forgiven her, but it was obvious Mathew couldn't. He had not fully recovered from the feelings of rejection he spoke of every time he mentioned her name and when he saw her at his graduation, he totally ignored her. He had the weight of the father's failing health on his mind then. Later that year when his dad died, and she visited to pay her last respects, he only spoke to her briefly on Susan's and his dad's dying wish insistence. The text from Claire put a slight damper on the night out and Susan drove them all to Mathew's for the night with plans for them all to visit Elizabeth's mum on Saturday, leaving her Sunday to be alone with Hazel.

For Elizabeth, the weekend went by like a flash. In a way, she was happy to return to work but even happier that she got a chance to spend quality time with her friends. She loved being a lawyer and didn't mind helping people like those caught up in domestic violence, and the children who were sometimes all but forgotten in the midst of the divorce settlements. She didn't mind arranging mediation or working collaboratively, it had long been said that, that was her calling; but at the firm, they took on everything or anything the 'big boys' thought was not juicy enough for them, which later landed on her desk. Not worth their time; did not bring in the big money. It made her sometimes impatient to start her own practice. She could not wait to be on her own, choosing and managing her own cases. To be a partner would mean behaving like one of them and she told herself she did not have it in her to be so cold and ruthless. Just then, she wondered what the new case that would land on her desk this week would be. She knew she still had a few cases to close before they had to pack and move the remainder of the office supplies into the larger space a few doors down and realised her new office block was now owned by her 'big brother'! She had insisted that no one in her company was to know of her relationship to the new owner and was very firm with Mathew about that. He could not understand her reason behind it, but she insisted on keeping her personal life away from the office.

On Wednesday when Richard called, she was surprised to be happy to hear from him. They chatted easily but briefly about their respective weekends and without mentioning her mum or giving too much detail about her friends, she told him it was quiet and that she was well rested and happy to be back doing what she loved. They both agreed that since Izzy's funeral, their main goal, was just to focus on each twenty-four hours as opposed to what could happen in a month or a year even.

"That's great." He told her. And before he hung up, he confirmed he would be picking her up at six thirty for dinner at Seven thirty. They were going a little way off, to The Ives. She had heard of The Ives but never been there before and was really looking forward to it. She had not been out on many dates in her adult life and only started some recent years back when in the second of her two-year mandatory training contract at Lansdowne legal office. Elizabeth had always said she was too busy with studies and besides, she had her dates with her friends, 'family' as she most times still referred to Mathew and Susan as.

The week went by smoothly with the estate agent coming around to value the house which she was happy to know the going price, and except for her wondering about Mathew's response to his mum's request she had nothing else on her mind. When Friday came, she left work half day to get a head start on her preparation for her date. Quickly, she attended her hair and nail appointment and was happy to have them all done in time for dinner with Richard. It had been over a year to be precise, since she had been out to dinner with anyone other than Mathew and she wanted to look perfect, *if only for one night*, she thought.

For a while, her main problem was that she couldn't decide whether to wear her hair up or down, then decided on down and when she saw herself in the mirror for the final glance, she was so happy with her choice and couldn't resist taking a selfie which she posted on her 'VIP' what's app chat which comprised of Mathew, Susan and Paul and to which since the funeral, she was thinking of adding Sarah although it was noted that she still hadn't removed Izzy. She smiled also at her intention to show it to her mum tomorrow, during her customary weekend visit. Love heart emojis came back from both her friends as just then the doorbell rang, at precisely six twenty-nine. Before long, she was holding a bunch of red roses as he greeted her with a kiss on the cheek and complimented her on how beautiful she looked.

She was wearing the dark blue midi-shift dress she picked up earlier and black pumps which she had for a while. She had always loved the flattering pointed toe of the shoes with its exposed heel to the sides which on this occasion matched her exposed shoulders. It also had an upturn bow at the back which Elizabeth thought, reminded her of the tail of a very playful kitten and rightly reflected her mood now.

Graciously, he accepted her invite to come in for a quick drink which also gave her time to put the flowers in water before they left out for dinner. Next time, she vowed to tell him where in her line of favourites they fall; but for now, she would show her appreciation - dwelling on, *it is the thought that counts*. He followed her to the kitchen and was very complimentary of the house too. Very quickly, she checked the back door adjoining the conservatory, and confident the lock was firmly in place, flicked on the switch to the outside light and picked up her small Gucci purse waiting on the island. With a quick glance around, led the way out as Richard held the door.

"Thank you," she said politely.

CHAPTER TEN

On Saturday while her mum took one of her many naps, she took the time to reflect on her night out with Richard. She thought he looked nice in his light blue blazer and crisp white shirt opened at the top leaving him modestly exposed. She concluded he had a nice smile but did not appear to want to make it an action he demonstrated often; and when he did, she wondered if it was a bit forced. She thought about how easy it was to tease Mathew but strangely Richard did not seem the type to take that well. That she put all down to possibly nerves. Afterall; it was only the first date; and besides, her friendship with Mathew was different with many more years to it. With a deep sigh she messaged Susan as she looked forward to hearing from them soon. Her message to Susan was all about how lovely The Ives was, that the food was amazing. She only remembered Claire's visit that weekend, when unusually, Susan's simple thumbs up emoji showed up in response. Just then, she wished Izzy were at the other end of the phone, she would love to tell her all about him. It did not cross her mind to speak of him just yet to Susan or Mathew. From experience it was not necessary to arrange introductions so early on, just after the first date. While she had concluded that he scored highly on choice of venture, she insisted the jury was out on personality. So, she really had no idea where it would go. Besides, she had been on a few dates before which died a peaceful death, for various reasons. As she was anti-guy-hopping, she was adamant that she would rather wait. On the way home from her mother's, unsurprisingly, Mathew called. She knew him well enough to know he would want to talk to her about seeing his mum at Susan's earlier.

"It was a pleasant meeting, and that's that." He paused. "What are you doing?"

"I am on my way home."

He was quiet for a while and when she asked if he was still there, he simply said goodbye and that he would see her soon. Her heart raced for her friend. She knew very well just how much he wanted nothing to do with Claire; and was quietly relieved when as the Uber approached, she spotted his silver Porsche outside her house. In fact, she was incredibly happy he was there. She knew how much he detested his mother and the potential effect that had on him. He had let himself in with the key she had given each of them a week after they took her mum to the Care Home.

He was asleep on the couch when she stepped down into the sunken sitting room and figured he must have already been there when he called. Quietly, she made her way upstairs to undergo her ritualistic bath after seeing her mum. The scent of the home she found she still needed to get used to. It had what she referred to as the scent of a hospital or of medicines; she couldn't decide which or was it both; and her mum would also sometimes spill things on herself and needed to be changed each time, which Elizabeth had become accustomed to. Confident she smelled of perfume instead, she proceeded to make dinner for both. Mathew entered the kitchen within minutes of her completing the thirty-minute salmon with pesto crust meal she had done on numerous occasions, one she liked doing particularly as it was quick and easy for her after a long day at work.

"You timed that very well, didn't you?" She teased. "I am just about to plate up and voila, he enters!" She poured two glasses of white wine and served a good portion of what she had prepared, to him. She knew that seeing his mother had taken a toll on him and they sat at the island where he told her, he did not want to ever see Claire again.

"And that's final." She could hear the determination in his voice and was not surprised, she only wondered what she had said to him this time. "As far as I am concerned, she is dead, and that's the way I want it to be. That woman is the most selfish, conceited, unrepentant person I have ever met."

She felt so sorry for him and left her stool immediately to hug him from behind. She thought how he too could easily have been a fostered or adopted child had it not been that he had an extraordinarily strong and caring father to look after him and his sister. Both he and Susan could be in a similar position to the nine-year-old twins she defended those months ago. For a moment, she thought he was crying.

"You know you have to seek counselling." She whispered. She felt him stiffened but he made no attempt at a verbal response. "You must! Or - this will destroy you." When he did not respond, she returned to her original position around the island, to look him squarely in the eye. All she saw was sadness and pain and realised he must have cried earlier because his face was stained, and his eyes were red. Her heart was breaking into unimaginable pieces for him and once again, she did not know what to do.

"You don't have to eat if you don't want to. I'll put it in the oven for later, maybe?" Just then, she could easily pass for the mum he so craved back when he was a boy and possibly still did.

He reached over and poured the wine she gave him in the sink between them and without speaking he went back to where he was when she came home. She texted Susan, to find out what had happened but got no response. Elizabeth was genuinely concerned about her friends. She went to sit opposite him in the couch. The one she had curled like a ball into when she was broken by news of Izzy's death and now, she wondered how to make his pain go away. She searched google for any counsellors away from the area that he could see. She thought that just a few sessions could help him put his feelings into perspective and help him 'remove the cobwebs' to figure out a way forward. After copying a few numbers, she walked across to kneel beside the couch he had managed to stretch his lean six feet body in, with feet hanging off the end handle and his head in the oddest position which Elizabeth knew he could easily get a neck strain from. Gently but firmly, she insisted, he saw a counsellor and to her relief and amazement, eventually, he agreed.

Excitedly, she offered to make the appointment for him and was only slightly bruised when he declined her services. "Send it to me and I will see when I am free." He sounded more asleep than awake which caused her to wonder if he would do any such thing, but she knew it had to be his decision.

"The guest room is ready when you are." She sat with him for a while before she tore herself away and slowly, as if counting each step, made her way up to her bedroom.

Elizabeth hated his mother whom she had met only a few times. Each time Elizabeth saw her, she could see how cold and uncaring and pretentious she was. Claire was the opposite of her own mum, Elizabeth thought, as she continued her ascension and shook her head in disbelief at another case of the awful effects of human selfishness. She figured something must have gone wrong in Claire's childhood for her to walk away from two young children and never looked back. Never one day did she have a fit of conscience to have returned, even if not to be with their father but to fight for them. She knew now Robert would not have given them up, not to her. Not to anyone. He was proud of his son and his daughter; and before he died, he told them so again as he made them swear to look out for each other. No one could ever say they did not live up to that.

Later that night, she had a dream. In the dream, she was walking in her garden with her mum, when she saw a dying orchid plant, she started to cry but her mum smiled and did not seem concerned at all. Her mum told her then, that one of reasons she loved the orchid is, "no matter how bare the orchid plant looks, sometimes one may think it's a whisker from its last ever season - like it's about to die; but honey, it's not. It is simply fine. It is waiting for next year's bloom. In the meantime, it's growing new leaves and new roots once all the mature flowers have fallen off and the old stems have died."

Her mum had dried her tears and told her it would be okay. "You'll see." They hugged each other but Elizabeth held on so tightly that when she woke, she was anxiously holding unto the pillow. Immediately she wanted to see her mum and wondered if something had happened to her. The dream was so vivid. She wanted to share it with Mathew but refrained from disturbing him. She called the care home and they assured her everything was fine. She wondered then, if by some miracle, her mum would be fine - but shook her head knowing that was simply impossible. Without thinking too much about what to wear today, quickly, she showered and dressed. As she evened her breathing and told herself. "It was just a dream."

The following weekend seemed to have come around so soon and before she realised, it was time to see her mum. She was happy as always to be with her and anxious to ask her about the orchid cycle, but Hazel was not having a good day. She didn't know who she was and refused to have her daughter come near her. Hazel shouted for the nurse to call the police and only settled when 'the stranger', was not in sight. Elizabeth knew she could never tell when or how long it would take and so she thought it would be better to go home. There was a mountain of work on her home office desk to catch up on and as she planned on seeing Richard again that Friday. So, she thought it best to get as much done as possible. She had thought of Mathew and if he would indeed seek counselling. She decided to call Susan whose returned call she had missed.

"It's so unfair for her to just walk into our lives when she feels like it, when it's convenient for her to hop across, especially now, when we no longer need her. What about when I was five and Matt was two? Who leaves a toddler and a young child to go trapesing around the world, chasing the next big story? Like, who does that? No wonder Mathew feels it is better not to let himself fall in love. For fear they would leave too." Her friend voiced what she had long suspected. "One would think he's old enough, but that woman has inadvertently thwarted any chances of her son ever being happy with the woman he loves!" Susan was livid and Elizabeth could understand but was shocked at the depth of Susan's anger and her obvious frustration at what sounded like not being able to help her brother. She told her friend how she encouraged Mathew to seek counselling and asked Susan if she would consider that too. "I'll think about it; although, I think I am fine. I am not bothered about that woman, but Matt is so hurt, he hates her! He freezes when she approaches him."

69

Elizabeth closed her eyes at the thought. She remembered the look on his face the night before and after Susan's call, she rang him to see how he was. He sounded hushed as he said he was much better and that he would talk to her later. He reassured her he would be fine. She wondered what he was doing that made him hurriedly put the phone down but decided against disturbing him again.

CHAPTER ELEVEN

Her dates with Richard had increased in frequency and recently, they had started seeing each other midweek too. Whenever they could that is, and called when they could not. She was beginning to rely on his predictable nature and saw him as a stable and welcomed break or an addition to what she sometimes referred to as her monotonous routine of work, home and visits to see her mum every weekend. His disposition could sometimes unnerve her, and she wondered if that seemingly grumpy state was synonymous with most neurosurgeons or surgeons in general. Over the Easter weekend, he took her to meet his parents and both Susan and Mathew were surprised when she told them she would be away on Good Friday coming back on Saturday.

While with her mum last weekend, she could see that she was falling asleep now more often than before and asked the nurse if she was sleeping properly at nights. Convinced by the report that she was, she requested to stay the night. But instead, of leaving on Sunday, she stayed until Monday. After going home for a quick shower and change, she hurried to a planned dinner with Susan, Paul, and Mathew. They had a good time and although she mentioned Richard, somehow, she still did not feel like talking about him. A part of her felt it was not the right time and she did not tell her friends either that she was considering putting the house in Knockholt up for sale. Finally, she had had the meeting with the estate agent and although somewhat lucrative, the Airbnb business was too inconsistent in a village like Knockholt. They told her it was slow, and she acknowledged she could not wait around for the seasonal tourists who descended on the area in droves over the summer period only. She had to be certain she had the money to look after her mum for the time that she had left with her. That was the sacrifice she was willing to make. She would not put a for sale out, for Mathew to see or for anyone to see and to alert her friends, and she did not talk to Richard about it either. She felt it was nothing to do with him. However, she was thinking of speaking to Pastor Lammy about her plans and about a suggestion for a possible cheaper living arrangement. It crossed her mind to board with one of his parishioners and that way she could pay a minimal fee for the furnished room. Several of the parishioners lived on their own and she figured she could be good company to one of them.

It was busy at work, and sometimes she wondered if her boss remembered that she specialised in family law. They seemed to pile more and more cases on that she sometimes felt under pressure. But, after the welcomed pay rise, she was happy to do what she could to prove she deserved it. After the Easter weekend, she told Richard about her mum and reiterated how disappointed she felt in herself for taking her out of their home to live in a care home. She told him that growing up, she thought she would never do anything like that. Amongst her relatives, it was not something they do. In the past, he had said he knew all about the unpredictable nature of Dementia disease and how her mum could experience any one of the many symptoms at any time. She thought he would understand; but when she spoke again about Hazel's full-time care requirements, the demands of which would mean, placing her career on hold, he insisted she could continue with her career later. She wondered if he was listening to her at all. She suspected he did not think of her job as anything to be taken seriously. She was taken aback when he reminded her then about his own mother and sister who had always been housewives and the calmness that added to the home and the balance it brought to family life. She knew that was something she would never be able to do and wondered if that was what he would expect of her should they make a commitment to each other.

It occurred to her then that she was right in taking their relationship slowly. Anyway, she felt she had enough going on between looking after her mother and work. Besides, he said he was busy too. They had missed out on seeing each other a few times as he had preparations underway for his consultancy exams and two months ago when he passed. She celebrated with him and his friends.

The trio had always celebrated each other's birthday and when Susan and Mathew threw a surprise birthday party for her early summer, she had no way of alerting them to her and Richard's budding relationship. Until then, she admitted to herself, she had not yet had the courage to tell all to either Susan or Mathew about the relationship. Instead she focussed on the sale of the house in Knockholt. Even she was surprised to learn that the buyer lived abroad and was generous extraordinarily rich, to have allowed her to stay in the house until end of the year. There was a small rent compulsory upkeep of the grounds written in the contract for her to uphold, both of which she was more than happy to pay and to do. Elizabeth could not believe her good fortune and wondered if she had Pastor Lammy to thank for the buyer's generosity. Relieved that she would not have to worry about money to look after her mother for a few good years, she thoroughly enjoyed her birthday celebration. Had she had time to mope, she would have confronted the deep seated sadness trying to make its way to the fore when she thought of the loss of the house, but she figured with time she would be able to purchase something else. Maybe even in the village and raise a family of her own there. But for now, gaining experience in her career and looking after her mother her reason-detre. The paperwork had only just completed earlier that day, and when she got home to - 'Surprise', there was nothing she could do. Susan demanded she changed very quickly and even made sure she wore the one shoulder midi black dress they bought a while back on one of their girls' shopping trips. "You've lost a lot of weight Lizzy, are you okay?" Susan looked concerned.

"I am okay. Seriously, I am fine."

Richard had come by because it was her birthday and not because he was invited to a party and he too was surprised to see the house full. Elizabeth could tell he was not comfortable with the gathering and her friends including Susan, were obviously shocked as she introduced him. Uncertain why, but she felt somewhat shy about her and Richard's relationship. They wondered why she felt the need to keep it a secret. She confessed to meeting his parents and his sister; and mentioned too that she had taken him to meet her mum who had randomly mentioned his name on occasions, on the few days when Hazel was somewhat lucid.

Susan was first to express how surprised she was at the big reveal and more so of the apparent seriousness of the relationship. Mathew appeared quiet and she wondered if when they were alone, he would host his inquisition. The next day when she spoke to Susan on the phone, Mathew was by her place and chimed in how he had been foolish to have attributed her scarcity, to workload. "But no, you have been rather busy with Mr. head-guy or Mr. brain man – I can't quite understand why he chooses to call himself either of those names. It is almost patronising – don't you think? Him assuming we mere human haven't got a clue as to what a neurosurgeon does." He snickered as she concluded, had she not known better, she would think he was jealous of Richard's achievement as a consultant neurosurgeon.

Mathew made clear his disappointment in what he saw as her lack of trust and much to Elizabeth's surprise, as if Mathew spoke for both, for the first time, Susan said extraordinarily little.

"I do trust you; it's just that I wasn't sure how I felt about him. Come on Matt, it's not really a secret, just a delay."

He reminded her how he would tell her everything, and that he would not have kept that from her. Elizabeth knew what she had done would test their friendship and she hoped it would survive, after all they were all she had.

"Thought we were a family." She could hear the disappointment in his voice and when she spoke again to Susan after work the next evening, Susan only blamed their mum for Matt's emotional state. Elizabeth was not quite sure of the connection but was happy for the distraction away from her and Richard.

A week later and for the first time in months, Elizabeth visited her mum for the first half of a Saturday only. Both girls had a day out, on Susan's insistence. Elizabeth was happy she suggested it. She so wanted to explain to her friend why she was less than forthcoming about her relationship with Richard, she felt she owed it to them to rebuild their trust. That afternoon, they shopped and chatted about Susan's IVF delay, Elizabeth possibly falling in love with Richard and about all her misgivings. Elizabeth was happy her friend did not seem to be holding a grudge.

At lunch they shared kibbeh and Fattoush at their favourite Lebanese restaurant in town; and Susan was obviously surprised when Elizabeth confessed to have sold the house.

I knew you had sold the one but didn't realise you were getting rid of Knockholt too." Susan had kept her face down as if studying something mystical in the cup of tea she ordered after their lunch.

"So, did you get the amount you need to keep looking after your mum?"

"It's enough for at least another two years or so."

"And what would you do then Lizzy? What if she lives for another ten?"

"I don't know, take out a loan or something?" She laughed out loud then, but Susan did not seem to find it funny, and she wondered if that secret was another nail in their friendship.

"You know you should have come to us?" Susan said quietly as she looked her in the eye. Elizabeth could feel her heart pounding but had to admit she was touched. "While we are in full confession mode, anymore secrets, Elizabeth."

"Please Sue, you know I never wanted to burden you or Matt. You have your own … family and soon a baby…" She welled up as she saw the disappointment in her friend's eyes.

"So, when are you moving or is that a secret too? Are you planning on moving in with Richard or something?" Susan was quick with her questions.

"No! definitely not. It is not like that. We are dating and I don't know but…" Her voice trailed off. She did not know what to say. She wondered when did her life become so complicated, or when it would be simple again. For the first time, she missed the regimented style of her childhood home where everything was predictable and safe and she knew what to do and what was expected of her and when her dad would be coming home from his work schedule that was posted on the notice board in the utility area. Not this downward spiral. Since he passed away, then the move to Knockholt, and then, Issy ... and now her mum's care which seems intent on eating away at every penny she had, some of which she wanted to put towards opening her own practice; life could never be more different than she had imagined. Suddenly, she longed for the death of the rose garden, with all its 'prickly-beauty', but knew that to kill the roses would mean death because after all, isn't life the rose garden, the one her mum spoke about time and again? And, she had to admit, she was warned, life was beautiful, but life could be prickly, sometimes more than others and now, she was only - sore. She thought briefly about how bruised she felt and wondered when would the orchid spring again. And for the first time since Issy's funeral, hopeful was the last thing she could bring herself to feel.

They were both sad when their time together ended and hugged each other as they said their long goodbye. On their way home, Elizabeth was a little surprised but happy that they continued chatting on the phone about work and their futures. The journey home seemed unusually short and as she turned the key to her front door, once again she could not shake the ominous feeling when Susan spoke of her fears for Mathew.

"I think that's why he works so hard and quite possibly may never settle down." His sister had said.

"You think that's why he broke up with Cara?" Elizabeth had been left perplexed ever since their breakup, and more so when Susan alluded to him being in love and not being able to be open about it or to even commit. She realised then that there was possibly something she had not been privy to and wondered what Susan knew, but had not said. Could it be that they were scolding her while holding onto theirs? She wondered.

"I've been thinking about that for a long time. I think he's trying to compensate, or something - when really, he should know he is enough, but I guess until you've been in his shoe one will never truly understand the effects of abandonment by a parent. By your own mother." Elizabeth had learnt a lot from the cases she was taking and knew that while Susan appeared to be taking things in her stride, Matt may never fully recover from Claire's selfish actions, and now, that was her primary concern.

"I reminded him about the counsellor you mentioned, and he said he was still *thinking about it*. I do not know, Liz. We cannot force him. He seems alright, I guess." Susan sighed and Elizabeth knew her friend was less than hopeful.

"No, we can't. Anyway, got to run, Sue. Richard will be here any minute and I need a shower, at the very least."

"You two are pretty serious, aren't you?"

Elizabeth realised then, that for some reason, it was taking Susan longer than she thought to process or to accept that they were a couple and wondered why that could be. She wished she could understand why it was so hard. She thought how her best friend's action reminded her of a dad or a parent finding it difficult to let their daughter go and smiled at her friend's concern.

"I like him, Sue; a lot. Like I said today, what happens next, I am not sure. Let us see. However, I would like to give us both a fair shot. Like you did with Paul, and mum with dad and you both have had… and are having in your case, you're happily ever after."

"I know, but please Lizzy… please keep your eyes open. A guy can tell you he loves you but he himself is not even certain what that means while another may not be able to say it but loves you more than himself!" Her friend pleaded. "Please, try not to rush into anything. When you are in love, it is an amazing feeling, not a guessing game; you do know that, right?"

"I promise, I'll take it a day at a time and no I have no plans to rush into anything. I mean, he is a very intelligent man. A brilliant doctor and all. I think my parents would be proud of my choice, don't you think?" She attempted a giggle which she realised had been lost on one of her dearest friends.

"I think your mum is very proud of you, and your dad would be too; irrespective of whomever you choose… but most importantly, that you are with someone with whom you can relate, you can be yourself. Someone who supports you and your choices. Lizzy, someone who knows you and really *understands* you."

"Thanks, girlfriend. My eyes are wide open, Sue. Got to go. Let us talk again, soon. Love you."

"Remember Lizzy, someone who has been burnt by life, or family or, you know - something, may have their guard up when it comes to giving or receiving love, may well not be able to talk about it, you know that don't you?" Susan made a final attempt to push her point home, Elizabeth noticed and snickered at what she described as her friend's ramblings.

"I am not sure what you are talking about, Sue; I do not get that impression from Richard." Elizabeth was puzzled at her friend's statement, which she thought was completely out of context and wondered if she was that bothered about her relationship with Richard to have been so strangely incoherent in her chain of thought.

"Hello?" Susan wondered if the call had been disconnected as there was such a long pause from her friend, and when she enquired if she was still there Susan simply said, "No more secrets." Just then, Elizabeth mused at how much she sounded like the big sister that they all say she is.

"No more secrets."

"Is that the apologetic voice?"

"It is the apologetic voice. Scouts' honour. No more secrets." The younger girl smiled.

Eventually, they said a quick goodbye and Elizabeth attempted to hurry but remembered they did not have a booking anywhere. She decided to cook that evening and when she told Richard of her plan, he was unusually overly happy with that.

"That's a nice surprise." He mused.

She was amazed to see the biggest grin on his face and before she knew it, he kissed her like they were kissing for the very first time.

She offered him a glass of wine, but he declined and surprised her when he chose to help himself instead. He reached for the bottle and she noticed then his shirt was out, hanging loosely around his hip.

"You look comfy," she teased.

"I am feeling comfy, oddly enough." And he kissed her again.

Later, he poured them both a glass and did the place settings as she plated her smoked paprika steak and lentils with spinach.

She lit the candles on the sideboard, in her attempt at recreating their first date night, and except for the dollop of fresh yogurt, he consumed the whole lot.

"Sorry, I am not a fan of yogurt; but that, was amazing." Just then he pointed at the plate. "You are a brilliant cook, Elizabeth." Obviously pleased, he pulled her to him, and this time, she was expecting it.

"I am glad you liked it." It was her time to light up her face with one of her trade-mark big smiles.

After instructing him to remain seated, she cleared the table and wondered off to get desert.

"Oh, dear!" She called out.

"What's the matter?"

"I think Matt must have raided my refrigerator, again! Well, the freezer is empty!"

"Matt? How? Does he have a key?"

"Yes, they both do."

"But doesn't he live like, an hour away? Why or what would he be doing here, and wouldn't you know?" She wondered if she was imagining the unpleasant sound in his voice.

"He tells me he visits their old house regularly for maintenance or something. I believe him so, I haven't pried."

"Oh, okay! Are you saying he comes by when he feels like it, without informing you?" She was sure now; he was not happy.

"Don't you think...?" She paused. She has never seen the need to justify giving both Susan and Mathew a copy of her house keys before, but from his tone, she didn't want anything to negatively alter the mood of the evening and hoped he would feel the same way. She really hoped he would understand. "You know, well anything could happen, that's all, and we are like – family, anyway." Silence ensued. The deafening silence which ensued, unnerved her, and for the rest of the evening, unhappily, she did all she could to restrain herself from talking about the two people who meant everything to her. The very two people who, along with her mum, were the most important people in the world and with whom she had so many of life's experiences. To Elizabeth, they were people she could relate to on all levels, they had a bond which made her wonder again why was sharing Richard with them such a challenge. Was it a bad omen? But, she concluded, that was the relationship she was hoping to one day have with Richard. Again, she recited in her mind, how important it was to give their relationship a fair try. Not long after and she very quickly succumbed to the thought that him being able to express how he felt, was a good sign. The opposite would be borderline oppressive, pure pretence which later, could only hurt them both. He had already made plans to stay the night and as she pointed him to the guest room, secretly she mulled over the idea that she could be treating him unfairly. Could it be that she had these grand visions of love that were unattainable and maybe she should be more realistic – less idealistic? As she enjoyed a leisurely bath, she settled in her mind that as her love for him grew, it would all become easier, clearer to her… to both. For now, she was happy for the companionship. It was a break from the constant worry about money and care home and her mother's illness – a welcomed distraction and for however long it lasted. She was determined to enjoy their evenings out and walks together when he could get away from theatre or she from the pile that seemed to grow each day on her desk. Completely immersed, she promised to think less about him as the disagreeable character he appeared to be earlier and more about him the professional focussed grown up with a hint of the romantic, she knew him to be.

On Saturday, they visited her mum, and again together, on Sunday. She noticed he was quiet on both days but knew he was a reserved character anyway. He also spent most of the time in the day room; but it made her happy that he wanted to be there at all; to be with her, and to see her mum if only for a short visit. She was pleased he made the effort. On Sunday afternoon on the way home, he surprised her when he suggested they stop for a meal. She had long suspected he was the traditional type. His strongly held views on family life left her in no doubt he was what he professed to be. He was clear about his preference for a home cooked meal as opposed to eating out. It was at the end of summer which for Elizabeth, was a bitter-sweet time of year. As autumn approached and winter with its shortened days beckoned; like William Shakespeare, she too thought 'summer's lease hath all too short a date'. She would do anything to hang onto her beloved light skirts, as she bemoaned having to once again don boots and heavy-set coats with layers beneath. She had always found Susan's eagerness to go coat shopping incomprehensible and a total waste of time which was usually accompanied by one of her disapproving facial expressions, that often caused her best friend to break out in a fit of giggles… and sometimes shop all the more. Over the years, Elizabeth had invested in a few which she had recycled time and again and was always happy to pack away as soon as spring peeped through. Just now, she wanted only to hang onto what was left of that whiff of summer air; and later, hopefully, walk along the beautiful cobble holes of her hometown village to catch a glimpse of the fallen leaves as summer waved goodbye. Roasted asparagus with pea and egg salad was Elizabeth's preferred menu, while Richard settled on miso salmon with ginger noodles. Together, they shared a small fruit sorbet as they chatted about his childhood and then explored the intricate nature of his work. When he paused, Elizabeth felt he must have just described a week in the life of a neurosurgeon as opposed to a typical day. She was even more in full blown admiration of him and the work he did. He, more than her, had a religious upbringing and like her had parents who ran a very regimented household. But look how liberal she had turned to be which made her wonder now if there was room for compromise, room to accommodate a modern feminist like her. It did not come as a surprise when she met his parents, how very conservative they were. She had listened as he spoke during their dinner dates about his upbringing and sometimes cringed when he described his mother almost cowering beneath his dad's cumbersome undertones which made her think her parents were pretty laid back and pale in comparison.

"Sounds like not much time for play or interaction with your friends, you know No sleep-overs or play dates? How does it make you feel, having missed out on that?"

"Elizabeth, getting good grades and a successful career comes with being focussed."

"…and I get that…" she interjected but was swiftly cut off.

"A man's worldview is different from…well, that of women. Besides, it is what it is and thinking or talking about it, won't change that." He uttered. "We have to move on with our lives, nothing just happens, there's a reason for everything, and had Claire stayed… Mathew would have quite likely had a worse childhood because she would be miserable. That's what your friend needs to understand. You know, life is not here to give us mums and dads the way we like them."

"Where did that come from?" As quickly as the words left her mouth, she thought better than to have made a comment which most often led to them having an argument, primarily as it related to Mathew. While deep down she concurred with only a fraction of what he said as it related to Mathew, somehow most of what he said did not resonate with her ideas of the way life should be. Again, she felt the need to defend someone with whom she felt she shared this 'secret fraternity', a fraternity borne out of loss and years of friendship; but quickly resolved, there was no point. She knew it was unlikely she would win a conversation of that nature, with Richard. She realised then how determined Richard had been to appear not to accept, what ordinary health professionals know, that an absentee parent can cause lifelong harm to any individual. She wondered what happened in his childhood to have made him so cold, so aloof towards Mathew; to show such indifference to her dear friend's plight. Was there something more sinister going on in his mind? Elizabeth sighed deeply and purposefully decided to be in the moment and leave all assumptions at bay, until facts moored in.

"My parents' idea of me being focussed and cultured, I guess, was to ensure I maintained a 'get on with in attitude.'" He snickered sarcastically as he shared what she thought was important insightful information he thought she needed to hear. As as the evening progressed, he made some insightful revelations: about his childhood and growing up almost in isolation. Elizabeth closed her plate, but opened her mind to the brilliant consultant sitting opposite her and wondered, if it were at all possible that he was insecure or even, jealous, of the attention Mathew got from Susan and her. She shook her head feeling sad for him. To her, suddenly he appeared like nothing but a lonely brilliant young man who made such success in his professional life but was hardly making headways in his personal life and she blamed his upbringing for his success as well as his thought process. Now she longed to show him there was happiness to be had if he could only relax and open a little. She vowed to show him how. Soon after, her resolve, she willed herself to focus instead, on the note the conversation commenced on and admitted, he was not usually this talkative. She suspected he wanted to tell her more about himself, as if to let her into his life. The not so admired part of him, and she smiled. Adjusting herself to be more relaxed in her chair, she allowed him the space to help her better understand him. *Well, if that's what he needs to do,* she thought as she leaned in. He reminded her how it was always his dream to be a consultant neurosurgeon and she noticed how similar to his mother he was, whom he obviously worshiped and although he denied it, she was adamant his views were shared with hers. Elizabeth had concluded her boyfriend's mother was very conventional, a traditionalist and wondered if the dynamics of that household contributed to him acting older than his thirty-eight years. Albeit, he looked like any typical post millennial. He took care of himself, that was obvious. As he spoke, she noted that familiar hint of melancholy, something she identified in his tone. Something about him as he explained his lack of relationship with his dad, whom he admitted to having this huge amount of respect for, but also who he said was never home.

"Dad, he gave himself to the ministry, always busy with his parishioners." Again, she was beginning to feel a new level of empathy towards him, and after the meal she was happy to accompany him out onto the terrace, where they were in full view of passers-by. Sated and relaxed, she ordered a pot of organic green tea and rested her head against the back of the chair. She had forgotten about the tea when she was disturbed by the waiter, and only then she noted Richard must have ordered the slice of pecan pie placed neatly between the tea set. The waiter poured her a cup and she inhaled the aroma deeply as she failed miserably in her attempt to resist a piece of the pecan pie which almost by magic, seemed to have made its way onto their table. Armed with the cup of tea in one hand, and half-a square of pecan pie in the other, Elizabeth squinted as she looked out over the makeshift picket fence like a wooden divider separating the terrace from the pedestrians. Peering across it, she rested her view on the people in the distance, the ones on the grassy path next to the basket-ball court, playing what looked like table tennis or something of the kind. She thought and wondered too, how best could she maintain a bit of this summer magic, during the winter months.

CHAPTER TWELVE

"Will you marry me?" She knew she heard something, a voice... but decided that is not at all possible. "Elizabeth, will you marry me?" In her mind, it came from somewhere – out there – out where she was looking, perhaps? Could it be that I can hear that boy's voice from here? With furrowed brows, she questioned herself. Then it dawned on her that she was not alone; she was in the company of the man she'd been dating for almost a year. Very slowly, she turned her head to meet his gaze but instead met his outstretched hand barely holding the box she somehow missed when he first asked.

"What, are you serious?" She chuckled. She was not quite expecting it; neither was she expecting it to be done this way, but she has come to accept that Richard was not the 'bells-and-whistles' type of guy. He had strong opinions; some she didn't necessarily agree with. So did her dad, but nonetheless her parents had what her mum said was 'an amazing twenty-seven years'. Now, she was determined to give her and Richard a fair shot. She accepted, "Yes, yes I will marry you."

"Yes?" He smiled at her and she smiled at him as they both leaned in for a kiss. He placed the ring on her left hand from across the table, and with another cup of organic green tea poured, they toasted. "To us."

She echoed that, "To us!". Afterward, like two shy little kids meeting for the first time, they were both quiet for a while. Not long, and her thoughts had once again sprung to life. As she admired the modest size square cut diamond on its thin gold band, she reflected on the stability that Richard would offer and how life with him would be different. At least she knew she would not be alone, and she welcomed that. She would find some way of getting around his idiosyncrasies, she was sure of it. She smiled at the thought of him going down on one knee for a conventional proposal and knew deep down, no way would he have done that. Instantly, the smile left her face.

Susan and Paul came to mind. She was surprised at her chain of thought but embraced it nonetheless, she reminisced on Susan's engagement on the night of her graduation from university. How everyone whose names were supposed be below hers were moved up and she was reallocated a seat at the end of the queue. Her friend was furious for not being told why and as she could not leave the hall to enquire, she could only sit still and be on her best behaviour. Until, finally, they said her name. Not one to hide her feelings, reluctantly, she approached the podium with almost lofty disdain but with the most practiced smile she could muster under the circumstances. The chancellor had just handed her the certificate when everyone in the auditorium, stood up, singing- "I think he wants to marry you", to the tune of Bruno Mars' and then she saw him, in the main aisle walking towards her saying how much he had loved her since he first laid eyes on her with her curly hair and big brown eyes. That he had never been able to get her out of his head. He had reached the base of the steps to the podium by then where he knelt on one knee and popped the question, "Susan Jane Roberts, will you do me the honour of becoming my wife, will you marry me?"

Susan had told them, the weekend after at Mathew's, how that night she experienced her highly probable once in a lifetime state of complete and utter speechlessness. And, both Elizabeth and Mathew nodded in agreement, as they gave their version of events. Susan told them how her brain froze and how thankful she was that in the end she managed to nod in response. Elizabeth chuckled as she described how it was obvious to everyone that her voice had stubbornly refused to return from whence it had taken flight while the whole auditorium found its' from somewhere within the hush which ensued Paul's speech. After awaiting her response with bated breath, they erupted in shouts of, 'YEAH!' and whistles and screams that were loud enough to pop one's eardrum. Amid tears and hugs, they all celebrated the end of an era and the beginning of two for Susan.

Elizabeth long suspected Richard was not that kind of guy. Another smile escaped her now and she looked at him again. For the first time since he slipped the medium sized rock onto her left hand, she could imagine herself being his wife.

"Let's go for a walk?" He urged.

"Why not?" She thought how tender he could be sometimes and concluded, He was actually okay.

They held hands as they left the black velvet box on the table and set out to wander, going nowhere in particular. She loved the quiet life, the predictability of the village. The spirit of community. Everyone looked out for everyone; and as they walked hand in hand, they nodded and waved and said hellos.

"Come on, young lady. I have a two-hour journey ahead, and an early meeting in the morning." He urged. Their walk had taken them further than planned but all along Elizabeth was acutely aware of his two-hour journey home.

"And, I can feel the evening chill," She quivered then, and briskly they made their way to his car.

"Happy?" He enquired.

"Happy," She replied.

There it was again, that search for a type of peace. The kind she suspected she would have in the ensuing days. This, like everything else would, she suspected, take some getting used to. With that, she managed to convince herself that from seeing her mum to suddenly being engaged it was hardly likely that she would feel any different than she did then. After all, leaving her mum at any time, always left her feeling somewhat bereft.

The short journey home occurred in no time and this time, when he opened the passenger door, he kissed her forehead as if he knew of her thoughts, and that was his attempt to put her mind to rest.

It was late in the evening, after Richard left, and she felt that familiar wave of loneliness. It was similar to that which she experienced after Susan and Mathew went to their respective homes and she was left on her own for the very first time. The day after they took her mum to the residential care home for people with Dementia. And, once again, she was looking forward to Monday. To be doing what she loves, with the team she had come to rely on which she told Mathew, 'cracks her up' in bed that night as she applied a large dollop of moisturiser to her face and hands. Smiling, she repositioned the simple diamond ring Richard had given her earlier that evening and wondered how everyone would react to the news of her engagement. She suspected neither Susan nor Mathew were even close to being enamoured with Richard, but she hoped her friends would eventually warm up to him, for her sake. At least, respect her choice. She knew her mum's routine very well; knew she would be snuggled in bed by then, and with her night light out she purposed in her mind to call the home first thing in the morning.

CHAPTER THIRTEEN

The usual morning meeting at Stevens and Stephenson's Solicitors was in progress. As she was skimming over the morning brief, Elizabeth's phone buzzed. It was Mathew.

"I thought you didn't like roses?"

"I don't," she texted back.

"When are you going to tell your boyfriend that they are *not your 'type'*? More secrets?"

"What are you doing at my house?"

"You need your house cleaned, don't you?"

"Oh no, I forgot to leave the key out for Lucille. Thanks, Hun. Anyway, you need to start telling me when you are coming by."

When he did not respond, she followed up with, "Richard and I are engaged!"

"Thanks for keeping that one a secret, too. Everything about you and Richard is one big secret." She could sense the emotional blackmail coming on.

"It only happened on the weekend, on Friday, no Sunday!"

"Make up your mind. The weekend, Friday, Sunday… whatever! Does not matter! Congratulations!"

"We can talk about it when we meet this Friday."

There was another long pause before he replied.

"I will be in St Bart's, with friends."

That for her, was a surprise. She was completely thrown by that. They had never forfeited their meet-up in all the years since university, a fact that had led even Richard to dismay. Somehow, they had continued, and now, for Mathew to renege on their agreement, and in such a nonchalant manner. She had to admit to herself, that hurt her deeply.

"Got to go. Lucille can let herself out. I have a meeting."

Frustrated and discombobulated, she laid the phone firmly on the page she had gotten to before he texted. It occurred to her that he had something on his mind which he needed to deal with and decided that texting was not the appropriate way to allow him to talk about it; "it will not resolve whatever is on your mind, Mr Roberts." She muttered to herself.

Elizabeth had remained puzzled at Mathew's obvious moodiness and again questioned what could be the cause. She knew he may not have forgiven her for keeping her and Richard's relationship a secret for so long. Especially, when they are meant to be best friends, family even; which had broken their -until now- unspoken, no secrets rule. Trust and loyalty had always been the hallmark of their relationship. It was the common bond on which they prided their friendship. And now, even after her truce-weekend out with Susan, she continued to wonder if by withholding information, she may have caused irreparable damage to their friendship. A possible damage to if not hers and Susan's, then quite possibly hers and Mathew's. She closed her eyes then, in utter dismay at the thought.

"Are you okay, you seemed very distracted in there?" Her distraction and subsequent lack of involvement in the meeting, had clearly not gone unnoticed by one of the senior partners.

"Sorry, it's my brother."

"Your brother, thought you were an only child?"

"I am. It's complicated."

"I am a lawyer! My speciality is, '*complicated*'! So?"

"I have been close to him and his sister ever since sixth form and they're as close to family as I may ever have." The thought of keeping work and private life separate, briefly crossed her mind, and she blamed her suddenly found loose tongue on the temporary lack of oxygen brought on by the considerable effort she now employed, in her effort to keep pace with the other party's questionable brisk walking, enroute to their respective offices.

"Well, whatever it is, in those meetings, 'we', we women, we either use our voice or lose it. Do you understand?" She could tell, Misha, the only female senior partner, was not impressed, and she blamed Mathew for his intrusion. "We, '*we women*', we have come too far a century on, to be knocked back another century by such silly moves. Moves like distraction, like not keeping your eyes on the ball, those can cost you a lifetime to put right." Ben, one of the two hoping to make partner sometime soon, had asked her out a few times, but she had turned him down; and for a while, the others were aware of his crush on her. He made it obvious, he could not bear to keep his eyes off her in the meetings, but she was never interested and made it equally obvious she did not find his advances endearing. Others, like Misha, who thought his attitude was highly unprofessional, praised Elizabeth for not entertaining that type of relationship at work. From experience at Lansdowne, she knew it could get messy, and besides, she had never been attracted to him. "You let up and those men," Misha was wagging her index finger now, "The Lionels and the Lucases and co. walk all over you and you lose all credibility. Before you know it, you are left feeling marginalised and inadequate. And you know the wort thing about it, with all your gift and intelligence, you end up sleeping with one of them as your meal ticket! NO! The feminist movement has made monumental strides, but there is still a lot of work to be done regarding our rights as women in the workplace. Do you understand what I am trying to say to you?" This time, she was even more forceful. Elizabeth could easily tell who was the fitter of the two as Misha, who was not long-ago milliseconds away from a trot, was nowhere as breathless as she had become.

"I am so sorry. You are right, I do understand. Thanks for that." Obviously out of breath, Elizabeth was close to shaking.

"Anyway, what's that, a rock?"

"I got engaged!" Misha was clearly in no mood for small talk, Elizabeth observed. She knew better than to continue the account of how it came to be on her left hand.

"Congratulations. Was that him being a pain, and causing you to be distracted?" Without waiting for an answer, Misha hastened on. "Maybe that ring will help you to get back on track – you know, refocused." They had reached the older woman's office now, where she all but ordered the younger girl to sit. "When you first came here, you were bright and witty and full of ideas; but somehow you seem to be a wilting violet. And yes, I get it, I know your mum is in a care home, and all that can be tough; but is there something else going on? Anything you are aware of that could have brought this new version of you to the fore? It's almost like you are always questioning your decisions; and don't get me wrong, they are primarily good ones. I mean right decisions, but you seem not to be sure of the attorney you are. Is everything okay, Elizabeth? Do you need some time off to deal with the whole engagement and mum situation?"

Elizabeth had always admired Misha for her strength and tenacity, like she did Susan, and although she thought they could both sometimes overreact... in a way, she was happy for that moment to be able to at least get close to the woman who headed her department. Someone she had admired, from afar.

"No, I am not particularly concerned about my mum except that I am …" She was tempted to say how she had been travelling to see her mum a lot more lately as well as making a two-hour journey midweek to see her now fiancé and together with Mathew's recent disposition, they must all be taking a bigger toll on her than she thought… but; she didn't wish to be at the centre of office gossip. Nor did she want to jeopardize working at one of the biggest law firms in the city. Not only did she love what she did but, she also needed the experience. Elizabeth knew that the wide variety of cases that were presented to the firm daily could almost guarantee she would get the experience she needed. It was a well-respected law firm, and she was lucky to have been one of the few to have made it past the third stage of the interview. Every so often, she remembered the gruelling process leading up to her receiving her first paycheque and smiled at being given the opportunity to work there. She was also hoping the name would help her as a good reference for luring her future clients to her own practice. "I promise, Misha, I will make some changes. There is a lot going on, but nothing I can't handle."

"Come and see me after lunch," She all but commanded. "We have a case to look over. Mark Lanely, ring any bells?" With a wave of the hand and a pointed stare, Elizabeth knew she was dismissed.

"How could it not. He's evil. What does he want now?" She muttered to herself, as she traversed the long corridor on her way to her office at the far end. *Must be the girls. Maybe he wants the twin back.* Her mind was racing, and suddenly she couldn't wait to meet with the boss after lunch. Very quickly, she instructed the office assistant, "Please reschedule Jason Mapp, I have a meeting with Misha immediately at one. Thanks, Pearlina!"

The rest of the day went by without her taking a lunch break and it was late evening when she remembered to tell her mum the good news. The thought of stopping by on the way home did play on her mind, but it later occurred to her that while it may not be too late to visit, her mum would have already been put to bed. She set a reminder on her phone to call the home just before lunchtime tomorrow.

Mathew's announcement weighed heavily on her mind. All evening into the morning she was left puzzled and began to blame herself for the apparent alteration to their friendship. On the way into the office, she texted Susan to confirm Mathew's plans to go to St. Bart's from Friday. The phone rang several times. Elizabeth was about to abort the call when her friend answered.

"Hmm, last time we spoke, he told me he would be leaving on Sunday. Unless I misheard. He can't go anywhere, we always meet-up. Except for me when I'm faced with the realities of, or shall I say, my fertility challenges." She could hear Susan's chuckle and knew that starting their family was always on her mind. The second round of IVF had failed to produce a baby and both she and Paul have decided to give themselves a break from trying for a while.

"I'm engaged." She wanted to get it out before she forgets.

"WOW, great! Are you serious? when did that happen?" Elizabeth heard a delayed squeal and was happy her friend sounded excited for her.

"On Sunday, after we visited Mum's. We had a late lunch, and then he popped the question."

"That's... that's great, Lizzy!" She could tell Susan was not expecting that. "You sound very excited and that's good. Look, I am happy for you and it goes without question, I am the maid of honour; but first, you have to come over later and tell me all about it. Details!"

"Thanks, Sue. And before you get your hopes up, Richard is a more conservative guy, you know that, right?"

"Is that another way of saying – 'socially challenged?'"

"Susan!"

"I'm just saying, Paul is the only crazy person around here so no surprise there."

There was a notable pause from Elizabeth which led Susan to ask "You're not upset, are you?"

"No, just looking forward to this New Year, and to my next chapter, that's all."

"This is meant to be the happiest time of your life. Please Lizzy, enjoy the moment. You are only doing this once, right? Remember our long chats about the 'till death do us part marriage? So, if you are happy, I am happy."

She managed to convince her friend she was happy and they proceeded to talk a while longer. Susan wanted to know if there were any possible dates, venues, and colours; but Elizabeth hadn't decided on any of that yet. The one thing she knew was it would mean the world to her if her mother were alive to see her walk down the aisle, "Even if she didn't understand but just to have her there, Sue."

"I understand, Liz, I do. And, she will be here to see you walk down the aisle. Just, please, don't rush into anything."

"I promise, I won't."

Elizabeth was somewhat relieved when the conversation took a lighter turn and they spoke mainly about their respective roles at work. Before hanging up, they made plans to see each other over the weekend. On Sunday, after a shortened visit to see her mum. They both knew now, and she felt much happier. She fumbled to find the allocated pocket for her phone and did another one of her deep inhale then exhale routines. Finally, she tucked her phone inside its holder which eventually made contact with her hand and somehow seemed much further on the inner aspect of her dark-red tote, than usual. Then, hurriedly, she made her way home. Along the way, she tried to, but couldn't shake the feeling that something was wrong with Mathew. She wondered what could have happened. He had come around since Claire's last visit. In fact, it had been a while since they spoke about her. He had not mentioned her at all, and neither had Susan, which led her to believe he was attending counselling. It was unlike him to be so unreasonable. She wondered if it was to do with any of his business ventures. He had problems before with last minute delays which threatened his relationship with some of his key stakeholders but he remained civil throughout. She could only conclude, it was all to do with Claire. Claire was at the root of all his troubles.

Mathew had once told her how seeing Claire made him so angry. He knew she was only after something. There was never a touch of the hand, or a kiss when he was a child or a meaningful hug. The few tender words at his graduation meant very little, in fact nothing at all. He knew they weren't ever going to be part of each other's lives. The emotional landscape between them was too wide and he had to learn to live with that. The only admiration he had for her as a young boy was how beautifully dressed she always was and not even her physical beauty appealed to him. The lack of a mother-son bond had affected him deeply and had an impact on every female relationship he had ever had too. And now, it made her sad to know not even theirs was immune to its effects. She wasn't sure what to do but she wasn't sure invading his space to hound him for an explanation, was the answer.

Six months until the wedding, and plans were in progress. Between several telephone conferences and three times in person, Elizabeth had her eyes set on a late spring wedding but first they had to get through Christmas, her favourite time of year. Already there was a firmly established relationship with the wedding planner Richard had, to her surprise, contracted, and who turned out to be one of his parents' parishioners. Although pleased with the progress, she remained cautiously optimistic. On the occasions they had met, Richard had professed to being too busy to join them but promised to be there at the next. She was aware of some dialogue between the planner and her fiancé but was adamant meeting as a team could not be substituted, and when she conferred with Susan, her friend declared, "That is not a good sign! All I'm saying is, Liz, if one partner doesn't care about the details, that is not usually a good omen." Susan said bluntly. Elizabeth's valiant attempt to refute her friend's insinuation, was met with cynicism. She told her friend that her fiancé did care, but was simply a terribly busy man. Susan told her, "She didn't sound convinced of that herself."

"He cares; he's just very busy that's all." She reiterated. "Anyway, he trusts me to take care of the details. Surely, I am mature enough to do that, don't you think, big sis?" Elizabeth's attempt at a caustic response did not deter her friend, who proceeded in the same vain.

"While I am not expecting him to be bogged down with all the minute details, he is expected to be *engaged* with the process. You know that right, Lizzy? It shouldn't be left to just you." Her friend shot back. "Or it will be you managing the house and the kids too and he – with his very important job- simply brings home the bacon and thinks that's enough. Don't forget, he already thinks your career is secondary!"

"Susan, please. It's not quite as dichotomous as that – there are some grey areas to this as well."

"All I am saying is, I understand that operating on someone's brain may not appear to be as important as representing a sexually abused victim in court but, it is – one is to do with fixing the person physically while the other is psychological in nature - but they are both of tremendous help to the individual, and it's about time some people stop seeing themselves as a demi-god and all else as mere mortals."

"Susan, that's not quite right. He is at a conference in Berlin." She did not want to add to her friend's doubts by admitting that Richard's parents told him, she is a bright girl and beautiful too but that they thought the relationship was 'potentially dangerous for their son.' A bit of fact Richard's brother in law was quick to relay. "Oh," he had continued, "They weren't too fond of me when I came along and look – twelve years later and his sister and I are still together." They had hoped he would have married someone actively involved in the church not a 'visitor', like Elizbeth, but according to Peter, Richard had insisted, it was his decision, and not theirs.

"Oh, sorry – but he does make you wonder."

"Why are you always so anti-Richard, what's that about. Surely, you want to see me happy, don't you?"

"Lizzy, I do. Mathew and I both do. But you have to promise to take things slowly. Be careful, that's all I am asking you to do."

"Speaking of your brother, any word from him yet?"

"Last time we spoke, he was busy with the renovation of his new office." She sighed, then chuckled. "His headquarters, as he calls it." Then sighed a louder version of the one earlier.

"Sounds like he's okay, then." Elizabeth probed.

"He is … kind of. Why don't you call him? Give him a call. You know he loves speaking to you, his voice of reason."

Susan had agreed to be maid of honour and was clearly taking her roles as longtime friend, adopted big sis turn chief bride's maid, very seriously. Elizabeth had threatened never to forgive her if she were to decline the role, for any reason, other than some *major illness*. Since Izzy, they had been careful to stay clear of the use of a 'certain word'. Both would rather not tempt death, as they noted a biannual trend in funeral attendance either in the family or outside of it.

"I know Susie, I know." Elizabeth made one last attempt to appease her friend, hoping to sway her – Richard's way. "He promised me he will be at the next meeting. I'll keep you posted." Elizabeth was near exasperated. She had long suspected that her longtime friend was not particularly fond of her choice of partner, but she did wonder about Richard's absence at the meetings. With just about six months to go before the big day, she was hoping he made more of an effort to be part of the planning.

She knew he was not particularly pleased with her decision to stand her ground and not give in to his demand. It was on account of his forceful way of asking that she stayed by his place that she recalled his cavalier attitude towards her career. They both knew the journey would entail a two-hour commute backwards and forwards to her office every day and she shook her head in determination to support his decision which was in the best interest of his patients; but was left baffled that somehow it did not seem to occur to Richard to offer her the same support. In the end, she knew being with Richard closer to his patients meant her being further away from her mother and from work, neither of which she was willing to sacrifice. Standing up for herself may have indicated defiance or a lack of compromise, but that was a chance she was willing to take.

He was on-call sometimes and she understood that which made his choice of location much more important. It had to be within half an hour or shorter for him to get in and scrubbed for theatre, in time to save a life. She had told him time and again, in case of an emergency, she wouldn't want someone to die because of her selfishness. He hugged her in celebration of her sensitivity while the inward raging debate grew even louder and she sighed between faint smiles wondering, *why must everything be so complicated.*

Elizabeth had told Susan that she was happy with a small wedding. In fact, she admitted she thought it would be just the two of them and a witness and that sometimes a part of her felt that that was what Richard would prefer. She did not tell her friend how hard it was to convince Richard to have the fifty guests. He was however, happy to have her soon to be sister-in-law as a bridesmaid and understood her choice of Mathew who appeared happy to be one of the Ushers; while Richard's brother in law had agreed to be the best man.

Together, they could not decide on a flower girl as Sarah could not confirm hers and little Maya's attendance just yet, while Richard's friend had agreed for his son to be the ring bearer. Elizabeth soon discovered that blue was Richard's favorite colour, and as he was not one for brighter shades, she confirmed with Susan, her decision.

"I have decided it's better to continue with blue as the main colour throughout."

"You do know a wedding is to, as far as possible; fulfil the bride's fantasy, right?" Her friend thought she was giving far too much thought to Richard's needs and not enough to her own and seemed determined to make that known.

"You bullied poor Paul; I am not about to do that!" Elizabeth told her. Laughing hysterically.

Susan reminded her of a few truths in any relationship, according to her. "A happy wife is a happy life. Please remind your man of that and by the way, don't forget there are many more fish in the sea."

"Oh! And what about compromise?" Elizabeth rolled her eyes at her friend then.

"Yes, but, not on my wedding day! I plan on walking down the aisle only once."

"I've already been 'down the aisle.'" Elizabeth muttered, and only then a hint of sadness entered her otherwise upbeat demeanor. Wedding plans had a way of increasing the frequency with which she thought of her late friend.

"Aww, honey you know what I mean." They knew Elizabeth would find any loophole to speak about Izzy's passing. She sometimes reminisced about the funeral too, and Susan was happy with that except for when she teared up, wishing she was with Isabelle to say goodbye. That was the part Elizabeth was finding the hardest, to which Mathew had always reminded her, in time she too would find her peace.

Had she been speaking to anyone other than Susan, she would probably have admitted her concern at his absence from all the meetings. Six months was no time in which to plan such an important event, such a big day, and she was becoming increasingly concerned. Days like today her mother's words would come back to her forcibly, and she could hear Hazel's voice telling her, "That's what you do", she told her daughter, "You will never find the perfect person, Orchid. Your dad was not perfect, but I made sure when he came home, after each of those long-haul flights, he came home to a happy home, quiet and filled with food and plenty of relaxation. He had an important job you know, he needed to focus. He had lives in his hands," and like her dad, Richard too, had lives in his hands. Hazel's advice had come a time long ago as they meandered through the well-manicured garden at their then new home. She knew her mum was proud of her dad and now, Elizabeth was more determined that whatever happened, she would give her relationship with Richard a fair chance. While wishing she could talk through her confusion with her mother now, or with Izzy even, she knew Izzy would have found something about the seriousness of it all, to make her laugh.

Susan was quite different: more forthright, unafraid and that was some of the things both girls loved about each other. The way they balance each other out, like yin and yang. The water – Elizabeth, helps to deescalate the fire – Susan, whom her younger sibling and husband often called the mum of the three, particularly when she had been reported on by Elizabeth. Both she and Matt had long concluded how much Paul was crazy about their big sister and would do anything for her. Everyone knew he had loved her since high school, when he stood up in the classroom in the tenth grade to claim her as his, and later, he did ensure she was.

They sometimes reminded each other of his very unorthodox method of proposing and applauded his efforts to have succeeded at convincing the faculty to go ahead with his 'out-of-this-world' engagement plan. Like Elizabeth, everyone who knew them, loved the way they looked at each other. The way they always held hands every chance they got and not long ago, she wanted that for herself too. She had long since resigned herself to the fact that, all men are packaged differently and that Richard was quite different from Paul, or even Mathew. Amidst it all, Richard was stable, kind and together they could make a decent home for their children, a life her parents would have been proud of.

She could see some similarities between Richard and her late father, and how unlike her mum she was and mused at the thought of Linette, no blood connection but so much a representation of the type of woman she would like to be. She snickered to herself as thoughts of a possible cross-genes being the only likely explanation.

Before they hung up, Susan had confessed to having cancelled another one, of her IVF appointments and Elizabeth was sad for her. Everyone in the circle was concerned she may have given up all hope of ever having a child of her own. Paul insisted that was not the case and that they wanted to wait a while before trying again. Although both admitted that she was still young enough to try, Susan wanted to wait. "I am looking forward to a, let us say, I'd rather not have a fretful Christmas. The year has been a very eventful one, I'd love to have a peaceful Christmas." She told Elizabeth.

"I hope so too, Sue." Finally, something they could both agree on.

They could not remember ever being strangers. As it were, they became instant friends. Both had always been happy to have each other and although somewhat strained in recent times, deep inside, Elizabeth knew their bond was stronger than ever and was hopeful Mathew would come around. In Elizabeth's world, real friends like Izzy and Sue and Mathew, did not come knocking on one's door every day. Many relationships are unidimensional, but theirs had always been reciprocal and in Elizabeth's view, she had been fortunate to have received so much from her friends. So much more than what she was sometimes able to give in return; which, in their view, that was so not the case.

Over the years, they had their share of spontaneous adventures and while Elizabeth was thought to be the quieter of the three, they nonetheless shared a similar humour, taste in food and set of values. They could sometimes appear to read each other's minds and could count on each other's honesty. And later, in the week when she next spoke to Susan, she was not surprised at her observation.

"I've been watching you become increasingly frustrated with the midweek journey when you go to see him; and I'm flabbergasted, to say the least, that you are even considering a possible change of firm. What – to please him? Lizzy, then what? You become his housewife? Why doesn't *he* retire, and baby sit then? When that time comes around?"

Elizabeth snickered at the picture her friend just painted. In fact, they both laughed out loud.

"Susan, you are used to having things your way all the time and no one has ever asked you to compromise. His job is important to him and yes mine is too and no I am not saying I am going to become a house wife for goodness sake. But what if I can work from home two days and two days from the office and get Fridays off, that could work, couldn't it?"

"I think you are giving up too much. You will have to travel all that distance each morning and evening."

She had thought about that a few times. She knew leaving Stevens and Stephenson's was not something she could contemplate right now, not when setting up her own practice was still one of her primary goals.

"I mean, can he compromise and stay by you alternate weeks or something? I don't know, but at least you'd get to share the challenges associated with such a long commute until you establish your practice or he chooses a hospital closer to you. Then relocates or something." She paused then "I mean, Knockholt could do with a good head doctor, don't you think?" She chuckled.

"I understand where you are coming from, Sue; but it's all hypothetical. Nothing is set in stone, and I could always set up my practice in his community, couldn't I? It's a nice neighborhood." Elizabeth could tell Susan was not about to make this easy for her and she was not sure she wanted it to be. There were many things she needed to think about and found herself procrastinating on. Sometimes she could even hear Misha's voice in her head, 'a fraction of yourself.'

"I think you are missing an important opportunity to have these discussions now. An opportunity to ask the difficult questions, to seek clarification and work out between you, your non-negotiables. Lizzy, after the wedding… it will be too late. I mean, why do you have to choose blue? Why not make it the beautiful autumnal hew you really want … with – a hint of blue?"

95

"It's too much, I don't have the strength. Work, planning a wedding, mum, Izzy; I am done. I am tired. You are right; this is a conversation to be had and I will, just not right now." She sighed exasperatingly.

Elizabeth knew her friend was right, and she wanted to address it all, but in time. She did not plan on having this conversation with anyone just yet. Not until she had had a chance to have it with Richard. She felt she had time, but to Susan, that time was now.

Her midweek battle with traffic during her two hour journey to see her fiancé' continued as did her telephone calls with Susan which had become increasingly focused on the goings on in Elizabeth's world; and while she was mostly happy to share her thoughts and feelings, hopes and dreams, she was less so in receiving the hard truths disseminated by her bestie.

After what seemed like a hard-fought battle, Elizabeth was happy to report that she had decided to stay at her place and Richard would travel up alternate weeks instead. Reluctantly, Richard had agreed to alternate. They both knew this may not work and that it depended on him not being on-call the week he was to come to hers, but for now at least, together, they had fallen the first big tree in the forest.

"You are a kind, caring and amazing person, Lizzy. You are above reducing yourself for the sake of companionship or out of fear or whatever reason. You deserve to be queen in someone's life, certainly not second to their needs." There was an unmistakable tenderness in her best friend's voice, and she knew all was forgiven.

"I Love you, Sue. Sometimes, strength fails me -but, very soon this will pass." Elizabeth was almost overcome by her friend's love and made a valiant attempt to save what was left of her mascara. Afterall, it was not yet end of the workday and there was another client meeting her on Teams.

"… and it is about time you put you first, Lizzy. He is not going to change; the Richard you see now is who he will be long after the dress is taken off. Already, he wants you to change your job and be a housewife, a replica of his mum no less and his dreary sister! What did his vicar parents do, cast a spell on their kids or something? Goodness me, they are both so bland. I mean, they are brilliant very educated but, hmm."

"Stop! Just stop, please, stop! Stop talking like that, please! One minute, you are kind and compassionate and the epitome of friendship; and the next, friendship appears inconsequential to you broadcasting your views. For heaven's sake, this is of my own volition; and Susan, you must respect my choice. And – my choice is to give our relationship a fair shot. That is all I can do. We have plenty of time to talk about everything, anything and I will!" Elizabeth was finding her friend very testy and her patience had finally breathed its last breath.

"You are right, I am sorry. I should not have done that. I have no right. I am sorry. Please forgive me. I must and I do respect your choice. Again, all I am saying is, grow some balls!"

Neither of them was able to maintain a straight face at the sound of that and together, over their WhatsApp video call, both were in hysterics. Elizabeth knew she could never be upset with Susan for any period. They loved each other like sisters. Nothing could change that. They would not let it. Besides, deep-down, Elizabeth knew her friend was right, and she wondered what if Susan was right about her being afraid. So then, what was it that she was afraid of, and where was the real Elizabeth hiding?

Since her mother's illness, she felt like she had been existing purely on autopilot mode, and the news of Hazel's rapid deterioration was extremely bothersome. When her mum 'went', all she would have was her two best friends and her career; and while she knew they would always be there for her, they had their own lives. After recent occurrences with Mathew, she wondered too if he was as dependable as she once thought. She needed to have her own family and live her own life and that too weighed heavily on her mind.

A month later, Susan and Paul invited her and Richard over to theirs instead, for their monthly meet-up. Elizabeth was both concerned and disappointed when Mathew texted to say he would be away; she was hoping to finally have a chance to talk to him. Their catchups were becoming noticeably less and less frequent. The trio finally had a chance for a belated engagement and pre-wedding celebration of her and Richard's engagement; and although there was no talk of Susan's infertility issues in the presence of the doctor, Elizabeth knew her friend was only putting her best foot forward.

Conversation was mostly sparse. Other than the weather and political drama, there wasn't much amongst them to talk about and when the girls spoke of not getting through to Mathew, Richard commented irritably that he was an adult and that they should not be imposing themselves on him. Neither Elizabeth nor Paul commented but, Susan was quick to point out that he was her little brother, after all; and that, she would always be concerned about him. Elizabeth was noticeably disappointed in his comment and later told him what she thought he should be more understanding. Afterall, she had told him about Claire's abandonment of both her children. She really hoped he would be more compassionate and that it would be sooner rather than later. It was important to her that they all got along.

Once again, the dynamics of their friendship, all four, now five, came to the fore and brought with it some troublesome thoughts. She reminded herself, to try not to discuss any matter pertaining to her friends with him. She wondered too if he

97

would truly fit into their relationship, like the way Paul had. To her, Paul was so much the 'older brother' of the group, someone she admired and loved.

Suddenly, a memory self-imposed. It was one of an argument she had with Richard recently about the possibility of reducing her hours at work once they got married. She had thought he was coming around and that he would no longer expect that of her. Afterall, he knew how she felt about her job and her plans to have her own practice; and when she insisted that being a housewife was not an option for her, he reneged and proposed that they talk about it... but after they had their first child. He tried to convince her she may or even would feel differently then and he was willing to wait for her to come around. He tried to convince her that he earned enough as it was, with him being a consultant his earnings were at least three times her salary. There was no doubt he could more than afford to look after both and a child, or even two; but that was not it for Elizabeth. She wanted her independence. She wanted the career she had worked so hard to achieve and wanted to feel proud of what she had accomplished instead of this constant feeling of not being on par or equal to him but rather having to live with this non-progressive backward view that she should be banished to the annals of a stay-at-home mom who did what her mother did not so many years back. It was clear that was what his mother wanted and prided herself on and it appeared that was the choice his sister, Rebecca, had made; but like Susan, who needed to accept her choice of partner now, she expected her partner to respect her choice of how she wanted to live. Rebecca was permanently exhausted and blamed either childcare, or house duties on her lack of energy. Elizabeth admired her for being the amazing mother and wife she was but reiterated, that was not the only thing she wanted to do with her life.

They settled on a compromise before the wedding but, Elizabeth knew Susan was right, they had many other things to settle before even the rehearsal dinner. And she made a mental note to discuss them later. When they were alone again, and after he had been fed one of his favourite home cooked meals. When the time was right; she knew she would convince him to see things at least partly her way.

It was obvious to Elizabeth, that Susan had taken a disliking to Richard and she vowed to get to the bottom of it. In her eyes, it just was not justified. "You are not prepared to even pretend to like Richard, are you, Susan? I mean, you would be honest to tell me how you feel, and why you feel that way, wouldn't you?" And, when Susan delayed her comment, "No more secrets, remember?" Elizabeth had noted her friend's tone earlier when she replied to Richard's assumption of them giving Mathew too much attention and had followed her into the kitchen. It was important to her that Sue at least tried, and she was hoping to speak to her about her concern but also to give the men time to get to know each other. Afterall, Richard would soon be fully part of 'the circle', and even though they had yet to set a date, she knew it would be soon. Her mum had always warned about being strung along by a man. "If he loves you, then it shouldn't take him long to make up his mind, Orchid!" She had laughed at the time, especially after learning of only a three-month gap between her parents' engagement and the wedding day.

Susan continued stacking dishes in the dishwasher. "Why on earth would you think I wouldn't?"

"I don't know, maybe your tone earlier." Elizabeth said cautiously. Suddenly wondering if she was imagining things. "Or your constant innuendos during our conversations over the past weeks."

"Come on, Lizzy. Matt is my brother." She said tenderly before she hastened on. "You know what, let us say, I have met more approachable doctors in my time; and, now I realise that that's just Richard's personality. It doesn't mean anything. Or does it?" Susan turned around to face her friend now. "I mean, you know him better than we do. So, is he friendly, approachable? Easy to get along with? Does he make you laugh?"

"He can be a bit traditional; you know that the stay-at-home wife requirement has never appealed to me and Richard seems to think that with his salary I can do that easily. Never mind the fact that I love my job, I love what I do just as much as he loves what he does. I also so desperately need the experience, and yes, his demeanour sometimes does makes him come across a bit unapproachable… but, that is just an affront. You know, he must be tough at work and sometimes all he needs is to separate work from home… sort of. Does he make me laugh? Yes, sometimes." Elizabeth knew she was rambling and may have said too much? The last thing she wanted was for Susan to start another one of her lectures about them having 'that conversation'.

"Well, you know, does he make you laugh like when you are with …you know, when we three or four are together?"

"I can't say he is hilariously funny, but he does have a sense of humour. Sue, he works extremely hard and his job demands a lot of him. I guess it's not easy being responsible for people's lives."

"But I think having a sense of humour would help. I mean, I've met enough doctors in my time to know, don't you think?"

"I hardly think a gynaecologist has as much demand as a neurosurgeon?" Elizabeth could not fathom her need to defend him when she herself felt so many conflicting emotions sometimes. However, she felt, she owed it to him to see what they haD together and where it would go. Susan had Paul and hopefully soon she would also have the family she had waited so long for; and if it went all the way, she too would be happily looking forward to a family of her own. Secretly, she acknowledged, he was an accomplished neurosurgeon and handsome as well and once again she resolved, to give their relationship the fair chance it deserved.

"Well... congratulations on your engagement. Please, just make sure you are genuinely happy, and - no more secrets."

Paul came to find them and was pleased to see them hugging. He too was concerned about the new twists and turns in their relationship. He knew his darling wife well enough to know when she started, she doesn't stop until she had achieved her goal; and he suspected what her new found reason detre was. He had warned her to be careful, being too hard on Elizabeth may backfire, and that was the last thing he wanted to see happen. "Hey, are you guys okay?" He smiled at Elizabeth as gently he stroked his wife's hair.

"Yea, we are good. Just missing each other already and Lizzy is not even married yet." Both girls looked at each other and giggled at Susan's hurriedly concocted tale; but Paul knew them well enough and wondered what exactly they were up to.

"Not to worry about the distance, I heard Mathew is thinking of getting a private jet I am sure he can give you a lift sometimes."

Elizabeth stiffened at the mention of his name and wondered what next was he planning to buy courtesy of Claire's abandonment. *I mean, hasn't he realised that 'things', cannot fix a heart or one's deep seated psychological issues?* She thought to herself.

"Jeez missy - lighten up, it's only a Jet. Everyone knew of Elizabeth's fear of heights and of helicopters, and they all laughed then.

"You know me and heights, so whoohooo!" She feigned a smile.

In the end it turned out to be a lovely evening spent with Susan and Paul and although Mathew's absence was noticeable, they managed to only mention him once. Afterwards, they drove to her house in silence. Elizabeth remained deeply in thought; as she was concerned about Mathew's mental health. Ever since Claire's visit some months ago, she felt he had changed somewhat – appeared to have returned to his state of youthful anger, more sensitive and noticeably less communicative.

The weekend with her mum was uneventful. Art on Saturday, a bit of swimming on Sunday or paddling in Hazel's case as she appeared to be quite tired from exceedingly early on and Elizabeth thought better than to push her. That night, minutes turned into hours, and hours into daybreak. All the while she chased the illusive dream, as sleep evaded her. Leaving her no choice but to mentally sort the pile of work on her desk, waiting for her arrival. Recently she has been thinking of employing her own assistant, sharing as they were now, was not working for her. Not with the increased volume of work. With any luck, her business case would be given the go ahead.

By morning, her lack of sleep was evident. Not least by the dark circles which enveloped her big light brown eyes, but she felt awful too, fatigued. Instinctively, she searched her phone for the 'greens' recipe Mathew WhatsApp to her awhile back. Richard, noticed the name and asked, "Why don't you call him?" Again, she thought he sounded a bit annoyed.

"It's not about that."

"No? Well; humour me. What exactly is this total silence all about, then?"

"It's about not enough sleep perhaps; or no, maybe it's about your insensitivity, actually."

"Oh, so it's my fault now, is it?"

"Yes, actually. I find you very insensitive sometimes."

"So, I am insensitive because I refuse to 'baby' a grown man? Who by the way, is perfectly happy getting on with his life while you my soon-to-be wife, appears to be pining after him! So, what's going on here, Elizabeth?" He had always insisted on calling her Elizabeth, stating that he did not find 'Lizzy', at all endearing.

"What do you mean - what is going on? He's not the same since Claire left. You know that. By the way, you are the doctor go figure it out. I am not going down that road with you again, certainly not this morning." The mental effects of lack of sleep could be blamed for her current disposition, but she had had enough of his accusations and was in no mood for another fight.

"Forgive me, but with all his money and success, he certainly doesn't look like a lost boy to me. If you'll excuse me; I think I'll clear my belongings from the guest room."

She knew her fiancé was a brilliant doctor, but times like these she wondered if he was mature enough to handle her relationship with Mathew. It was a while before she was dressed and ready to leave. "Oh, coffee." She muttered, just as the phone rang. It was the care home.

Her mum had been blue-lighted to the hospital, the manager told her, "… she was restless overnight and this morning we noticed she was finding it a bit more difficult to breathe." For a moment, Elizabeth herself forgot to breathe. Without thinking, she was about to ring Mathew, but stopped herself. He was away, anyway; and then she remembered Richard being around… somewhere in her house. Hysterically, she called out to him. He called back, alerting her to his presence in the living room. Unbeknown to her, he had made his way downstairs, and was in fact, having a croissant. Quickly, she told him what had happened, what the call was about adding that he did not have to come, but he insisted. He wanted to be there.

Even she was surprised he knew to ignore the speed limit. They drove as fast as they could give the early morning traffic and when they arrived, Hazel could barely breathe. "Mum, I am here." She said, as she rushed to her mother's bedside. She was hopeful she would at least know she was there… know that she was not alone.

It wasn't long before the nurse entered the room and picking up her notes, she told her that Hazel had a very bad chest infection, "C.A.P" the nurse called it, then hurriedly explained, community acquired pneumonia. It had caused blood poisoning. Elizabeth found her inhale/exhale routine particularly helpful again now. After another quick intake of air, she exhaled slowly when she learnt that the doctor was on the way in and she would get more details shortly.

"They'll explain everything, Ms Dawes; and you will also be able to get your questions answered." Elizabeth knew she spoke but decided to wait for the doctor as the contents of her statement were less important to her in that moment. She proceeded to call her mum, to reassure her that she was there. Richard attempted to fill her in on the treatment plan with names of some antibiotics she thought better than to memorise. Quickly, he introduced himself as her son-in-law and a consultant neurosurgeon and when a team of doctors came in, he spoke to all of them, as one of them. It was hard to miss the obvious respect and admiration they had for him and for a moment she got a glimpse of him in his world and admitted, she felt proud of her choice. She could imagine him being in-charge, as he would be if he were her mother's designated consultant.

Amidst the admiration for her fiancé and her mother's obvious struggle to breathe, she felt everything just a little overwhelming and to bring a sense of calm to her roller-coaster of thoughts, she lightly rested her head on her mum's shoulder, hoping to steady her fears with each cycle of the rise and fall of her frail looking rib cage. Hazel had lost at least a few stones since she moved into the care home almost a year ago, which Elizabeth knew was associated with her disease process. The consultant had mentioned anything from depression, tiredness, and changes to her medication to an inability to communicate hunger as some of the reasons for poor appetite and ensuing weight loss. The home was incredibly good, they monitored her for signs of constipation and if they thought she was becoming depressed that would be flogged for attention by the visiting therapist. She was kept active, Elizabeth knew that and with the many different types of medications she was on, Elizabeth was assured they were doing all they could for her. But now, those were not her bother. The menacing threat of losing her mother, was.

Refusing to open her eyes, she closed them even tighter, now. All the discussions had died down at that time, leaving only the whistling sound of the Oxygen making its way into her mother's lungs. There was a strong need to embrace the stillness, if only that was all Hazel needed and then she could take her home, but from what the doctor just explained, she knew her mother was very unwell. It had long been decided that should she take a turn for the worst; Hazel would not be a candidate for resuscitation. Elizabeth had cried at the time, wishing her dad was there, but happy to have had Mathew and Susan's company and wondered briefly if today was the day when they would say to her, 'we can only make her comfortable' and shook her head to rid it of that depressing thought.

There was also a new admiration for the man she had fought with only a few hours before, and thought she had done the right thing by giving their relationship a fair chance. *He'll come around*, she thought, *And hopefully, so will Mum.*

She refused to leave her mum's side and was happy to see that dawn brought Susan and Paul with it. They were on their way to work but left out much earlier so they would have enough time to stop by and support their friend.

"You know what our evenings are like." Paul was very apologetic for not coming straight away at the news.

"It's okay, you are here now, and that's all that matters."

Both girls hugged as Susanne reassured her that there is no place else, she could be. "Where's Richard, thought he was with you?"

"He was. He has gone home to change and check in at work. He is hoping one of his colleagues can cover his clinic. If not, he will have to go in." Elizabeth was hoping they could see that he was a decent man. One with not much of a sense of humour as her friend knew, but a nice guy anyway.

Neither of them mentioned Mathew and Elizabeth insisted on not talking about him. If there was any news, she knew Susan would have said. Richard was unable to find cover and had not returned for the night, but Elizabeth understood and was happy to have Susan with her. The night was a buzz of activities with people introducing themselves as specialist nurses and physiotherapists coming in alternately and sometimes together. Between asleep and waking moments, Elizabeth thought whatever medication her mum was given was helping, and by morning she seemed more relaxed. Paul had gone to her house and first thing in the morning, he brought what he found for her to change into.

Later, they left the room to have a coffee and something to eat. When they returned, they saw what looked like everyone who was anyone in the room. Elizabeth knew immediately that something was wrong. A nurse explained how they tried to call her, but she was out of range, immediately she checked her phone to see her battery had died. Susan's phone buzzed then and when she looked, she noticed it was Mathew. She quickly told him she was at the hospital and he said he figured because the nurse had just called him. All three were listed in line as Hazel's next of kin and when they were unable to contact Elizabeth or Susan, he was next in line to be called. Susan closed her eyes, listening to him. He told her he could be back but questioned if Elizabeth wanted him to. "I know she has Richard now. It's not like she is on her own anymore. Susan and I have to, we have to make room for that."

"So, is that what you call friendship?" She whispered, not wanting anyone to hear her frustration. He attempted to continue but Susan would not let him. "Well, Richard is not here." She told him pointedly. "He has a clinic and even if he were, family and friendship supersede all else, or have you forgotten that!" Elizabeth pretended not to be listening. "Do you want to talk to her?" Susan sounded like the older sister that she was, then relayed Mathew's message. "Mathew said how sorry he is and that he will be here tomorrow."

Elizabeth could only nod her head in response. She did not trust herself to speak.

Susan and Paul left for work but not before confirming they would be back later. Richard called to reassure her and to say he was still trying to find cover for his clinics but with some key people on annual leave it was proving more of a challenge than he previously envisaged.

The day was pretty much like the night. Specialist teams coming and going. Very polite but worrying nonetheless, Elizabeth thought. She waited with bated breath for some good news, but none was forthcoming. Not just yet. Susan assured her when she called to say she was on her way home and would be with her later in the evening.

By nightfall, the lead doctor was on his way home but decided to stop by before he left for the day. He entered the room and headed straight in her direction. Without delay, he asked her to come with him and he ushered her into an adjoining waiting room. He reiterated his conclusion of her mother's condition and asked if there was anyone else, she would like to call. When she said they were on their way, the Mediterranean looking middle-aged man was pleased to hear it. "That's good," he told her. "Your mum is extremely sick. Her breathing has improved but the infection is still rife. We are giving her all the right antibiotics and hope for the best but just in case she takes a turn for the worst, we would do all we can to make her comfortable."

Elizabeth nodded in agreement as she fought to hold back the tears and before she knew it, she was hugged from behind. It was Mathew. He had come earlier than Susan or she had expected, and she had never been happier to see him. The consultant paused while she cried with Mathew holding her. He could only look around in bewilderment.

"She's dying, Mathew."

The doctor looked at her as if seeking permission to continue and she nodded her head in response.

"I have seen the documentation around the conversation you had with her doctor at the Home." He reminded her gently. "Given her bad heart, and advanced Dementia, should her heart stop it is best not to attempt resuscitation." Elizabeth only nodded and fell into Mathew's arms again. "I have prescribed all the medication she may need. So, should she need them overnight, the night team are aware and will keep her pain free and comfortable."

At first, she had no reaction to his words, but when he left, she exploded. She sat at Hazel's bedside and refused to leave except to go to the toilet when pressed. She knew she should be prepared but, somehow, she was not; and all the new feelings were too much for her. Overwhelming somewhat. She wondered how she would cope with losing her. The one person who kept her together. It was all too surreal.

Later, when everyone came to visit, she found herself completely alone, even in the midst of them. Nothing could shake the intense fear she felt, not even thoughts of marrying Richard. Not even the closeness of her dear friends.

Just past midnight, and everyone left the room. First the healthcare team and then her best friends, which gave her a chance to be alone, alone with her dying mum. No one could be certain of when the end would come but she knew more than anyone that it would. Grateful that it would be different for her mum than it was for her dad or Izzy, she smiled and stroked her hands then applied moisturiser to her lips. Happy for the time to be with her, happy to have this moment to say goodbye.

Richard had finally found someone to cover part of his clinic and had made the two-hour journey back to be with her and after a while, he too left to get a drink. Alone by the bedside, she sought her mum's forgiveness. Quietly she pleaded for her forgiveness for placing her in the care home. "Away from the beautiful house you bought for both of us," and promised to see Pastor Lammy sometime soon. She spoke to her mum about her conflicting thoughts around Richard and asked what she should do. Elizabeth knew deep down her mum would say pray about it and decided that too, was something important she wanted to speak to Pastor Lammy about.

The night was pretty much the same as the others had been but with less interference. The following morning and evening were busy but with relatives and friends visiting. By late evening, all her friends had been and offered their support. There were cards and Teddy Bears everywhere. The manager from the care home had been too and brought some of what she said were Hazel's favourites. They all left and finally, she was on her own with her mum again. Thankful for the show of support but equally grateful for the time alone.

She must have dozed off because a tap on the shoulder with the gentle sound of her name alerted her to life in the room. It was early in the morning and Mathew had made his way back as quickly as he could. They held each other for a long time with only the words "I am so sorry, Elizabeth," coming from his deep bass-baritone.

The next day, they spent the day together at the hospital. He realised the gravity of the moment and had cancelled what plans he had made for the day. Richard was back at his place and had promised to come as soon as was able to.

For a long time, neither Mathew nor her spoke very much; and when they did it was all small talk like when she enquired about what his latest exploits were and then to confirm the 1959 edition of his Breitling Navitimer, was the watch his dad had given him. "Is that the watch your dad left you?"

"The one and only, why?"

"It looks new, that's all."

"I had it reconditioned. You know…"

"It's your pride and joy. Yeah. I know it means a lot to you. I wish I had something from Daddy, you know, or Isabelle."

"You do. You look exactly like your dad; and Isabelle, she left us so many amazing memories."

That must have broken the ice for them. A reminder almost of how much they knew about each other and how much they meant to each other. She was happy to see him but thought he had changed so much that it was difficult to tell what he was thinking.

He refused to leave and every time she looked across the bed, she could see him looking at her as he held on to her mother's hand. She could not tell what he was thinking, but she was desperate to know. Everyone was surprised but happy to see him when they did their return visit late that evening. Richard was busy in theatre all day and promised to come but in the end, was unable to. There was an unmistakable quietness about Mathew which she had not noticed before, as if suddenly he was this mature young man, a gentleman no less. She saw his eyes and every time she wondered if the stress of her ill mother was causing her to see things that were not there. She shook her head. Determined to focus on her mother. He left briefly to get food for both, which gave her time to whispered to her mum, "I think he's wearing contacts, mum." She applied the wet sponge to moisten Hazel's lips, then reapplied Vaseline with a little chuckle.

With not much of a desire to do anything other than to sit by her mother, neither was surprised at her lack of appetite. Only out of gratitude, she managed to have a small amount of the vegetable soup he brought. Once again, she told herself, he had changed so much, she was afraid to pry into his life now. She had to know he had forgiven her just in case any other actions on her part may push him further away. She valued his friendship more than so many things or people and more so now than ever.

"I am sorry," she told him.

"Life happens, Elizabeth; which only makes it more interesting. I guess. You know, the roses."

She smiled thinking of her mum then, she glanced down at her remembering her famous analogy of the world. Life being a beautiful rose garden with all the varieties of roses; some prickly, others not so much and still some that had no spike at all but one could never tell who or which is of the prickly variety.

"Hmm" She mused and this time when she looked at him fully, she thought he had gained a few pounds but that too she wanted to keep to herself.

"Don't worry, there's nothing to forgive. You are ... well, let us just say; you are a rare kind, Miss Elizabeth Savannah Dawes."

She had not heard him called her name fully in a long time, not since almost a year ago when they had his celebratory dinner at the Fairmont – when he announced his and Cara's separation. She smiled, thinking of her reactions then; and somehow, she knew their misgivings were behind them now.

"I am happy to go when Richard comes. I know there is a somewhat disconnect between us. We are not quite at friends come brother-in-law just yet. So, if it would make you happier, I'd wait downstairs."

"No Mathew, I am happy to have your company. Mum is happy to have her son here too." Holding onto her mother, she took his hand with the next as she whispered to him from across her mum. She jolted upright at the rather serious or expression he displayed or was it 'pensive'? it was difficult to decide. He had already told her he had forgiven her, so she thought better than to make a mountain of his expression.

"Do you love him, Elizabeth?"

That was the last thing she was expecting to have been asked. But anything for a conversation – *let us talk*, she thought. She did not particularly enjoy the silence and would rather they did not just sit there. In time past, whenever they were together, they would always have fun. Finding something to talk about was never a challenge, they could talk about anything. This new dynamic was unnerving, and with all else happening around her, she longed for some normalcy. It was in search of this normality that she thought *why not just tell her best friend how she really felt? Why not start over - with honesty?* "I admire him, Mathew. He is absolutely brilliant at what he does." His eyes were searching now, imploring her to continue "He can be really gentle and nice, but sometimes he can come across to be very cold and insensitive. Uncaring almost; but he's been great with mum and ..."

"How does he fit into what you want for your future? You know, your own practice, children? Have you finalised that yet?" He sounded genuinely concerned.

"We do have a few things to settle, I must admit."

"Like what?" He sipped his hot drink as he looked at her above the lid.

Sighing deeply, she confessed to travelling two hours backward and forwards in the middle of the week, albeit alternate weeks being a win for her and had relieved her from the usual weekly routine.

"Are you moving in with him?" He asked calmly.

"No. Well kind of. Well, you know my values."

"I liked your values. Sounds like... well, like they have they changed?"

She thought she knew what he was thinking, then. "No! Well, we have to compromise in relationships, you know that." She whispered forcibly. Suddenly she felt uncomfortable having to justify herself.

"So, if we have to compromise, what is he compromising or let me guess wait until after the wedding?"

Her mum took a deep breath then, and they both looked at her with breaths held, then she settled once more.

"In relationships we must sometimes give up something for each other." She continued thoughtfully. "I knew when I went to law school that it was a choice that would entail long hours, and that it may possibly lead to no relationships and I hoped not but, there's a real possibility of no children too." She sighed then "But, so too when I said yes to Richard's proposal, I knew that I may have to give up somethings and …"

"Law school, how did we get there?" She could see the puzzled look on his face and realised then that she must not have made any sense. "Some things? What are you planning to give up Elizabeth?" He continued.

"Well, we haven't finalised anything yet but he's asking if after we have children I would…you know stop working. For a while that is, and focus on our family and …"

"And you are prepared to do that? What about starting your own practice?"

"Yeah. Eventually, I guess."

"I thought that was important to you. Like, a deal breaker almost."

"Sounds like we are playing a game of - finding Elizabeth."

"I don't know. You tell me, are we?"

"Sometimes, I do like talking to you." She whispered.

"And now?"

"I don't know. Suddenly you seem so mature and grown up."

"Well, I have learnt very recently that I have to be true…honest with myself and I…"

"And are you?" She pressed, remembering Misha's bluntness the day she was less than participatory in the meeting. Since then she had been working on her assertiveness skills, remembering her dad's words to speak up respectfully – never to be rude. All of which she found easiest with her clients, and in the courtroom; but thought herself as passive outside of it. She was happy to turn the questioning to him.

"I was about to say, I am working on it. I am getting there. You know, the whole Claire situation really threw me, and I must admit for a while I guess, I was a lost boy... but I am working on it." He looked down in the cup then and she wondered, what exactly was, 'working on it' supposed to mean.

Nonetheless, she was happy for him, and when she came around to hug him, she was certain he had changed. She just wasn't sure how much or when, and for how long it would last; but in that moment, she was happy he was at least getting the help he needed to get past Claire until he could forgive her, and move on to embracing his true self.

Susan had called before going to bed and Elizabeth promised to keep her abreast of her mum's condition. Her friend was obviously incredibly happy her brother was there and said as much to Elizabeth. They whispered about how much quieter he appeared to be, and Susan reassured her friend, "Mark my words, Lizzy. Like the orchid, he's died and now he's going to bloom. I know my brother and I know his worst days are behind him now. Onwards and upwards."

Elizabeth smiled at her metaphor and remembered how she made fun of her the day at the barbecue when she told her all about her orchid and roses philosophy, according to her mum that is.

"Guess you believe in the good old orchid theory then, huh?" Elizabeth teased. Her friend agreed. They both chuckled.

"I guess I do, my love. I guess I do. And you will be okay too, Lizzy. Take all the time you can with your mum. She is so proud of you, of your strength. You have been through so much. Just call me anytime. If anything changes, or just ask Matt to call."

She told her friend that somehow, she believed Mathew would be okay, and that she was happy for him, for both of them. The rest of the night they took turns watching her mum and by daybreak, they could both tell she had stopped breathing. Elizabeth held her for as long as she felt able to, while Mathew stood by her side and stroked her hair offering whatever comfort he could.

Both Susan and Paul were called in and came in to pay their last respects, and to ensure their friend was okay. Paul went to work while, Mathew volunteered to take both girls home. On the way to Elizabeth's, Susan rang her school to say she was unable to come in, "My aunt died this morning." Elizabeth heard her say, and was so moved, she reached out to hold her friend's hand which she held onto for the rest of the journey, and without speaking, they both knew that their bond was unbreakable. Richard was unavailable. He was in theatre, the junior doctor told her. She left him a text message instead.

They got to her house and as she alighted from the car, Mathew came around to open her door. He told her, "Seriously, Lizzy, Susan is right, your mother was a mother for us too. My only regret is not meeting you, her, earlier."

Elizabeth was truly touched, and she hugged him. "Thank you, Matt."

As soon as they were inside, Susan made them each a cup of tea while Paul called from work to check in, and afterwards, both Elizabeth and Mathew went their separate ways to shower and change.

"You slept down here or something?" Susan was curious as to the state of the sitting room.

"I couldn't sleep, so I had just stayed here. You know, to hang out for a bit." Elizabeth looked away as she spoke. "And then we got the call." Elizabeth had not been home since Monday morning and could see the effects of her restless Sunday night almost a week before, the night before she got the call. Now, so much had changed in a week. Again. She wondered when, if ever, would she get some reprieve from the roses' pricks. When would she be truly happy again?

"I am so sorry, Lizzy; but at least we know your mum is at peace now. No more anxiety attacks. Remember the early days when she first started to forget who you are, that was tough to watch. You know, to see you go through that. You have been very brave, Lizzy. You have done so well. I know she was so proud of the lady you have become." She hugged her friend again, and together they shed some tears.

Elizabeth knew deep down that although she cried, a part of her was happy that her mother was out of the suffering and for a moment she remembered the words from the minister who officiated Izzy's funeral service. She knew not even death could separate her mum from God's love, and that her mum was finally at peace in God's arms. Stevens and Stephenson's were good to her. She was given a month off and told to keep in touch. Should she need more time, that could be discussed. She was happy to know that Misha's tough exterior housed a very humane, empathetic soul, and thanked her mentor for her understanding. The whole department sent her cards and flowers and called to make sure she was well.

The thought of making funeral arrangements filled her with dread. Pastor Lammy lessened the load for her. She knew him very well and he knew her mum even more, so it was easy to choose their Pastor to officiate. He had been to the hospital a few times, but she knew he had gone to the care home for weekly Pastoral visits. She long knew he sometimes shared Holy Communion with her mum and that

111

he too had been at the receiving end of some of her outbursts. While at other times, it simply had to be abandoned because Hazel was either asleep or was not feeling very well. She could recall him being the most patient and kind man she had ever known and his wife being no different. Like Susan, they had not been blessed with any birth children and when they knew that time had passed for them, they adopted a pair of twins. Both of whom they had from birth and who have so far turned out well.

Her friends refused to leave. Mathew hugged the guest room, Susan and Paul stayed in her room, and she could not bring herself to be anywhere else but her mum's old bedroom, and that night, as everyone finally retired to bed, Elizabeth busied herself in Hazel's old room. It was another sleepless night, pretty much like the last night she was home, only this time, it was for a different reason. Mathew was there and they were friends again, Susan was there too and she knew Richard would be coming in the morning. She busied herself unpacking Hazel's closet while all the time she recalled the journey they had been on together over the past three years, until when cruelly, dementia forced her to have to leave her beautiful home. She could not help but cry as she felt the heartbreak all over again. Like the one she felt as she watched her fade away, so quickly, right before her eyes. She sobbed even harder clutching at the Chanel purse she had bought along with the pearl necklace for her university graduation, thinking of its menacing persistence. How it pursued her, relentless, until finally, it had taken her.

She recalled too, how sometimes her mum would become so anxious, and only the childlike clutching of a toy-doll could calm her troubled mind but hazard a smile as she remembered her kindness. Although less gregarious or charismatic than her dad, Hazel was known to be of a kind nature, nonetheless. Always sought to help out at the local church; she could be seen either with the homeless, serving meals or visiting those who were sick. She was also known to volunteer at the local charity shops. Forging through the many photos tucked safely away in Hazel's walk-in closet was possibly the hardest to do. Some were as recent as four years ago, just before she began to seriously forget she was even at home. Elizabeth knew how much her family and friends meant to her mother, almost as much as helping others, and from her own Google research since the diagnosis, she also knew it could have happened to anyone. She resolved to spend her life helping to raise awareness and wanted to make a monthly financial contribution to the charity. They did a brilliant job, offering excellent advice in such a compassionate way. Elizabeth smiled then and put a note in her phone to start as early as this month end.

Thinking about it now, she sat at the end of the huge king-sized bed, realising how relieved she was to have received the diagnosis. Just being able to name what was happening to her mum, helped somewhat in dealing with it. She sighed deeply as she could see in her mind's eye the reality that presented, how it made her acutely aware of what was to come. She felt a new wave of guilt as she remembered the suggestion by one of the carers to have all of downstairs, or the conservatory even adapted and have full time carers coming in or living in. She recalled a conversation with the specialist who stressed the need for social interaction and while she would have been more than happy to make the adjustments, Elizabeth wanted the reassurance that the carers were trained and skilled in meeting her mother's needs.

She heard a sound along the hallway. Cautiously, she peered through the small opening, only just realising that she had not actually locked the door all along. It was Mathew, making his way downstairs. Adjusting her vision in the dimly lit room, she noticed then the time on the antique clock, the one by her mum's bedside table closer to the door. Suddenly it dawned on her that she had been up all night. Again.

By the end of the week, everyone kept coming and going; pretty much as they did at the hospital. There were times that she longed for some peace and quiet, time with her thoughts, and very quickly, night-time became her sanctuary. Although the Pastoral team at her mum's church had kindly taken on the planning of the funeral with only limited input from her, she had a lot to check on, to make sure it was the way her mum would have liked it to be. She still had to speak to the insurance companies which was a surprise to her because she knew only about one of them; but after going through the myriad of documents in Hazel's closet, she had unearthed another. They were all written in complex language; the grieving lawyer was finding difficult to decipher and thought it better to wait until she had the mental capacity to read through everything she had found. No surprise was expected to come from the reading of the will. She figured that would be the easy part and she was certain she could easily disperse of her mother's belongings as she saw fit.

By week two, she and Richard had somehow managed to see each other every day but he had not stayed over again since the night before Hazel was taken to the hospital, and she had not asked him to. She had enough going on without another argument as to why Mathew was there all the time or why not; and in the evenings, when he left, she would go to Susan and Paul's. Some nights, they stayed at hers. They had the wake a week before the funeral, which was a beautiful celebration of her mum's life where she was able to catch up with many of their long-time friends and extended family. She was happy to see so many people from their old neighbourhood and at the end, when they had all dispersed, her closest friends all crashed at hers. For the first time in a long time, she was able to sleep throughout the night.

So peaceful was her rest that it was not until midday when she awakened to a commotion coming from somewhere downstairs. Familiar voices mixed with unfamiliar ones filled the air and gone was the feeling of loss and melancholy. Almost like behold, life and vitality. It was Sarah. The unmistakable high-pitched sound became more audible as stealthily she made her way downstairs. It was none other than her late friend's little sister. Without informing her, she had travelled over from the United States with her young daughter. She wanted to support her late sister's friend in her time of bereavement. Elizabeth was so happy to see Sarah she almost choked up and when she enquired of Lynette. Sarah told her she could only make it to the funeral.

"Glad that you have come, so happy to see you!" They hugged each other tightly for a long time as if they had an unspoken bond, a unity in grief.

"She's rapping things up and looking to retire." All eyes were on Sarah's three-year-old daughter who was keeping everyone entertained. Amongst the mothers, Hazel was the eldest of the three. Claire did not work as much anymore either; but like Linette, continued to do some freelance work. Last time she came, she told Susan she was going to Turkey to cover an uprising there, and that she would head back to her home in the south of France right after. Neither child was impressed or even cared. Elizabeth was surprised but happy to hear that Lynette would be coming over. Their support meant a lot to her.

Everyone came together to add their culinary skills to the meal and after that, they came together again, to put the final plans in place for the funeral. Not long after they ate, Richard had to go. He told her he had some last-minute errands to run. She felt he was being a bit vague but thought better than to question his motives, not in front of her friends.

The next day, they all went shopping with Mathew as their chauffeur; while they picked out appropriate attire, and on the way home Elizabeth and Susan checked in with the church team for finalisations. Elizabeth was so happy to have the help of her mum's church family; she knew it would have been hard on her. She would not have known where to begin.

They had always been helpful to anyone in the village who needed help and she suspected they would anyone outside of it too. She had seen how supportive they were to both Susan and Mathew when their father, George died, and as Knockholt was such a small community, all the neighbours offered to help too. And even long after the burial, they still looked out for his children who lived there all their lives and never thought of leaving until Susan got married and moved further. A thirty-minute commute away while, Mathew's penthouse was situated in the city much further, an-hour's journey, in fact. Their family home laid empty as neither could bring themself to sell it, keeping it almost like a retreat from their current homes. Susan had always said it would be the perfect place to raise her children with all the fond memories of times with her dad and her brother.

Elizabeth had never thought of moving. The Residential care home her mum was in was only a maximum thirty-minute journey in the opposite direction to Susan's; another thirty, and she was at work. Besides, there was no way she could bring herself to being further away from her mum at the time. It was difficult enough for her to forgive herself for not being able to keep her in her own home and hoped that in time she would come to feel somewhat 'vindicated'.

The care home had said they had packed everything away for her to come by and collect whenever she felt able to, but with Susan and Richard back at work, it was Mathew only who was able to help and before she even asked, he agreed. She felt like something had changed between them but still she was not sure what it was, and until revealed, he remained an enigma. She thought of how confusing it must have been for him all those years not knowing what to make of his anger at his mother, while all the time trying to be the son his dad demanded. They said extraordinarily little while they busied themselves with packing and organising boxes for charity. Some for the care home, other things they thought would be perfect for the church endeavours. There were a few pictures too that Elizabeth wanted to keep.

Mathew handed her a book about various plants. Thinking of her mum's famous orchid and roses theory; hesitantly, she opened it. There, in the front cover, she recognised the handwriting and noticed it was a gift to her mum from a long time ago. It was from her dad. She smiled as she read the title, 'Orchids and Roses: the conundrum'. She brought it to her chest and closed her eyes as if that action would somehow, push back the lump forming... the happy-memories lump. The one that could make her cry right there and then, and she did not want to, not this time; but concluded it was a useless wasted effort. As the tears flowed, she ignored them, much the same way they ignored her silent request and once again made their appearance, anyway.

"Are you okay?" She could hear the gentleness in his voice and thought about the orchid her mum mentioned. The part about it blooming after it appeared it had died and wondered when she, her mum's little orchid would 'bloom' again, because at this precise moment she felt trampled on. Ran over even, by a huge bolder, or something of that weight and had no idea when or how or what strength of fertiliser or frequency of exposure to the sometimes glorious sunshine or if indeed there was any amount of watering, that would bring her back to life again. She would have responded but a nod was all she could muster as hesitantly he took a call just then.

"Yes, Mathew speaking." quickly, he left the room and once again sorting took priority. As she proceeded with the matter at hand, she could not help but wonder why he had to leave the room and wondered if their friendship had truly been restored. In the past, he would not have left the room, they would have no secrets. "No secrets. Thought we had past that," She whispered, wiping her tears with the back of her hands then depositing the droplets on the white jumpsuit she chose that morning. Not only was it the easiest to find, but she thought it would be most fitting to reflect the purity of her mother's heart. "Guess I'm not the only one then, huh?" She hurried on checking each drawer to ensure everything was emptied.

Mathew was back in time to help her carry the boxes she had packed, the ones she wanted to take with her. She alerted the charge nurse to what she had gifted to the care home. They were very appreciative, especially for a painting she had left behind. She knew her mum would have wanted them to have it, she always said she wanted it to find a good home, somewhere it would be appreciated. On the way home, they drove along mainly in silence and stopped firstly by the church, then the local charity shop. Everyone they met expressed their condolences and showed their appreciation for the gifts.

"My house is empty, how about it if we stop and get something to eat?"

"If you want to get something, we can stop but I am heading to the old house, I have some leftovers." He stammered.

She wanted to show her gratitude for the time he took to help her and thought dinner would be fitting. She was taken aback when he mentioned his leftovers as opposed to a freshly prepared meal and time for them to sit together, as friends.

"Leftovers, are you kidding me?" Now, he had her wondering if he was trying to avoid her.

"I am going to be at the house – alone, anyway, so how about it if we picked up the 'leftovers', if that's what you really want, and if not, we can have omelettes with some home-made smoothie or something ..." She knew he must be hungry; they had been gone longer than they thought they would have and neither of them had anything to eat in just under eight hours.

"For starters, you will not be alone. The call I took earlier was from Sue, she said she saw Richard's car outside and wanted to know if he had a key."

"She called you to tell you that, why didn't she call me?" Elizabeth was furious and confused. "I could tell her he has a key; he is my fiancé for Pete's sake."

"…ahm, no. She called to find out how you were holding up, going through your mum's stuff and all. You know Sue, like a mother hen. She thought it would be hard for you so she…"

"She called you. That was nice of her. I am sorry for shouting at you." Without expecting it, she hugged him; and a few tears fell as he just about put an arm around her as opposed to his full big bear hug which normally hugged her like an envelope. Amid the myriad of emotions, she felt him stiffen, and thought it best to compose herself. He behaved as if he had closed the account of trust and no longer wanted to make a deposit. Lately she had this uneasy feeling that they had somehow both violated the account of trust, and neither knew how to re-open it. She questioned herself aloud. "Have I been untrustworthy all this time?"

"No Elizabeth, that's why I am so disappointed now that we have survived so much and still you didn't think we could deal with this together," She recalled his scolding before he left, the time he called while she was in the board meeting. The day she came face to face with the real Misha and discovered the real Elizabeth had gone into hibernation, a bit like the orchid.

He took her home as she decided against his professed leftovers and after leaving the lone box in the hall way, he waved good bye to both her and Richard.

"How was it?" He attempted to give her a hug, but she slipped away.

"I need the toilet, sorry."

"I made us something; let me know when you are ready." He called out behind him and made his way into the kitchen.

She emerged from the washroom, headed straight upstairs, and when Richard came to bid her goodbye, she complained of a headache and assumed the foetal position in her mum's bed.

CHAPTER FOURTEEN

Sarah, like everyone else who saw her, thought Elizabeth exuded such regal dignity and beauty. It was the day of her mum's funeral and she was determined to have everything done impeccably.

"Oh honey, how are you? Silly question I know, but you look so beautiful?" Sarah had always been one to speak it as she saw it. The highlights had long gone from her hair and Elizabeth was now left with her long black mane. With no time to spend all of two hours or more at the hairdresser's, she had decided to just leave it to grow to its full length. And now, it was thick and full and healthy. Susan had volunteered to spray and style it for her. They both decided in the end to simply let it fall to frame her face naturally. With Sarah's insistence, she had bought a black Givenchy dress made of a square neckline to the front and a 'v' shape to the back. The sleeves were made from the softest mesh, complete with rows of tiny butterfly patterns to add a feminine softness from shoulder to wrist. A plain midi skirt formed the rest of the dress and she completed her ensemble with her black Aquazzura pumps and one of her old favourites, a small Gucci black clutch.

She had declined a lift from Susan and Paul and had opted instead to travel with her mum's only sister and her three children, two other cousins and Richard filled the rented black Bentley. She could hear the organ playing as the car pulled up outside the entrance to the church. Mathew was leaving his brother-in-law's car when they saw each other. She waved at him and with a faint smile, he waved back. She thought he looked handsome and wanted to tell him, but he made no attempt to approach her just then and she was being called over by the Reverend. Having taken her customary deep breath in and exhaling through pursed lips; she led the way up the aisle with only the Minister ahead of the queue. Mathew and Susan were seated to the left of her, next to her aunt and cousins as relatives of the deceased, while Richard sat to her right. Taking her seat, she remembered the last time she was in that church with her mum. It was the Christmas Eve before she took seriously ill the following year. Elizabeth remembered then how both she and her mum thought of her memory lapse as age playing its cruel tricks; and when Elizabeth came home to find an empty oven and hob on and her mum could not remember turning either of them on, she knew she had to do something. She shook her head then, she didn't want to be present in body only, like at her father's farewell service. To this day it was still all a blur. She wanted to be truly present with nothing but happy memories and her friends and relatives beside her.

The service ended much quicker than Elizabeth had thought it would. She was incredibly pleased when Susan agreed to do a Bible reading; followed by her aunt, who did a beautiful reflection. She knew there was no getting away with not saying something about her mum and she did. She spoke fondly of her and when she felt the tears coming, she looked up to find herself face to face with Mathew. Until then, she had not thought of him except for when he texted her to say he had managed to find somewhere to sit, which she suspected was a subtle reprimand. But she wouldn't let him, and he gave in when she insisted, he sat with her. She smiled briefly as she thought of him being there. Somehow, that gave her strength and although he did not smile back, she convinced herself he wanted to.

"...So, rest now, mum, I know nothing can separate me from your love or you from God's eternal love."

The Minister complimented her on her chosen ending for her reflection and told her, "Elizabeth, you do know that, like your mum, God's love extends to you as well?" She nodded, in agreement as very measuredly, he continued, "We would love to see you in church sometimes." Pastor Lammy had been saying that for quite some time; and recently, Elizabeth had been thinking about arranging a meeting with his secretary. She had some pressing questions she thought he could answer and knew he would be honest, like the dad she so missed.

"I will. As soon as all of this is over, I will make more of an effort. I know mum would like it if I did." She hoped to honour her mum by attending more often; she knew she would have loved to see her, if only to keep an eye on her moral compass. Neither her dad's nor Izzy's funeral prepared her for the reality of her mum's coffin being lowered into the ground and she felt her legs being reduced to jelly as the dirt was thrown on the lowered coffin. Richard caught her in time but when he attempted to move her away from direct view, she successfully made a valiant attempt at standing firmly on both legs which convinced him, she was alright. Susan, Paul, and Mathew all came closer to her then, and as she looked up to acknowledge their support, she could see Lynette and Sarah in the distance. She managed a smile but at this time, holding back the tears was much harder. Mathew moved in closer still as the last of the flowers and wreaths were being laid out and he held her hand.

She squeezed his in acknowledgement. Discreetly, he did hers; but she did not look up at him. Instead, she kept her eyes firmly on how beautifully the flowers were being arranged. The number of people in attendance surprised her. There were those from the church, friends from their old neighbourhood and what felt like the entire inhabitants of Knockholt village who showed up. She was touched and said so to Susan.

Except for her relatives, almost everyone had now dispersed. They each said their own goodbyes and after when she was left with only Paul and Susan, she noticed too that Mathew was still there and when he attempted to leave, she asked him not to. In the end, she was left alone to say hers, to be alone with her mum for one last time as they looked on from their vehicles parked nearby. Distraught but composed, she knelt by the grave to place a single white orchid on the fresh earth and promised her mum that she would be okay. She had Susan and Mathew to make sure of it. In that moment, she did not realise she had forgot to mention Richard.

It started to rain as they made their way to the hotel for refreshment. Her aunt had agreed to oversee this part of the arrangements and when she arrived, she could see her talking to one of the waitresses and everything seemed to be going well. The hall was beautifully decorated with all different types of orchids and a large beautifully arranged centrepiece filled with all different types of roses, which made the room look far grander than one would usually see at a funeral. But Elizabeth wanted it to be as beautiful as her understated mother would have liked it. Susan accompanied her to the bathroom, where she reattempted hair repair and tear-stained face make-up removal then reapplication.

Mathew was on his way to the gents when she made her way out. "Hi Matt" she reached out her hand to hold his and somehow, she expected him to pull away but was relieved when he did not.

"Sorry you have to go through something like this again so soon after …"

"…After Izzy. Yes, I know. It's kind of different now though." He knew what she meant.

"What have you done to your hair?" She could feel his hand in her hair.

"Why, what's wrong with it?" She reached up to touch it and touched his hand instead.

"Nothing, its fine. You look beautiful. It- it looks lovely, that's all!"

"Forgive me for interrupting. Oh, hello Mathew." Just then, Elizabeth thought how much Richard could be mistaken for the quintessential school headmaster

120

interrupting truant students who should really be on their way to the next class. "I have been looking all over for you, Elizabeth. Obviously, you are in safe hands, so I am going to go. Call me when you are not as occupied." Elizabeth noted his accusatory tone and hoped she did not have to deal with his pettiness today, not on the day of her mother's funeral.

"I am not – occupied, Richard. Matt and I have only just had a chance to catch up."

"And I am heading to the gents." Mathew said hastily pointing in the opposite direction.

"Hurry and come and get something to eat, Matt." She called after him.

He only waved but did not look back.

"That seemed pretty intense, is everything alright?"

"Richard, I just buried my mother …sorry if …"

"I know, I know. I just can't get over the way you two…" He pulled her in for a hug, and she did not dare ask what he wanted to say.

"Oh, there you are. We have been looking all over for you!" It was young Sarah with her little daughter in toe.

"I had to go to the bathroom. Sorry."

"It's okay. Have you seen Mathew? He does not look well. He seems so withdrawn. Is he okay? You know, like, everyone is used to jovial Mathew who is ready to pay for everything and give everyone a treat; but of late, he's noticeably more reserved and less playful. He's not unwell, is he? Or broken up from a bad relationship or something?" Sarah somehow missed Elizabeth's eyes indicating for her to, please, stop talking, and simply carried on without as much as a pause for breath. While Richard, who seemingly had no such interest, had long released her hand, and was now headed towards the bar.

"Did I say something wrong? Is he okay?"

"Who Sarah, Richard or Mathew?"

"Both." Sarah smiled.

"I don't know, Sarah. We are all going through this roller coaster of emotions right now. It's kind of hard to be 'okay' when we have all … you know what I mean?" Elizabeth felt tired and took care to not say anything to indicate she was a tad bit annoyed with her late best friend's sister. She was tired of having to second guess what everyone else was feeling. Tired of crying and having to wade through the myriad of emotions she has encountered since that faithful Sunday evening almost three months ago when Richard proposed.

"I understand. I can see the way he looks at you. Poor you what are you going to do about Richard?"

"What?" Elizabeth was unclear what Sarah was alluding to and was anxious to clear up any misconceptions.

"Mathew, he looks at you so tenderly. It is obvious, he's in love with you."

"Sarah, that's absolutely not the case and that's not what I was alluding to. We all knew my mum well enough to be affected by her passing, nothing to do with Mathew. Well, not like that." Elizabeth was not convinced of Sarah's observations for a moment and quickly set out to clarify things for her late friend's sister, someone she was usually quite fond of.

"Oh, sorry; from the bar I saw when he touched your hair and that unmissable gaze. Anyone could see the look on his face, as I did, watching from across the room. I was hopeful for both of you, but you are right, you are with Richard now and there's nothing to think about. You are happy and that's all that matters."

Elizabeth's mind had taken flight at that precise moment in time, and all she could think about was when would Sarah take a breath. Surely, she would be next to collapse from asphyxiation and it would be of her own doing. "Breathe, girl. By the way, you are too funny. You are just like your sister. Come, let's get some food." Hand in hand, they went with Sarah's little girl, Maya, to the buffet where both forego the main meal and opt for a small portion of quinoa and avocado salad instead.

"I'll give the tahini a miss," Elizabeth wanted something light just to feed her brain. "But I'll have the water, thanks." She told the waiter, as she drizzled some extra virgin olive oil onto her salad and acknowledged guests who handed in cards or flowers or simply words of comfort.

"The Tahina dressing is spot on, hmm thanks Sarah for the suggestion."

Sarah winked at her late sister's friend and left her purse at the side of the table opposite and when Richard took the seat, Sarah confessed to have left the purse deliberately with the hope Mathew would emerge from the gents and join them. Elizabeth rolled her eyes and wondered then if Sarah secretly had a crush on her friend. Mathew was no longer anywhere to be seen for the remainder of the evening, except at the end when they were all made aware that their allocated time was over, a wedding reception was to happen in an hour.

Richard took her home, and as they bid each other goodnight, he suggested they take a break.

"A break, like us, taking a break?" For a minute, Elizabeth's mind was racing. She knew they had some issues to work out but – take a break? That hadn't crossed her mind.

But he was quick to clarify, "No, a holiday break! We could relax in Venice or Maldives or Seychelles, what do you think about that?"

"That would be nice." Somewhat relieved, she smiled nervously as he kissed her cheeks.

"You haven't had a holiday since your mother … you know."

"No, not really. But where would we go for our honeymoon? I mean, those places you mentioned sound like perfect honeymoon destinations.

"That's something we can talk about another time."

She was happy he had suggested it and thought about fleshing out the details in the coming week. She made her way upstairs but surprised herself to find that the entire journey up, she wondered how she would feel if they were to take a break – a break from the relationship. That too, she decided would have to be another thing on their now growing list of things to talk about.

The will was uneventful as she has suspected with the exception of a small trust fund she never knew existed and one she could have accessed at her last birthday when he turned twenty-eight, had she known about it, she wouldn't have sold the second house so quickly. She sighed and smiled, knowing her parents were always thinking about her. It was the beginning of the second week that the letter from the insurance companies came and so too two big surprises. She knew her mother had one for her to access in the event of her passing, but she had no idea of the exact amount. The second was an even larger sum than the first. It was enough for her to re-approach the estate agent hoping they could convince the kind couple who purchased her house, to sell it back to her. They said they would but that she should not get her hopes up. Her mother's second insurance money had been handed down from her parents and she had only rolled it over while adding monthly to it.

Elizabeth could not believe what she saw. The thought that she had enough to repurchase the house cash and still have something left over to set up her practice, was not what she was expecting in the midst of this sadness; and for the first time since her mum's passing, she prayed a prayer of thanksgiving to God. Between her staying at Susan's or them at hers or Richard, when he was able to, he would also make his midweek visit, she was never short of companionship, at least for the first month.

Mathew called every day, although most times brief, but she applauded his efforts and knew whatever had happened between them would also need time to be rebuilt. He did his best to make her laugh at times and he too was surprised to see her mother had left him an original oil painting on canvas and a similar one to his sister, Susan. They were both so pleased, he immediately took his from the safe and placed it in his sitting room, vowing never to sell it while; Susan placed hers in her study, as her way of evoking the peace that Ms Hazel brought with her.

Mathew took her out for lunch often and when Susan could make it, they all went out together. One day, he surprised her when he brought her a pair of waterproof trainers, and insisted of eating they went for a walk. She had no idea they were heading the hour and a half walk to the nearest beach. He had everything they would need for the journey; water, his specially concocted homemade smoothie and two portions of pecan pie. They held hand sometimes as he helped her traverse the more challenging terrains. When they eventually made it to the beach, she collapsed on the sand and he did the same, beside her. Finally, she was finding it easy to laugh and talk with him again and he seemed relaxed too. That night, as he slept in the nearby guest room, she wondered if this was the glimmer of hope in their relationship.

After almost three months of a well-established routine, she found weekends particularly difficult and Mathew suspected that too. He tried to leave his Sundays free just for her. They went out on Sunday evenings for late lunches, somehow, not wanting to call it 'dinner', he labelled it their 'late Sunday brunch'. Very slowly her appetite was making its way back and maybe it was the company, but she admitted to eating a bit more, which Mathew could see whenever they went out. He was enjoying his time with her and was happy he took Susan's advice about this. Over their last late lunch just, before Christmas, finally he admitted how much he had missed her. Missed their friendship but that he thought it better to give her and Richard space to grow their relationship. She appreciated his confession and without saying too much, reassured him, he was never in the way.

"Richard, he's not accustomed to forming relationships outside of his 'bubble' – meaning, his family or work, and clearly, he doesn't have any friends himself. It's clear he finds our closeness a bit mindboggling and I don't know, maybe he's even …"

"A little jealous?" He said that a bit too seriously for her.

"Why would you think that?

"I don't know, just a thought, I guess. We are adults aren't we – anything is possible."

"Hmm, but you, you and I, we are different."

"We are different." He echoed, which made her laugh a little louder, wondering why he had to put an emphasis on the word - different. He smiled then and covered her hand on the table with his, which was when he noticed again, she wasn't wearing her engagement ring. She did not wear it on the day of the funeral either, but like him, Susan didn't ask why. Neither of them thought it was appropriate at the time.

"Don't you wear your engagement ring anymore?"

"I will, eventually. I am just not in the mood to plan a wedding now and thought, 'oh well, wearing it won't change that fact' so, its somewhere safe until, I can …"

"… figure things out, outside of grieving." He interjected. "But you won't know how long that process will take so have you been speaking to Richard?"

"We talk, when he's not in theatre or running an outpatient's clinic or a preassessment clinic or whatever it's called on any given day. His job is very demanding, and we have a lot to work through. We will see."

"Yeah, when your mind is in a better place – yeah."

She attempted a smile and nodded in response.

"But Lizzy, not many people have what we have – this friendship and I know we had a bit of a bad patch recently and the truth is I was taken aback by the whole Richard situation. I wasn't sure how to handle that." As soon as he said it, he wished he had not, but he needed to know how she felt.

"What do you mean? What about Richard – you are so like your sister. Susan thinks he's – well, I don't know – who knows what Sue thinks." She chuckled, thinking about his sister, her sister – 'sort of'.

He realised then that she had not heard what he attempted to say and thought, clearly, she didn't or may never feel for him, what he had begun to admit to himself. *So much good was that bit of counselling.* He thought.

It was much later than they had realised. They were both sitting there for a long time and the waiters were beginning to see the last of the Sunday evening customers go; and had either of them been looking anywhere other than in each other's direction, they would have noticed that they were about to be the last of the couples to leave.

125

S. P. Scott

Christmas was fast approaching, and she willed herself to feel the Christmas spirit, to embrace some of its festivities. It was now fully three months since her mother died and she was not feeling any way festive.

She and Richard spent Christmas eve together. He insisted he had to be back in time for Christmas at his parents', it was their family tradition. But Elizabeth did not wish to be with his family at this time and told him the loss was still fresh in her mind. She promised to try to see them in the new year.

The trio were all at Susan's from Christmas eve and on Christmas day, they exchanged presents and plenty of hugs and kisses. Elizabeth was glad she decided to be with people who she could trust and not with Richard's family who she felt would possibly judge her for – something, anything. With them, you would never know, she confessed to Susan.

The day after Christmas, she refused to leave her bed at Susan's and they all understood - going in and out of her room, checking in on her then giving her time alone, while all the time she could hear their voices coming up from downstairs. She spoke to Richard again that day, but only briefly as he insisted, he would not be coming by her friend's house. She knew she was in no mood to give in and when he hung up, she could tell he was not pleased with her decision.

Suddenly, there was an urgency to arrange another meeting with Pastor Lammy. The first meeting was to thank him and the church for everything they did for her mum; but this one would need be of a different nature. She needed someone – someone totally unbiased, whose sound judgement she could rely on to take the right decision. Sleep was ever so near now, and she promised herself to make an appointment in the new year.

CHAPTER FIFTEEN

The new year came and went for Elizabeth, with all four of them attending church as the only exception. Richard still could not get away for the holiday and she did not push for him to. This rendered their plans for that much needed break, void. By the middle of the third month following the funeral, she was on an emotional roller coaster and now in month four, she was desperate to talk to someone. Without a second thought, she finally spoke to Pastor Lammy and by the end of January, she had already been in his office, all of three times.

Richard had visited less frequently and with her period of mourning fully underway, she was relieved he understood her reluctance to do anything now including planning a wedding or travelling two hours to see him. This time, her appointment with Pastor Lammy was for just before lunch time and she arrived in time to see his secretary going into the building.

Their session started as they usually did, with Pastor Lammy opting to say a prayer, only this time he asked her if she wanted to; but she felt she couldn't, and he understood.

"Some days, I feel just fine and then, for no apparent reason, I am totally overcome with grief." She knew she didn't cry so much now but acknowledged it was still a tumultuous time for her, something she never wanted to become accustomed to.

"Elizabeth, with grief and grieving, there's no warning and there is certainly no timetable about the end time but, there is a promise that eventually you will have more good days than bad ones. So, there is hope. But the important thing is to take care of yourself. Are you eating, or sleeping at all?"

She nodded to sleeping which most nights she just about got over five hours but was a little more honest as she shook her head to confirm a slow return of her appetite. He enquired about Richard and although she knew she could trust him, she was uncertain how to reply. "I don't know." She told him, and before she had time to think, she was relaying to him something she had been thinking about since the morning of her mum's death. "Maybe Richard and I should just be friends like, Mathew and I are. It's less complex that way, I think. I have enough complex issues with my job and everything that has happened. I need simple- I need seamless -

Richard bothers so much about what his parents think - you know? Pleasing them, like I am secondary and that concerns me; but when we talk about it, he has a way of making me feel silly. Like I am overthinking or overreacting- I do not know - something just doesn't add up; but it's hard to put my logical fingers on it. And it frustrates me - no it infuriates me. I hate feeling like this ... I need, I do not know, simple. It's all too complicated right now." At risk of repeating herself she had to use the word which best described what she was feeling.

"It's okay, Elizabeth. So sorry – but, you know, no one, even I cannot promise you, that life will be simple. I guess you have noticed that since your dad died. Life has a way of - how did you say your mum would have said it, presenting itself like a rose garden? So beautiful sometimes but, in its own season, it produces a certain variety that has the potential to prick you the hardest, and that is usually at a particular time when you least expect it to." He paused, then quietly told her that she was not alone and that with time it would all get easier. He encouraged her to pray, which she said she would, and he was pleased to hear.

They explored most of what she had on her mind then, but particularly 'Richard's peculiar disposition'. Pastor Lamy, who after listening intently, made his own observation.

"Sounds to me like you need to stop, and … give yourself time. Correct me if I am wrong; but am I correct in saying that you are no longer certain of your feelings - what you feel for Richard?" She nodded as he hastened on. "And, that's okay, especially at a time like this when you are going through bereavement and loss, that's another time when things can easily become blurred - muddled. So, you said you have taken some time off. Let's see when we next meet, how useful you find that break."

By the end of the session, the one which was meant to last an hour, they had finished three cups of her favorite organic green tea. Pastor Lammy turned out to be exactly as she thought. A good listener, someone she found easy to talk to; and before she knew it, she had done just as he had suggested. She had booked a doctor's appointment and was meeting with a group of ladies from the church at dawn, for a run. What started out as a month's break from work was later extended to become four. But still not quite ready to face socializing or even seeing her clients at work, she was filled with dread. Hesitantly but assured she needed more time, she made the call she had been putting off, to Misha. But when she did, she was again a little surprised at how supportive her mentor was in without hesitation, granting her an additional two months off.

"Six months should do the trick." Misha said playfully, which was unusual for her. "We need you here. No, we need the real version of you here. I've had enough of these crybabies pulling at me to solve their ..." Elizabeth could not stop herself and for the first time in a while she laughed like the old Elizabeth would. Something about the way Misha said that did it, and she was grateful 'grumpy Misha' was back and it looked like the real Elizabeth was trying to make a come-back too.

The time off was exactly what she needed; and she was happier still to know that she would be able to afford to and that her job at the firm was not at risk. No longer did she need it so much for the money, but more so for the experience; and besides, there was no doubt that she loved what she did. She wanted to use the time to get things into perspective, but most of all to revisit some goals and rebuild some relationships particularly with those she held dear. When she last saw Richard, she knew she could not continue. An indefinite break was what she proposed but a definite one was what he said he could offer. She never wanted to hurt him, but she had had enough of hurting herself and compromising to her detriment and she wanted to start the new year with less thoughts about who or whatever else but more about her. She needed that time to find her – Orchid amongst the roses.

She and Mathew were pretty close to old times; with the exception of the elephant in the room, Richard, they had quite a lot to talk about. He didn't ask again when they met-up for the first time in the new year, and she didn't volunteer any information. She figured Pastor Lammy was the only unbiased voice of reason and that Mathew was too much like his sister. Besides, finding herself did not include worrying about either Mathew or Susan, but about her and she was not ready to share that bit of information just yet. Should they accuse her of keeping secrets, that was a chance she was willing to take. Only Pastor Lammy knew of the break-up and she wanted to keep it that way; well, for a little while at least. She respected Richard and wanted that to be her way of showing it. "We are still friends." She told Pastor Lammy, but from what he knew of Richard, he knew better than to think that friendship would last. He knew Richard was a focused man, no wonder he was ready to get married and although things didn't work out between them, he still thought of him as a brilliant mind, and a good person; just not the one for Elizabeth.

The end of January was Susan's thirtieth birthday and Paul did not hold back. Everyone who was anyone was there. Government officials he met on his travels and in his line of work, made their appearance.
"Remind me in my next life to choose a career in international cyber security." Elizabeth muttered to Mathew. She thought he looked handsome in his dinner suit and bow tie. It was not often these days that she got to see him all dressed up, and

wanted to tell him how handsome he looked but was mindful of his guest, someone he introduced as an old friend from Uni.

"You look beautiful", he told her just as all three reached for their drinks and it appeared his guest thought so too because, she smiled in response. Elizabeth was out in red. She had been to the hairdresser for the first time in months and although simple, her hair suited her couture dark red dress, superbly. It was left black, sleek and chic with every strand in place, flowing backwards over her shoulders. She had her mother's build and although her weight loss was noticeable, the dress suited her complexion and her frame perfectly. She smiled as Susan approached but was taken aback when she appeared to know Mathew's guest rather well. She appeared not to notice as they whispered in French interspersed with English. Without thinking, she headed straight for the ladies' room.

Everyone was shocked at the guest list but not at the elaborate party; while, for Susan, it was the total opposite. Due to the nature of his work, she had never made a big deal of her husband's connections but knew him well enough that when he threw a surprise party, it was big. All along, she thought they had first class tickets to the Seychelles only. The food, the wine, the decorations, everything was just as Elizabeth had imagined it when she met with the men and the planner to organize her friend's due.

"It's beautiful, don't you think!" Susan was pleased, beaming from ear to ear and Elizabeth was happy that her friend was genuinely surprised.

Mathew enquired about Richard.
"Couldn't make it." She said nonchalantly, between sips.

"Hmm, I only brought Leanne as I thought you had a plus one."

"Oh, what are you saying?"

"Oh, I am saying you could have told me. She is Susan's friend, not particularly mine." She almost spilled her drink trying to hide her relief.

"Oh well, blame me for not telling you. I will be at the party we helped to plan, without, a man."

"Elizabeth! Not just any man, he is your fiancé. You could have said something. Like, Richard is working, can we go together, or something!" She could tell he was annoyed and that made her smile inside. It felt like old times.

"Oh, and save you using someone?"

"I am not - using her! She was invited by the lovely Susan." He waved in his sister's direction to see her busy meeting and greeting, while Leanne made her way over to them.

For the rest of the evening, Elizabeth's attempt to pay more attention to his guest than to him was ruined. Starting with the cutting of the cake when Susan had Mathew and Paul positioned on either side of her and was about to cut the cake, only for her to pause and beckoned Elizabeth to join them. Not long, and the music was blaring once again, and they all danced; she with Mathew and Susan with Paul. Afterwards, they all donned coats and umbrellas to watch fireworks in the winter showers. The snow caused the reflection and shifting of colours which made the whole show spectacular. They all agreed it was a fitting end to an amazing night. One that was almost like a coming-out of sorts for Elizabeth. For that one time, only briefly did she think about Izzy and how much fun it would have been to have her there.

On the way home, she remembered always sharing her party shenanigans with her mum afterwards and tonight, she would have loved to tell her how she felt when at first she saw Leanne on Mathew's arms.

Valentine's day was not long after Susan's celebration, and after finally admitting to have broken off the engagement to her friends, they made plans for Valentine's dinner which included Mathew's business partner, the one who owned the house in what Elizabeth referred to as the 'show house neighbourhood', the night Mathew detoured.

She had met Marcus a few times but never met his wife, a well-known model. They had a lovely evening. She had fun getting to know Tiffany, Marcus' wife; and although she found his and Mathew's business ventures rather interesting, she knew more than ever that was not a road she wanted to take and was relieved to know, the other ladies shared her view.

After dinner, when it was time to dance, she did not feel much like it and Mathew took turn to dance with Tiffany and his sister instead. In the end, after much persuading, she agreed to one dance only with Marcus. Not long in and Mathew became the subject. Marcus made it clear how happy he was for his longtime friend. He was proud of his achievements and that he had finally rid himself of Claire's demons. Elizabeth shared her joy too but, was a little puzzled how he managed to do that. Desert arrived as they returned to their seats and in time for Marcus to ask his friend, "So, what are you waiting on to 'pop the question'?"

Mathew stared at her while Susan pretended to be busy fixing something on Paul's perfectly framed jacket as all along Elizabeth looked from Marcus to Mathew, puzzled.

The case involving the nine-year-old twin was the first thing to land on her desk, as she returned to work after her extended six-month break and was still what she was working on, a month later. Glad the Monday morning board meeting had nothing sinister to flag, she returned to her office. Just then, Mathew came to mind, and she made a mental note to ring him in the week when she was certain he was back from his business travels. Their longest conversation had been a while back, shortly after the awkward valentine's meal, and after that when she had requested the services of his real estate team, to help her get her house back.

She had hoped that with some clever negotiating on their part, the new owner would agree to an above market value price. Most of the money from her mum she did not need to use anyway, and now even less so as she would be back at work and could easily live off her salary. A part from spending a small amount to transform the outhouse into a large open plan office, she knew she could put the vast majority of it in one of Mathew's less risky ventures, if he would let her that is. He had refused in the past and offered to help her invest in rental properties only instead.

Admittedly it did take a few attempts to get to him and when she did, she confirmed it was a good time to talk. Marcus hinted at him being in a better place; in fact, he said it was the best he'd seen him in their years of friendship and she wondered also if he had started the counselling sessions she had recommended those many months ago. They had not been on their monthly meet-up in ages and she was hoping they would be able to do so soon. She missed them, and their time together. Both her and his sister were always cognizant of him being very busy with his business and Susan was always reminding Elizabeth not to take his actions personally, he had a lot going on. In fact, the day she returned to work was the day he flew out to Dubai and a week ago when she was hoping to see him, she learnt from his sister that he would be staying a while longer in Dubai after this trip to South Africa.

Now in her third month of her weekly meetings with Pastor Lammy, which truth be told, she quite enjoyed, his neutral ear and her faith in his integrity made talking to him so much easier than speaking to either of her best friends. She always wondered where the answers she gave him came from, when on her own she sometimes felt so confused. When today's session ended, she was a little sad to say goodbye to the safe space they had created over the months. Quickly, she readied herself to make her way to meet the 'family'. Like Susan, she was excited to see

Mathew. He had said he would be in town only briefly and Elizabeth was looking forward to their meet-up albeit with mixed feelings. It was all planned out about a week ago when his schedule made them miss out that night, and the same looked set to happen, had Mathew's last-minute flight not brought him in from Dublin on time. At his request, they decided to meet at his place instead.

Elizabeth was first to be picked up, while Susan and Paul would be waiting there. Enroute, they could both hear the buzz of her phone, but she had thrown her bag on the rear seats and was in no mood to reach for it now. She mentioned about the fight she had with a client earlier that day. He challenged her decision, but in the end had agreed with most of her actions. Mathew gave her the proverbial listening ear and right after, as if wanting to be alone with his thoughts, the music came on. Not long and on schedule, they were all exchanging hugs and kisses as they greeted each other in his living room. They were all happy to be at his place, they loved it. Susan always saw it as a treat. It was always immaculate which was in perfect contrast to her 'impeccably untidy home' and laughed out loud as the words rolled off her tongue in perfect phonetics. She too had a busy week but would agree she had had more gruelling ones. But she would do anything for her brother and making her way to see him after more than a month away, was the highlight of her week.

Very quickly they settled in. Hair down and jackets off, revealing nearly toned arms. The skirt Elizabeth wore became more of a mini having to sit in Mathew's well-chosen extremely low couch while; ironically for Susan, she was convinced her trousers were much tighter at the end of the day. Typical of the older girl, she had them all in hysterics as Paul looked at his wife with dreamy admiration. They chatted briefly about Lucille who was away on a tour of the Caribbean with her children, and had not been around to clean any of their places in a while, which gave Mathew time to get showered and dressed for their planned indoor evening together. He too was happy they were there and punched the air when they all agreed to spend at least the evening at his place, for a change. He loved his penthouse apartment but sometimes wished for a voice other than his in it. "In time," he told Susan and more often these days, Marcus.

Elizabeth promised to organise the cleaning schedule for their place in her neighbourhood when next she had Lucille over. Earlier she had seen Paul's eyes as he looked at his wife and for a moment she wondered if they had given up on having the third round of IVF treatment but thought better than to spoil the mood. She decided instead to wait until she and Susan were next out together, alone, and to avoid a strain in their conversation, she dismissed it immediately. They ate sushi, played card games then a few rounds of scrabble, as they chatted amiably. The music was on and appeared to have gotten louder as they played, because now Elizabeth was convinced, they were shouting to hear each other. But no one cared really, they continued with the next game of cards and when it was time for her to take the one-hour journey home, she was exhausted and confessed to feeling drained, which they all blamed on her caseload at work.

"Why not leave in the morning? It's already quite late as it is." Susan quickly suggested, as Mathew sneezed immediately followed by a fit of coughs. Paul offered to help with his recovery and they both left for the kitchen.

Yawning, the thought of a nearby bed was most inviting and without much prodding she conceded, adding, "If it's okay with Matt, I could hang around and aim to leave first thing in the morning." She yawned again.

Paul knew of the weather forecast prediction of at least three days of torrential rains which could make her leaving the following day, nearly impossible, but he too was having too much fun and didn't want to be the one to put a damper on things. Admitting he had to be the one to drive, he agreed with Elizabeth to have her stay the night saving him or Mathew having to drive another hour in his case, while the added return journey would mean two hours for a tired Mathew who had only just arrived home earlier that evening, he reminded them.

"Thanks for calling me a burden, dear Paul." She shouted back. "I will remember that when next you or your wife invite me to your perfectly impeccable mess of a place." She spoke but what she said, and the sense it made did not matter then, she was too tired to care and luckily, amid her ramblings they found the humour hinted at. Susan consented on behalf of her brother in his absence and headed into the kitchen to join the men, leaving Elizabeth dozing on the couch. She was barely awake and could hear her friend's voice.

"We are going to go before the rain comes," Paul pitched in almost too chirpily, and a little too quickly for dozing Elizabeth's comfort which led her to think her friends must be all too happy to leave but, admitted that she was too tired to protest.

She too had had a long week. On none of the days had she been home before dark. Besides, she had not been at Matt's in almost a year and for a moment was looking forward to all of them, together, if not for the weekend, at least for the night. For a long time, she longed for some semblance of what she missed, what she called normalcy and was happy to have found it again. No backwards and forwards and trying to figure out how to get Richard to understand that she enjoyed the rigors of her job, of helping people, children and that she never wanted to have to give that up. Even if they should have a child themselves, and at twenty-eight, she was looking forward to having one fairly soon, but not if it meant saying goodbye to her career. To her friendship with the two people in the world whom she had loved and who had stood by her for as far as she could remember and she was damned if she was not going to have it all. She just had to figure out how. As she closed the bedroom door, she sighed at the thought of not having to justify her staying at Mathew's, to Richard and fell asleep within minutes of her climbing unto the bed.

"Lizzy, it's okay. Shh." She could hear her name in the distance and felt a shaking. It was Mathew. He heard her crying and had come to see if she was okay. She was still asleep, and when she became fully awake, she told him about being with her mum, at their old house.

"...and mum was brushing my hair and calling me 'her orchid'," she whispered exasperatingly. "She was trying to tell me that I am strong and ... well, beautiful ...and her little orchid. It felt so real. I miss her so much." And once again, she felt the tears and wondered if they would ever truly cease. When would she recall fond memories of her mum, dad and amazing friend and not feel the flow of water down her cheeks? The kind that was now so torrential, they were making their steady streams down another one of her best friend's exposed back.

He held her and she felt silly but knew he understood, and he confirmed as much when he told her, "I miss dad too so much sometimes, I ..." he didn't say the words, but she thought she knew exactly what they would be.

"You wish he was here, to see the man you have become, and enjoy some of what you have worked so hard every day for. I know, I feel the same way too about my parents and Izzy." She finished for him.

"And it breaks my heart every time, but your mother is right. You are strong, and beautiful and equally as delicate and graceful - just like the orchid, and, that balance is so important. Just believe in yourself and the values she has placed here," he pointed at her heart then brought his hand up to ever so gently, rest on her head, "...and time will heal. When time wants to. All you have to do, is just let it."

Once again, she was happy to be there and later, after she settled, he put the light out and went to spend the rest of the morning in his home office. She slept for most of the day and awoke to mayhem outside. It was blistering showers with lightning and thunder and when she checked everywhere was under siege. No sign of life in her line of vision and when she enquired from Mathew, he said it started from before she woke up the first time around.

The downpour was unmissable and almost worrisome. There was lightning and thunder and reports of flash flooding. Mathew reached under his desk and located the remote control for his heavy-set floor to ceiling brown-grey window blinds. After closing them, he prepared lunch for himself and Elizabeth; some assorted sandwiches, but when he checked in to alert her, she had already gone back to sleep.

When finally, she became conscious, it was late evening and Mathew was as surprised as he was relieved when she insisted on not having him drive her home.

"Shame it's not a dry day, and had you gotten up earlier, we could have had a picnic. But…"

"It's pouring down outside! Besides, I was so tired, and you know I am not a fan of thunder or lightening." She clapped her hands as if to applaud his recent performance and without intending to, the lights came on. Surprised, she burst out laughing. She had forgotten her friend was a gadget geek and a big fan of the simple high-tech life.

"You, my dear, will be the one to wash these." He offered her another one of his white T-shirts and threw her phone closer to her on the bed. His nonchalant attempt was not lost on her.

She could see there were two missed calls and wondered if Susan and Paul were okay. Puzzled, she enquired, "Have you spoken to your sister"

"Well, briefly. They are home safe and sound and warned me not to leave the house but to let you walk, crawl or, I don't know run the way there if you attempted to leave."

"Spoken like your sister indeed. Somehow, I cannot imagine Paul saying any such dreadful thing." He did not respond. She watched him as he walked barefooted towards the large open plan kitchen and disappeared in the direction of his huge integrated refrigerator, and she smiled happily in the moment. Just then she attempted to call Susan but when she returned the call, she was unavailable. So, she texted Paul instead, to tell him how awful his wife was and that he was to get out before he became just as dreadful as she was. His red-faced emoji only made her laugh.

Fully rested, Elizabeth was happy; happy for the first time, in a long time. Happy to be with him and his remote controlled everything; clap and the lights were on or, they'd go brighter or off completely. All of which she called his toys. Happy to have him share although brief, but once again stories of his girlfriends. It continued to trouble her, though, that since Cara, he had not introduced anyone officially; just as friends in passing or as a one-off accompaniment to one of Susan's barbecues or to one of their friend's parties. Still, sometimes although not often, she had that annoying feeling that they were not as close as they used to be. Before Richard that is. And sometimes, for fear of widening the distance between them, she thought it better to let him have his space and maybe, just maybe, they would find their way back to how they used to be; carefree, and open and honest with each other.

She left everything on the floor and without thinking, stepped under the body heat sensor-controlled shower of the En-suite. She squealed as she felt her hair become completely soaked. Mathew rushed in.

"Are you alright, and why did you not close the door, woman." Very quickly, he did so vigorously.

"Why couldn't you have a hair sensor-controlled shower cap dispenser or something, and then I wouldn't get my hair completely soaked!" He thought she was crying but realised it was only her high-pitched squeal coming through the fire door.

"There's a place called the hairdresser's madame, where they would be happy to fix that wet mane for you." He hissed.

"I do not want to have to go to the hairdresser. I haven't got the time, for goodness sake!"

"Why did you scream like that anyway? You are not seriously crying, are you? Remind me to add that toy next time. Thought you were hurt." He hissed.

"I am hurt! You can be so insensitive!" She hissed back.

But he had already left the room and was on his way back to the kitchen where he could no longer decide whether to have a cup of tea or one of his favourite kale and moringa smoothies he had picked up from Nickleby's Smoothie Bar, on his way home the evening before. Shaking his head, he chose a glass of filtered cold water which, thanks to his lack of focus, over spilled onto the heated tiled floor.

She had always loved his place and the few times she had stayed over with Susan, there was always plenty in the refrigerator and just then she felt the need for food and smiled in anticipation. She smiled too at Richard's face had he been able to see her now and all but laughed out loud at what Mathew concluded that Richards consistently unhappy appearance must be a neurosurgeon's inherent disposition. She reminisced over the course of the year on the numerous heated debates she had with Richard. Arguments about Mathew and his money and that he was a grown man to be left to his devices. In the end, Richard had insisted on her not spending too much time with him. In his view, between her and his sister, they treated him like a 'baby' and that he was just a spoilt kid. She had never thought of him as spoilt and had many times reiterated to her then fiancé, how hard her friend had worked to achieve what he had, but she knew Richard never understood and the strange thing for her was, she hadn't yet figured out why.

The large open plan living area was just off the large guest room, and as she entered, Mathew approached with the biggest grin on his face.

"Why are you laughing at me?" She retracted wondering what she must look like or what she could be exposing.

She was wearing one of his white Burberry cotton T-shirts while another one was piled high unto her head as a makeshift wrap-around for her hair.

"Well, I am just thinking of the huge laundry bill, you know - that any discoloration of any kind, and I mean any weird dyes or oils, on any of my Ts will be charged to you, right?" He was centred fully on her face and was making small stealth-like steps towards her. These days she wasn't sure if he was serious or annoyed. Once again, he was becoming increasingly difficult to read.

"Okay, calm down. I can do that."

He had reached the doorway now. For a moment, it felt like old times and without thinking they were encircled in one of his man-hug embraces, and like a little sister who was overjoyed to see her big brother she grinned and laid her head on his chest. Immediately, she felt him stiffened, a reaction she recognised from the day of her mum's funeral, and confused she stepped back.

"I'm calm." He said wide-eyed extending both of his long arms like an eagle's wings in position for flight. "Come, let me help you dry this thing."

"Thing, uh, how dare you!" Ignoring her protest, he grabbed hold of her hand and led the way down the corridor where he later turned right to the main bathroom located in a hidden section of the Penthouse, which happened to be at the farthest end.

The tiny sunken sensor lights came on immediately, but left the layered chandelier in the centre of the large room unlit, and with a tap on one of the black suspended drawers on the right, beneath the black and white marble topped surface, the drawer slowly opened to reveal more of his toys. Again, he touched something and like a magical scene out of 'Once Upon a Time', she watched as all her hair would ever need, appeared from where they had been nicely stored away, in a multi-shelved cupboard complete with more small round lights. Then voila, a hair dryer.

"Oh, where did that come from? I didn't know you had that."

"What, the hairdryer or the cupboard or both?" He continued as she peered inside in obvious admiration and bewilderment. "Well, you never needed it before so now you do…"

"It emerges. At the touch of a button. What else have you got hidden in these walls, Mr. Thomas?" Her voice was deep and hushed as she looked at him with eyes half opened.

"It depends; what do you need Ms Dawes." He mirrored her tone and demeanour.

She laughed. She was happy. She felt it was a bit like old times and suddenly she acknowledged how much she missed him, missed their friendship.

"Missed you, Matt." She reached up and without touching him, kissed his right cheek.

"Why? It's not like I've gone anywhere?" She could tell from his furrowed brow and cessation of his handwork from assembling everything he thought she would need, that he was taken by her question.

"Not only physically, but for the year, there were sometimes when it felt like it emotionally." She made herself comfortable on the stool nearby as she hastened on, "You know, like we are not friends like we used to be. I wonder if maybe it's taking you longer this time around to get over Claire and Cara, and if you are drowning yourself in work because of it? You know?" She was happy to be able to say this in what she hoped was a non-threatening tone.

"Stop! Stop overthinking things." He whispered while he very gently separated her hair in preparation for drying. They looked at each other from the wide mirror covering that entire wall. She could see the light and dark shades of brown with the hint of green of his eyes, as his mood changed with the depth of his answers. She was becoming awfully familiar with those hews. "I am always, always here for you. You know that, don't you? There is no one else in the world that …" He stopped himself.

Faced down, she could not see his face as he attended to the back of her hair first, but she could tell he was about to say something about their friendship, and she wondered why he stopped himself. She thought how unfair it was that Claire's selfishness had even prevented him from talking openly with his friends, and his family too, sometimes. "So, go on. What no one else in the world could do or...?"

"Here she goes. No one else in the world could get me to dry their hair but you and this big head. Like, look at the size of it. Huge. Massive!"

"Hey!"

The noise of the blow dryer prevented much conversation after that. Together, they got her hair dried and moisturised. He watched her as she sat dutifully while he sprayed some sheen on for her at the end. She thought of Richard then and wondered why they never got to this stage. Maybe if he had just lightened up, she thought, maybe they would do things like this. Like what Matt is doing, just allow her to be childlike sometimes. Thought dismissed, she searched for Matt's eyes in the mirror, but found his back to her.

"Thanks, Matt." She looked back to see the hairdryer making its way back into its hidden holder and within minutes the wall appeared once again, seamless.

"That's pretty cool!

"You know me, I hate clutter."

"You know me, a little clutter is good. Makes the place - shall I say, more homely." Looking into his eyes, she laughed as she encircled his elbow and they made their way back to the sitting room.

"I had thought of us going out for dinner but with the heavy rain and all…There are still some sandwiches which I made while you were asleep. If you like we could have those?"

"I am not sure about sandwiches currently." She smiled, knowing full well he could not read her mind. "Never mind let me roam that refrigerator, see what I can find for both of us." They both knew how much she loved cooking and she was looking forward to being all over his man-sized kitchen.

After rummaging inside the huge monstrosity called his American-style refrigerator, she had gathered a few small tomatoes, brought out a medium packet of deveined king prawns, some scallops which she wanted to cut into half, some mussels and was disappointed when she could not locate any shells.

"Any shells? And where can I find some olive oil, and some white wine would be good too."

"Over there, if you are tall enough that is."

She was obviously startled. "Have you been standing there the whole time?"

"No, not really. Just about the time when you realised that there were only cherry tomatoes in there."

"That's like, the whole time and, didn't it occur to you that you are best placed to find the items in your own refrigerator than anyone else ever could!" She threw the lemon she had not long taken out, at him, and continued to make her demands. "Well, you can make yourself useful by getting me two cloves of garlic, a pack of pasta, the olive oil I asked for earlier; and please get me the wine. You are driving me insane."

After they each had a small glass of wine, he teased her to get on with her dinner-lady duties. "Come on, get moving young Lawyer lady cook, I am starving." He winked and headed back to his home office.

She heard his phone ringing and wondered why he was not answering. She removed her now completed 'Saffron Seafood with Pasta Special', from the heat and headed towards his office. She was surprised he was not there, and that his phone was unattended. She noted it was from an unknown caller. A little concerned, she made her way towards the master suite, calling him as she proceeded. It was not until she entered that she heard him singing and realised that he was in his shower. She noticed the door was ajar and quickly, she almost shouted as she told him he had left his phone in the office and that he had several missed calls.

"You can keep it. I am done for the day. Unless it is Marcus or Sue, that's it for me." He emerged from the shower now and walked across the room wet but towelled. She threw the phone on his bed and told him dinner is ready whenever he was.

"Finally!" He shouted.

Unbeknown to him, she had stepped back and could see him putting on his boxers with one hand as the other poked through a stack of folded Ts in his walk-in closet next to his En-suite.

"Careful, I may just have to add a few more ingredients, how would you like that?"

"Go away! Go on, get out of here. He threw a cushion from the chaise lounge at her from across the room, which she caught in time and threw right back at him.

"A pillow fight, now? bring it on." His phone vibrated again, and she ran.

She left him to change into another one of his T-shirts, this time one from Calvin Klein. "Well, all my Ts worn and now I think I am about to be poisoned by whatever it is she has concocted" He said with a chuckle. He approached the sitting room as she stepped out of the guess room barefooted with her lanky legs hanging out below his T-shirt. Her now dried black hair hung loosed, cascaded mindlessly past her shoulders. He saw her but quickly looked away. It turned out to be Susan who had called, she wanted to speak to her, and without looking at her fully, he handed her the phone and returned to his room.

"I don't know what's wrong with him, I loved him in his teenage years, now he's so moody." Mid her complaints, she could hear Susan's signature belly laughs.

"What's so funny?"

Susan only continued laughing – harder and harder.

"Well, it's pouring down outside, and I can't go home. Imagine Mathew putting us both at risk by driving in that weather."

At the sound of that, Susan seemed to have sobered up immediately. "Please, whatever you do, please stay indoors." She pleaded, "The neighbours called to say a tree had fallen down and is now blocking our drive to the house in Knockholt. I asked another neighbour to check on your place as soon as they can. I'll let you know when they do."

"Oh, thanks, Sue! You are a real big sis, aren't you?"

"Don't know about that. I am glad you are with him, Liz. I'm glad you are together and happy." Elizabeth heard the gentleness in her friend's voice and for a moment was worried, *was something wrong with Mathew. Was he ill,* she wondered?

"Are you okay? Is he kay? I'd love to see you both more often, but life gets in the way, you know that?"

"I know, Hun. You two must have a lot to catch up on; so, I am going to go now. Tell my brother I love him, and he is to do what I told him to do before it's too late."

"Talk about no more secrets." Elizabeth was confused but Susan had hung up which Elizabeth thought she had done deliberately.

Annoyed, she threw the phone down in the couch as she shouted at him. "She said you are to do whatever it is she told you to do before it's too late."

"Shouting, is un-lady-like and in this case totally unnecessary, I am right here." In a few long strides he was close enough to extend his long arms, retrieve his phone which he turned off immediately then headed into the kitchen. Elizabeth knew then that they were hiding something from her and whatever it was she was determined to get to the bottom of it.

"Wish we could sit on the terrace, don't you?" She asked coyly.

"Hmm that would be nice. White or red what would you like, or which would you recommend, chef?"

"White for me please. And tell you what, as the lightning and thunder have ceased and all that's left is just the sound of the rain, what do you say we move the smaller of the two desks in your office to that end of the sitting room next to the window, open the curtains and enjoy the view of the city in all its rainy dimly lit glory."

"Hmm, brilliant. Yeah, we can do that. Tell you what, you serve, and I'll see to the table." She thought his parting smile was somewhat sarcastic, but she was on a mission and she wanted to remain focussed.

She was ill prepared for what she saw as she made her way to the desired destination and he could see her face totally lit up as they past each other going in opposite directions across the room, past the couches facing the huge fireplace and the beautiful paintings in different sizes elegantly displayed on the immaculate white wall stretching all the way to the opposite end of the room. Immediately she recognised the oil on canvas from her mum to him and she was happy to see it displayed amongst his prize collection. He was destined for the wine rack and she to where once there was only a standing lamp which was now accompanied by a small table big enough for two, placed strategically to soak up the full view of the city below. As he approached with a bottle of wine and two glasses, she placed both plates down, one at each end while all the time wondering when he collected the place mats and cutlery.

Together they were mesmerised by the view from the forty first floor, voicing simultaneously how beautiful it was. Other than the night before when they were all together, she couldn't remember a happier time in a long time and for a moment she felt hopeful. Hopeful for all that life had to offer and as he pulled out her seat and placed the napkin on her lap she smiled at his playful ways and clapped like a school child as she said again, "Wow, this is so beautiful. The views are simply breath-taking." She echoed.

"Thanks to you. I would never have thought of this. I would have crashed out in the study or sat boringly by the island or pigged out in the couch." He smiled as he raised his glass, "Thanks for showing me what I truly have. I wonder if one day you too will see what you truly have. Cheers!"

"Cheers. I do sometimes feel like I am missing something but, we won't talk about all of my well documented losses tonight – let's dwell on some wins, like – now, being here with you and this," she pointed again to the view. "By the way, you could leave this here and during the winter months or when it's raining or too windy, you can still enjoy the amazing views without being exposed to the elements. How about that?"

He simply nodded in response. "Hmm this is delicious, Lizzy. Hmm mmm. This is good." He pointed at his plate then.

"Mathew, do not speak with your mouthful." She scolded.

"Sorry, ma'am."

"Are you rolling your eyes at me?"

Cutlery down. Hands up. "You got me."

"Susan told me about the tree, was that all she called about?"

"And to remind me that your birthday is in a few months."

"Really? like you are in a habit of forgetting my birthday. And, like almost a year is the same thing as almost a few months."

Somehow Elizabeth was not at all convinced and thought she would try again later. She poured him another glass.

"Susan said she had asked someone to go by my place. That is sweet of her, I hope everything is okay." He was always quite stern when he talked business and as she was enjoying the lightness of the moment, she hoped her statement just then did not alter the mood. She did not wish for it go heavy. "Have you ever thought of adding some colour to the place?" She added quickly. "I mean it's nice, but the stark white walls make what is, a beautiful place, appear somewhat clinical."

They had finished eating now and were both full. Like her mother, she enjoyed cooking but even more so when it is enjoyed. That was one of the things she had learnt from her mum and which she had prided herself on.

"You should come by more often. No, I take that back, I may live to regret it. Because the frequency with which you are hopping in and out my Ts, very soon I'll have nothing to wear to work." He did not look amused and again she wondered if she had upset him. She knew he loved his white T- shirts and jeans with a pair of trainers but she was in a happy place and so she decided to push back at his accusations.

"Well you will just have to go naked and show off that body you hang out with your personal trainer three mornings per week to maintain. Remember the 5am work out you were showing off about – yes that one …it's about time the world sees the fruit of your labour, don't you think?" She teased, straight-facedly. She was on her feet now and she pulled him to stand opposite so she could lift his vest and sing, "take it off, take it off, take it off" as she clapped to the rhythm. He obliged and lifted it off, and she went "ooooh!" They were alone, just the two of them, and for a moment she forgot about all her issues, her mom, and Izzy and the sadness of the cases she was working on at work. She felt free. She wondered if Richard could be as relaxed and fun as Mathew was. *Was it the demands of his job? Was it that he simply wanted her to be there when he got home, after a long surgery or a hectic day? That was not too much to ask was it?* It was too late now she mused. She would never know. She had decided to continue seeing Pastor Lammy and together with the changes at work, she was more ready to embrace the new Elizabeth, the orchid was coming back to life, about to bloom again, after being pricked by life's roses.

"Elizabeth; now, payment please."

"Pay you, for what?" she was distracted with her own thoughts and though present in body was absent in mind. She missed his performance.

"Don't they pay strippers these days."

"Not if it's as poorly executed as what you did just then!"

He lounged at her, knowing full well she hated to be tickled. Not long, and to make her get-a-way, together they collapsed on the couch. It was then that suddenly it dawned on her. Her being there may have prevented him being with anyone he was seeing then.

"Oh Mathew, I am so sorry. I hope I am not intruding or putting a dent in your love life?"

"No, no. Rest assured, you are not. I am not seeing anyone." He could hear her breathing heavily. "Not until Tuesday, anyway." He added.

The ending was totally missed on her. She told herself, she wanted only the best for him and acknowledged then that she had found herself becoming increasingly protective of him. She had often thought of what he had been through to get over his mother's abandonment and his success in business and felt she did not want anyone to take advantage of him. And now, she wanted him to be happy and she wanted to wait until she found someone, like his sister did when she met Paul.

She put her head back on his shoulder as she gave herself time to catch her breath. He stroked her hair. He had told her he loved her hair.

"Is she coming here, or will you go by hers?" She was desperate for them to share everything again, like they once did and, there was still that little 'need to know' - the answer to what Susan had told him to do before it was too late- that she needed to get to.

He paused. He was not expecting that. He stuttered. He hated lying to her and realised he had done plenty of that already. He closed his eyes just then and as if voluntarily his head went backwards to rest against hers. "I'll go by hers, I guess."

"What's her name? come on, tell me."

He looked across at the painting a gift from his dad. It was the Japanese foot bridge painting by Monet which his father kept in his study and had been in his family for years, and somehow, decided on not lying anymore. "Sorry. I am sorry, Lizzy," She was puzzled at his apology. "I am not seeing a ... I am not dating now.

I am working on some projects in Dubai which as you know takes me away lot, and now, I am looking to go over into Abu Dhabi. It is not fair to anyone to travel around with me or wait for me until I get settled or change their lifestyle just for me. If I meet someone and she is happy with seeing me whenever and we can make a go of it then fine, but I am not going to deliberately mislead anyone."

She could hear the sincerity in his voice and was happy he had decided to be honest with her. She wondered why he appeared not to be able to do so in the beginning but settled for 'better late than never'.

"But you are here this weekend and we were not planning on being here, it just happened so, couldn't you make the time for that someone if you had to? If she means so much to you?" She wondered if she had touched a nerve and although she could not see his eyes, she felt him tense.

"I have, I mean, I am in love with someone."

She employed every effort to remain still, thinking, finally, finally it is out. "I am confused. Is it that you have let the one you love go in favour of a career?"

"No. It's a bit complicated, Lizzy."

At that moment, she changed her position; forcing him to change his. "Well let's see what we can come up with to uncomplicate it. You know 'heads together'?" She nudged his head just then, and he closed his eyes again as if wishing she would stop, and she knew she could not let him just walk away now.

"She's beautiful, Lizzy. So smart, loving, funny with such a big heart, so loyal and sometimes she drives me mad, but I love her. I have always loved her. And the fear is, I think I always will. I need to find a way around her and at this moment in time, it is proving extremely difficult as she has proved in recent times the type of person she wants in her life, some one that's − I don't know, a bit of a nerd maybe and boring as hell. And you know what, Lizzy, I should do the same. It's about time I acknowledge that I am not her type and move on with my life."

She was happy with his attempt at honesty and hugged him sympathetically. "I am so sorry, Matt. Thanks for your honesty. I can't believe you have never said anything about, oh what's her name?" She had thought all along that his mother's absence was the primary factor, she had no idea he had a lost love. She wondered if it was Cara and he didn't want to say.

"No, that I will not say." He untangled his hand and repositioned himself to face her.

"Elizabeth, Please. Do not ask me who it is. I will promise you this, when the time has come and I have had a chance to get her out of my head, you will be the first to know." He raised her hand to his lips while never taking his eyes from hers.

"Were you in love with Cara at all?"

"Cara?" He sighed, "You know me, Lizzy; I don't think I was or ever would have. Sometimes, I felt she loved what we could afford to do. She is driven by the lifestyle she has known from childhood while we - you, me, we care about the people by dad's old church and you, about the people you serve every day, and who you intend to serve when finally you get your practice up and running. One could say, I met her during a period of 'youth inflicted mid-life crisis'." He smiled as he said it and she couldn't help herself smiling back at him.

She knew Cara was from the Goldhorn line of family, all well-known socialites, but she had no idea she was as shallow as Mathew now said.

"Cara's lifestyle is not how I want to live. I'm not a show-off, am I, Lizzy?"

"No, absolutely not." She wondered where that came from and did her best to reassure him. She was now certain from her line of questioning that Cara was not the lost love and had every intention of finding out who was.

"So, what is it Sue told you to do before it was too late?" He thought she had forgotten about that, and now he could not remember what he told her when she first asked.

"It's a surprise, I am not going to say. That too is something you will be the first to know about. I promise. Scout's honour."

"Whatever! I know you are both hiding something. So much for no more secrets. I am going to bed." She was not happy.

He could see that and although it hurt to lie to her, he felt he needed time. Time to clear his own head and could tell that she recognised him almost as if giving with one hand and withholding with the other.

"Bed, it's only half nine…" He looked disappointed, but she chose to ignore any sign of penitence and without knowing it, they both blamed Susan for sending him her cryptic message, which had now aroused her suspicion and placed Mathew in such a precarious position.

"… and I am hoping to leave early in the morning, should the rain abate. By the way, I am happy to take the train. Travelling backwards and forwards, that is unfair on you. I am off to my assigned sleeping quarters and see you in the morning. If you are awake when I am leaving, that is."

She laid in bed reminiscing on love letters they let each other read, letters from others who liked them, and she smiled when she remembered how although she would throw hers out, she would always insist he replied, until she found out he was writing to tell everyone he already had a girlfriend, and that her name was Elizabeth. She remembered too, being so upset with him for about two weeks when he stopped talking to her without so much as a word and later, he confessed to hearing from his mother for his twenty first birthday and how upset it made him. He had gone into hiding that summer break. She thought of how they made faces at each other, while they danced with their respective dates at their graduation and laughed out loud then when she heard a knock on the door.

"And what may I ask is so amusing in this particular room?" He was happy to know she was not still upset but was curious as to what brought on her fit of giggles.

"Just musing over another one of your bathroom 'toys'." She rolled her eyes then, when he held out the phone indicating another call from his sister. Susan had requested they both joined in a conference call where she reported having received a call from one of the neighbours, who had gone to check on both houses for any damage from the heavy wind and rain earlier.

"It turns out that a tree had fallen in and broken the window to your mum's old front room, Lizzy, which leaves the place..."

"Totally unsecured and potential for severe water damage" Elizabeth interrupted, eager to see what damage had been done.

"Paul is happy to go by and see what he can do. We will let you know."

"I don't mind. I could get a sheet of ply and nail to the outside and tomorrow ..." Mathew added.

"The insurance company can be called in." Elizabeth quickly chimed in.

But Susan would not hear of it and insisted neither of them left the safety of the apartment to venture out into such treacherous roads, which as far as she knew, many parts were still blocked and needed clearing. "No Matt, an hour's drive in this weather, is not safe. I am just letting you guys know. Between us and the neighbours, we will take care of it."

And once again Elizabeth could never be happier to have them as her friends. Many times, she had thanked her mum for deciding to move to Knockholt. What would she have done otherwise? Her only aunt lived hours away in the quaint rural village of Inglewood; and the cousins she only saw during rare family gatherings, gatherings which she knew would now be fewer-if any, as her mother was no longer around to invite them over. Besides, she was busy with work and preparing to start her own legal practice, and very soon would have a non-existent social life.

Later, when Paul texted to say it was all done, both Mathew and Elizabeth breathed a sigh of relief. It was Monday morning and Mathew was up early. He had made one of his large egg-white omelets with spinach, while she helped herself to organic green tea and watched as she sealed a container with one of his homemade green smoothies for lunch.

She thanked him for an amazing impromptu weekend. "It's still raining and for a bright spring day, it is bitterly cold but weirdly, I'm the happiest I've been in a long time." She confessed, then decided to stop talking. She wondered if she should say how complicated life had been lately and how much she wished it could just be seamless like before Izzy died. Even with her mum's memory lapses and her lashing out when she became anxious due to the disease, Lizzy still felt it was simpler then.

"Hello, where are you, Lizzy" Mathew tried to get her attention, but she was deep in thought.

"So sorry, lost in thought for a moment." She didn't realise she had gone off daydreaming and smiled at the tenderness in his voice, designed to bring her back from her reverie.

"Try to be in the moment as much as you can, young lady, or life can slip by without you ever enjoying it." He warned.

"Yeah, I am learning to do that."

"Have you thought of speaking to anyone?"

"About?" It was his turn to suggest counselling. He had noticed her drifting off in thought on more than one occasions that weekend and wondered if the grieving process was taking a further toll on her mental health.

"Your mum. You know, life."

"I've met with Pastor Lammy a few times, a bit more actually."

He almost choked on his omelette, and quickly she went to his assistance.

"Are you okay?"

He nodded, then helped himself to some water. "How- how do you find that? I mean him, the sessions?" He stammered.

"Very good, he's really nice. He listens and I am quite sure he'll maintain confidentiality. He is well spoken of in terms of integrity and decency and that is so hard to find these days."

"You are right about that. No one has a bad word to say about Pastor Lammy, and he's quite funny too." To which they both agreed. "Do you see him often?"

"Each week, pretty much."

He almost choked again. This time, she wondered if he was surprised at her seeking help or, was he truly that clumsy.

"What's wrong with you? Maybe you should stop eating. Whatever you put in that omelette does not agree with you." She rolled her eyes then.

"Don't roll your eye at me, woman!" He scolded. But petulantly, she did it again. "Elizabeth, that's not even funny." He approached to tickle her, but she managed to escape in time. "Pastor Lammy was quite good to both my dad and us after Claire left and when he was ill; even long after he was gone, he continued to check in on us." He paused then made his confession. "I see him sometimes too. We talk a lot. Pretty often to be honest. He is really a nice guy." He deliberately looked away as he spoke. He knew she would be surprised to hear that and hoped she would be pleased.

"You do?"

"Do what?"

"Talk to him, a lot?"

"We do. Yes, why you seem surprised?" He feigned innocence. "I never said, that's all but he makes time for people and I agree, he can be trusted to hold one's affairs in the strictest of confidence."

She was surprised and happy. At least, now she knew Mathew was getting the help he needed. Well, she hoped so; and wondered if Pastor Lammy was responsible for the changes she now saw in him. "I'd never guess."

"Neither me you."

They looked at each other as if with the new revelation came a new understanding and at the same time a mystery which neither of them could put their finger on. They were quiet for a while; pensive, with an awkward smile plastered over each of their faces.

He looked outside then as he told her, "Lizzy, what happened with Claire was somewhat debilitating for me. I blamed myself at first." He chuckled then. "Imagine a little kid, two years old is responsible for loving his mother too much, or not enough, for her to choose to stay… choose to work around him and his four-year-old sister even if she no longer loved their father. I could not understand it. It led me to being somewhat functionally dysfunctional! Not trusting, afraid to love, then to have that person leave. Silly me! I have had some difficulty speaking up or speaking my mind. Claire doesn't seem to be aware of that pain she had caused us and thinks that a card and gift at Christmas and one for our birthdays somehow makes up or compensates for her absence." He was shaking but just a little and she could still feel him loosening and tightening his grip on her as he described what Claire had done, and all she wanted to do was to listen to let him, to let him know that she was in this with him and that she had always been. "I've decided never to see her again; and since her last visit, I have been seeing Pastor Lammy." He didn't look at her while he spoke and as he turned around, she could still see the pain in his eyes but not as deep as what she had seen in her kitchen all those months ago, when she had not long left his sister's house.

She could not resist hugging him and time for them both stood still, as they held each other. Very slowly she admitted to why she really broke up with Richard. If Mathew was surprised, he showed no sign of it. She told him about the pressure she felt from his parents and him to do things their way and how unrelenting it had become. Almost like she was to be morphed into one of them and their way of life and how it had affected her work with Misha calling her a shrunken violet. The conflict of trying to be a woman fighting back in her male dominated workplace while the man she was to marry represented that oppression she was up against. That backward 'woman be seen but be docile' 'be in the house and I work', like back some centuries ago way of thinking and living. That after the funeral, she had started seeing Pastor Lammy as well as coaching and mentoring at work and how she was finding herself once again.

She told him that she realised now that maybe Richard was jealous of them after all. Of what they had; he quite possibly could not understand it. She was on a roll and like a burst dam, she could not hold back. She told him too of her recent plan for an employee engagement project. "To leave as my legacy there." She had started looking at properties as office for her practice should the owners of her house refused her over market value offer.

He spoke up then to say how happy he was that she was working hard to start her own practice by the end of the year.

"Particularly the female staff," she continued. "I would love to motivate them, influence them, even to be more involved, more aware of their rights, roles and responsibilities within the company. To be empowered to use their voice. To engage."

And when she finished speaking, they were still standing in the middle of his kitchen, in each other's arms; for both lives had taken on a new trajectory, a new focus, a new meaning. Purpose.

"I'm so proud of you, Elizabeth Savannah Dawes. You have been through so much, but here you are!"

"No, I am so proud of you, Mathew William Roberts. You have been through so much and yet, here *you* are."

For a moment she thought he was going to kiss her and had to blink a few times to clear her vision, he kissed both cheeks instead. Her phone rang then causing them to separate. It was Sarah. She held her breath and looked at Mathew.

"It's Sarah. what if it is something terrible, my poor heart cannot take anymore just yet, Matt it's only just mending." She whimpered.

He whispered back. "Go ahead. I am here, whatever it is, we will always have each other. You are your mother's orchid remember; you are stronger than you think.

She used both hands to create a heart-shape by her heart and he touched both hands as they held each other's gaze for a moment.

"Hello?"

The high pitched voiced was full of elation and when the conversation ended, she was visibly relieved and shocked.

"Sarah is getting married and asked me to be one of her bridesmaids."

"That's amazing, Lizzy." Without warning he picked her up and she screamed, she hated it; heights of any kind scared her, and he knew it.

She knew he would be leaving again for Dubai later that week and she was happy they had had that chance to be with each other just like old times and except for the 'secret' lingering on her mind on the way to work, Elizabeth admitted to Susan, who had called her on the way to work, that it was an amazing weekend.

"I did not get a chance to catch up on any work, Sue; I will need to work late all of this week, again." She chuckled.

"At least you rested." Susan wondered if there was anything her friend was not telling her and wondered if Mathew would.

"I rested. That's true."

"What did you guys get up to, anyway? Was Matt alright when you left?"

"He was good, we cooked and talked about all sorts." Suddenly his confession came to memory and hesitantly she mentioned to Susie, hoping he had told her, and that she could shed some light on the mystery lady.

"Did he tell you about this person he's been love with for years, who appears to be with someone else?"

"Guess he didn't tell you her name then, huh?" Susan commented dryly.

"No. Well, he said something along the lines of not asking who it is and promised to tell all when he has had a chance to, *get her out of his head*', oh and, apparently, I will be the first to know."

"Hmm, my little brother." Susan sighed then paused.

"I take it he hasn't 'shared' her with you yet?"

"Well, yes actually. Well, no - not really. We talked about it a little, no detail but he is an adult, he has to say. What am I saying? I do not know, sorry. I am waffling but he's, ... well, let us wait and see?" Susan sighed again and Elizabeth thought she sounded disappointed or was it worried.

"You know what, Sue? He's the happiest I have seen him in a long time. I am hoping he does get that person out of his head so he can really enjoy life to its fullest and not have to walk around like your dad did, with a broken heart."

"Or maybe he needs to speak to the person, otherwise he will not get that person out of his head, I don't think!"

"You sound very annoyed with him, are you?"

"I want him to be happy, Lizzy. That's all. He knows what he needs to do. I will love you and leave you. Call me after work or see you on the weekend. Chow."

They hung up but that question of, 'what are you hiding'- still rested on Elizabeth's mind and just then she remembered when Susan had dropped what Elizabeth could only describe as a bombshell. The time she told her that he would

153

not be here for long after his return from South Africa. She was not expecting that at the time they spoke. She was happy to have him home and was looking forward to, at least having him 'around'. Elizabeth had enquired as to the reason for this and had wondered why he had chosen not to tell her.

"What sort of time will he be there for, you think?"

"Minimum a year." Susan said, matter-of-factly.

"Will you be seeing him at all?" Elizabeth felt, at first, a little confused and as the conversation persisted, that state of mind deepened.

"Yes, Lizzy. We plan to pop over and you are too of course." Susan hastened on.

"Oh, I guess he was going to tell me eventually."

"He will. So, try not to say I told you first."

Elizabeth was baffled first at her own reaction and then, admittedly somewhat relieved. She was trying not to think he was keeping her out of his life and was now very curious as to this change of heart. She could only conclude business was either doing better or worse than he thought but whatever it was, he must've felt quite strongly about it to want to stay away from his home and Susan and friends for that very long period of time. Nonetheless, she remained puzzled and if she allowed herself to acknowledge it, she was disappointed.

With the weekend behind her, Elizabeth threw herself into her work. Misha had committed to ongoing mentoring and both were happy. Towards the end of last month, she had single handed obtained two injunctions in favour of her respective clients. She wanted to continue taking on tougher cases and quite recently was assigned one involving the financial management and property arrangements in the Winter vs Smith case; the consensus was that her confidence is much improved, to which Misha agreed. Misha was proud of her progress and told her so, and recently without asking, her boss appointed a friend of hers from university, to coach her. Elizabeth was happy and since that morning meeting misdemeanour, she had stayed clear of her phone in morning meetings and ensured she was always well prepared.

"It's amazing how empowering and confident one can feel when we talk about and explore different ways of dealing with our various challenges." Elizabeth recognised Misha as the fighter she was not, but wanted to be; and with the end of the year now approaching faster than she anticipated, her new year's resolution was to open her own practice. It was something she knew would demand a high degree of tenacity and determination, but she knew she could do it. Misha had suggested getting ready for a promotion, but she was not keen, stating that she had too much going on now. Still, Elizabeth did not want to speak of her plans to start her own practice, just yet.

Before long, she was once again settled into her work/home routine and sometimes she would talk to Richard; but she no longer made the effort to return his call or to meet him for lunch on his few free days. She wanted to use that year to find her, the Elizabeth who Misha spoke of the one who came to the interview four years ago. The time when she had the world at her feet and her future all mapped out. Before her mum became ill and her foray into a complex relationship.

Mathew had called the minute she had gotten home from work. He confessed to having to leave for a while but was looking forward to having her and Sue over sometime. It was only for a year, he told her hoping she would understand and like Susan, hoping his cowardice wouldn't lead to her finding another Richard. He had settled in Dubai as he said he would be, and although they spoke less frequently of late, they still managed to text or Whats app every day. She would have missed him more had she had the time to think about it, but she had been too busy being intentional about making progress at work.

It was midweek and she was happy to be going home on time; and this was only because her case had been cancelled due to lack of preparation by the defendant's team who requested more time. As she walked the fifteen minutes journey home from the train station, she had a myriad of ideas mulling over in her mind. First, she reviewed what she had not long admitted to herself, how increasingly concerned she had become about Mathew and his – life. She also thought it was about time she purchased a car; not that she had ever really seen the need for one, in addition to the fact that she hated driving. But, the more she worked with Misha, the more she wanted to do much more with her life, her time and her voice. She thought about the lack of staff engagement and once again she vowed to make that her legacy when she left Steven and Stephenson's. She was about to make a note on her phone, when surprisingly, Pastor Lammy tooted and offered her a ride home.

They quickly spoke about her recent attitude towards Richard after he accused her of misusing him which she thought was baseless and that he had initially given her the silent treatment. And now, once again, he started reaching out to her, but she had become mentally detached. Gently he told her, "Love is patient and its kind, it perseveres, but bear in mind that one going through some sort of adversity such as grief with another person can intensify romantic attraction. The central dopamine may be responsible for this reaction too, because research shows that when a reward is delayed, dopamine – producing neurons in the midbrain region become more productive."

"So are you saying, I have done the right thing breaking off the engagement.

"I am saying, Elizabeth, that the body has physical response to an emotional state and vice versa. Better decisions are taken when equilibrium is reached."

"So how, may I ask, will I know when 'equilibrium' is reached? What are the signs?"

"You will know, my child, you will know. God has a way of preparing us. He prepares us for each other."

"I am sure you are very capable and very intelligent, but should you decide to re-engage, so to speak, it's worth talking about it and getting to grips with the more nuanced aspects of a potential new union. I am always here for you." He advised.

"I'll bear that in mind." She mused more at the way he spoke than at the seriousness of his advice.

Pastor Lammy had always appeared to be happy for her and was the first to mention a few times during their meetings about marriage being an honourable thing to do. He always told her he was happy for her and had always reminded her, not to forget it was a big step, a very important step. He would say sometimes, "One that must be taken very seriously and after much thought."

She would usually smile and promised herself, never to forget. They chatted as he slowly made his way to hers. She realised he was even more humorous than she had given him credit for. He had a way of making each person feel comfortable in his company; like her dad, she thought. He reminded her to make a follow-up appointment before he left, and if not, they could meet up for coffee. Their short talk made her think, *'what about you, Elizabeth, how do you really feel about where you are now?'* She reminisced on some of the cases and when she had to ask the child, "And what do you like?" And as she reached into her mailbox, just outside her door, she made a note to ask herself that question more often.

She continued meeting with the ladies from his church for their morning run, something she has found most inspirational. Together, they chatted as they ran. All the women were kind to her. But one of them, she had become quite fond of, Evelyn. Evelyn always waited with her when she felt the pace was too much and would always seem to know the right words to say. Every morning, Elizabeth looked forward to running with 'the pack', as she called them, she looked forward to their laughter and chatter. But it was Evelyn who encouraged her the most; who took her under her wings, almost like a mother and who encouraged her to stop and help in the homeless ministry, something she had found extremely rewarding.

Elizabeth loved talking to people and found that the two hours with them gave her that opportunity. It was interesting listening to their stories and how they came to be in their unfortunate positions. At first, she did it in honour of her mom but now, it felt good to give back. She wanted to always keep Hazel's memory alive and going there one Saturday afternoon per month was one way of doing that; but there was more she could do, Evelyn understood this and she wanted to. It often came up in their chats and sometimes when the absence of her mother became overwhelming, it was Evelyn who would comfort her. They were not yet sharing secrets, but she had that feeling that she could talk to her. For now, she trusted Pastor Lammy, that was important; and it was enough for her. Maybe one day, she and Evelyn would be closer, but for the moment they were getting to know each other. That was enough

Evelyn had introduced her to a burly middle-aged looking man called Carl and told her privately that she had been trying to get him to come with them on the morning run, but he had not yet agreed. She was hoping Elizabeth could talk him into coming. Elizabeth was happy to help her friend but for a moment, questioned if it were to do with a certain type of attraction. Evelyn had simply told her his soul mattered more, which she was not sure if that was a 'yes' or a 'no' but was even happier to help. Elizabeth smiled, thinking there were already enough single women in the church, and if Evelyn could find her happiness, that would make her happy too.

Overtime, Elizabeth unearthed some sad details of his divorce and how misguided and unfairly he was treated and for the first time, she took a pro-bono case and brought the firm he had contracted, to court. The charge was, 'failure to act in their client's best interest'. When she won, they all went out for a meal including Pastor Lammy, who was obviously impressed and elated at what Elizabeth had done. Elizabeth was beginning to see them as an extended family. They made her feel comfortable, and already she was looking forward to how she could use her knowledge to help the parishioners.

Susan was pleased to hear about her charitable endeavours, but hastened to remind her, "You do know you need to be remunerated to keep your own business afloat and too many pro-bono cases can affect the bottom line." Susan went on with what Elizabeth recognised as her motherly monologue. "...after running costs, deductions, staff salary payment, payment for the lease or, I don't know, mortgage on the property... you will need the money, Lizzy."

Elizabeth had long since acknowledged that, and to appease her friend, only insisted on taking one every now and again. For her, that would be her way of recognising her corporate social responsibility.

Above all, the team there meant the world to her. They had helped her with so much psychological support, she would never be able to repay them but she was sure that coming alongside them at a time when they needed her most, would set her well on her way to giving back.

"Sounds like you will be baptised soon, Lizzy. "Susan whispered

"What did Pastor Lammy say? 'It is good to do good works but to do good works only is not good enough."

"Okay, that sounds like something my dad would have said." They could both recognise a bit of their father in Pastor Lammy and smiled at their conclusion.

She managed to take a pro bono case for a gentleman who was left with nothing after his divorce. She could see again the dangers of taking key decisions when one's mental health and capacity to process information was questioned. She was happy to explore this.

It was not until about a month later that Elizabeth was able to ring Pastor Lammy for an appointment. A week later, and when the day finally came, she could tell he was happy to see her, and she likewise.

They chatted at first about all things and then pointedly but gently he enquired, "How you are doing, really?"

"Honestly, I feel like finally, I am finding myself again."

"Tell me a bit more about that."

"It's like I am rediscovering or reacquainting myself with me." She chuckled and then hastened on. "I guess in the past several months I have had a chance to revisit all the things I set out to do from when I entered University, and they have not changed at all and each day I am feeling happier with my own company and just realising how much I have changed. I can't say when that turning point occurred, but something has."

"The thing is Elizabeth, life, like roses has the potential to change us like the rose in the vase changing the water red – therefore it's not unusual to have been changed by situations."

"But I am less accepting, and more thinking of how what I am being asked to do or to embrace fits in with who I am, and what I want for my future. At one point, I only knew I wanted companionship and that I never wanted to be on my own – afraid even.

"And now?"

"Well, I was left on my own and it turned out to be a period of growth, for me. To rediscover my goals and dreams and a newfound confidence to challenge as well and defend, total empowerment." She recognised it had taken for her to arrive at this point.

"Maybe, caring for your mum and then dealing with such a major loss." They both knew it has been a build up to here. Layers piled upon layers. "You have been carrying around the death of your dad, your best friend, who might I add was so young, and no doubt you felt cheated and possibly out of control. Then, your mum. That, must have rendered you totally helpless – particularly, not forgiving yourself for doing what you had to do." He was referring to when Hazel was taken to the care home, he knew how difficult that was for Elizabeth. "Which, might I hasten to add, looks like it was the right thing to do. You were so strong to have given up all your weekends to be with her." He always knew the right words to say and how to say them and she appreciated his listening ear and all the support he gave her.

"So, tell me, what is your friendship circle like."

"I have Mathew and Susan."

"The Roberts, yes. I know them very well. Their dad was a generous man. Shame about his ex-wife."

They spoke about so much as the weeks ensued.

All of them had made travel arrangements to go to Mauritius. They were all excited; until a month later, when Susan had to cancel, claiming to be swamped with work in preparation for an OFSTED inspection. Lizzy and Mathew were both extremely disappointed, and more so when she declined being with them on their usual night out. It was not lost on them and quickly they recalled the last time that happened was when she had the first round of IVF. This time Elizabeth wondered if this was a repeat but for fear of bad luck, even she was afraid to ask, afraid of the disappointment.

The weeks turned into a month and there was no letting up for Elizabeth. She was busy with her project at work and enjoyed the distraction. Setting up her own practice made her busy as well, but she was determined to forge ahead. The first challenge was to locate a suitable place for her office. By now, Mathew had made several attempts to help her, but she insisted on doing it on her own. He loved her sense of independence, but she drove him crazy when she got so stubborn.

Both girls called each other regularly and with Mathew back in Dubai, Elizabeth was alone finding her place. She heard from Richard a couple of times and met with him for lunch just out of kindness. The last time she saw him, he was as handsome and youthful looking as ever but she felt nothing for him and knew she had taken the right decision. He knew she wouldn't have given up her independence and for her it was a lot to ask. She was not sure his parents saw it that way and was certain they both hated her even more but she was so far away from them to care; and she knew that no matter what she would be fine.

Pastor Lammy continued to check-in on her as often as he could. Sometimes, as often as a weekly call, but he too had come to realise how busy she was. When she could not see him, he would still call when he had a chance. The morning run was now an established part of her life and one by one she watched as what was initially a small group of ladies having a run and a chat grew into what looked sometimes like a mini marathon; much to Pastore Lammy's delight, he now calls it 'an army of ladies with some men thrown'.

Running every morning almost like living life, with each going at their own pace but finding friendship and support as they went along. Elizabeth vowed never to give that up. She continued to help too with the homeless feeding program and wanted to take on some more of their cases, volunteering to help them access the services they needed to get their lives back on track. She even thought of one day setting up the 'Hazel Dawes Foundation' in honor of her mum, and the work she did in those communities. She knew her dad supported her mum and was very proud of her but he was a pilot and a very good one too; he just didn't have the time to commit. When he was off work, he would take her mum away; usually hiking or to a quiet country side somewhere, while Elizabeth had a sitter for the time as her aunty lived too far away and her parents didn't allow her to sleep over at friends'. He too would be proud of their efforts to help make life better for others.

Suddenly, it dawned on her that she had a huge land space at the back of the house in Knockholt, and she could use some of the money from her mum to build a fairly large open plan office there. Without wasting anymore time, she quickly emailed Mathew her thoughts and he too was happy she had decided on that. She realised that it would have been too expensive to purchase an office block or to rent one of the very few and far between ones located in the neighborhood, which would have been too small anyway.

Both the architect and the builders were adamant it would be ready in three months; and best of all, she would still have her beautiful garden, undisturbed. In the end, the building project was a week overrun but she was pleased with the results and already she had sent out business cards and had contracted Cara's advertising agency to help her get the word out. Mathew did not mind her using his ex-girlfriend; he had long said she meant nothing to him and that she was nothing more than a youthful crush. That as beautiful as she was, they had nothing in common. He still stood by his decision not to have prolonged the relationship; but they all admitted she did an amazing job both getting the word out and the extremely high standard to which each of those very expensive thirty seconds adverts was done.

Finally, she was able to hand in her notice at Stevens and Stephenson's two months before the project completed, and although Misha was happy for her and was pleased with the growth and the strides she had taken at the firm, she knew Elizabeth was not after partnership. The older woman had long realised that Elizabeth had a heart for her community and even though they both knew she would make far more money practicing with them; they also knew in the end for one to be truly happy, they had to be true to who they were.

Time went by so quickly and before she knew it, it was her last day at the renown Stevens and Stephenson's. The Law firm that had been in the city for almost seventy years with a flawless reputation to boot. Elizabeth was happy to have gotten a job there and counted herself incredibly lucky. And on this, her last day, they held a big party for her at the firm. They opened the dividing walls and everything that could be pushed out the way was. There was no sign of any documents anywhere, filing cabinets covered and shielded with white orchids. They had chosen the fourth floor which was known to be less cumbersome as it was where the largest offices were, the ones belonging to each of the partners and their personal secretaries. It offered amazing panoramic views against the backdrop of what looked like a sea of white orchids.

Throughout the day, she could not escape seeing herself everywhere. Misha had placed her picture on the Firm's intranet, and everyone got a chance to wish her well. She was both sad and happy all at the same time. As she had hoped, her legacy would live on in the networks she formed, the internal communication team she developed and the monthly magazine which everyone now looked forward to. Amongst the commendations, were promises to send her some clients to help her get off her feet. She was surprised when even Ben said he would miss her and asked if she would now consider them going on a date as she would no longer be working at the firm.

She could tell he was smitten with her, but she wasn't quite there and after Richard, she realised how dangerous it was to 'settle' out of fear of loneliness or depression or worry about age and feeling of being made to feel incomplete. She knew now how to make herself feel fulfilled, through enjoying life one day at a time and being her best self. Her coach had always alluded to and encouraged her to look after her psychological health. She warned about taking the time to cherish and look out for her loyal friends who were usually irreplaceable and were many times better than even family. Happy with the feeling that she was complete and in her mum's words stronger than she thought, she was ready to face her next challenge. Thinking Ben was a partner and may one day turn out to be an asset to her practice, she thought about keeping him in her network. He may just turn out to be another feather in her bow, she thought and so she gave a less crass reply than the one that came to mind. "Maybe one day, but not now." Besides, she had too much to do and was, more than anything else, looking forward to getting settled into her new office. Her own office. More often than she wanted to admit, she had envisaged the sign, first her picture then: Elizabeth Dawes, Attorney-at-Law in black and gold writing.

The party was in full swing and she had changed into a simple off white Givenchy gown and her favorite glass-heel-slipper stilettos, with her hair piled high on her head accentuating her five foot-six inch height, her slender neckline was left bare, with only a pair of Tiffany's platinum diamond stud earnings, which were a gift from Mathew for her last birthday. At twenty-nine, she was happy. Happy for the chance to wear them; which she had been dying to do so for a while. They went perfectly with her simple strand platinum and diamond clasp bracelet, a gift to herself when she landed her job at the firm.

Everyone was milling around with lots of laughter and chatter and lovely messages coming her way. There was so much food, Elizabeth could not believe the spread and felt truly special. Dinner was a mix of finger food and small plates for hot meal. She had a portion of confit duck at one time then a small portion of caviar the next; and as the drinks flowed, so did the trays of fruit and vegetable salads. There were trays moving through the air like little spaceships policing the skies as a dozen or so waiters served with utmost precision and charm. Overwhelmed, she looked walked away to the edge of the building to looked out at the city she had called her second home for just over five years; and as if to say goodbye, she smiled as her brain told her eyes, *Look a trickle of rain along the surrounding glass*, which luckily wasn't enough to obscure the most amazing views the surrounding glass offered from anywhere in the office. She smiled again, this time at the heavens as if acknowledging God's blessing to her with the showers from above. With one of her trademark deep inhale in and exhale slowly out through pursed lips routines, she turned... and their eyes met. He was in the middle of the room but was suddenly obscured by Susan, then Pastor Lammy; and as she adjusted her vision, her smile deepened as her steps hastened. She could see better now, and covered her mouth with both her hands as she spotted the ladies from 'the pack', her running mates from her morning runs.

Confused, not knowing who to hug first, Susan saved her by reaching out almost immediately as she approached, then it was the Pastor Lammy and each of the ladies followed suit. After that she was not quite sure where to look and for a moment she wondered if her mind was playing a cruel trick on her. She turned again to ask Susan, but like a wall, there he was. Just in front of her, as if to shield her from the onslaught of the maddening crowd. They held each other. Misha, never to miss a beat, thought and even now suspected there was more going on than Elizabeth either knew or wanted to acknowledge. And not long after, when they were alone in the bathroom, she told her so.

"That handsome guy who hugged you for dear life isn't that your 'brother'? What is his name Matt- Mathew?"

"Oh, Matt! Yes, he's Susan's brother but we are ..."

"So close, yes you've said that; but the blind can see he's in love with you." Misha had never been one to mince her words or to hold back but Elizabeth did not see that tornado coming.

"Come on, Misha." She laughed, refusing to entertain the thought. She knew and often admitted to Mathew being a handsome and sweet person, but always said he had his eyes on the Cara's of this world. She never thought ever that she looked like the Cara's or would ever look anything like the Cara's; nor did she want to. She did not want or have the entrepreneurial genes either, she didn't want to be the head of some big money spinner like Cara's Advertising Agency complete with her name as well, and in the very best part of town too.

Not long, and it was Susan who entered the bathroom, who once again, rescued her. Misha gave her that look of "don't forget I told you so," as she left the room to go mill about with the crowd which gave the two ladies some space to catch up. They hugged each other again immediately.

"You look amazing! I have missed you. I haven't seen you in years." Susan blurted out.

"Oh, it feels like it, doesn't it? I'm so happy to see you."

They managed to pull away from each other.

"Have you gained a few pounds?" Elizabeth asked wide-eyed.

Susan whispered to her friend that she may get even bigger, but she did not want to jinx it.

Elizabeth was so happy for her friend and without saying a word they hugged again and for the rest of the evening their roles were reversed with Elizabeth being mum for Susan while everyone watched as Mathew ogled Elizabeth. Everyone but Elizabeth could tell he was completely besotted with her or so Misha and the secretaries and Ben and anyone else who was not too drunk or self-absorbed could see. Susan's heart pounded for her brother and silently she prayed he would at least ask her friend out; but she had been warned and never wanted to interfere in that aspect of his life. As difficult as it was to watch, she knew he had to do what he had to do when he felt it was right. She would hate for something to happen and for their 'family" to be broken up, and even more fearful if it were to be her fault. Besides, Paul had always warned her about being match-maker and maybe, that was the only thing she had managed to pay any attention to that was coming from him. She loved her brother, and she loved Elizabeth like a sister.

Pastor Lammy came into view then, and as she glanced at the Pastor, she wondered if a visit to church could be the answer to her prayers, and smiled as Paul looked at her. She raised her glass of apple juice at him and silently she vowed it was about time she started praying about a few things. Paul had taken Susan home in good time, with everyone's fingers crossed for an uneventful pregnancy.

On the way to Elizabeth's, Mathew told her how proud he was of her and when they pulled onto her driveway, she thought about how wise and trusted Misha was and so she had to ask. "Well, Misha thinks you are …"

"Misha thinks I am …"

"Hmm," How shall I say this-" she paused. Unable to bring herself to say it – or think it. It was simply not possible, she told herself.

"Is it that, I am – gay, does Misha really thinks that I am gay?"

She realised she could not and so she nodded and then neither of them could stop laughing. They had dinner the following weekend, as Mathew was busy in the week, and would be leaving again for Dubai at the start of next week. They spoke almost every night before she went to bed and again, he would call her during the day, as he said, to check how her new practice was coming on. But for her, although she had not said, she did not stop thinking and replaying scenes from past times and now as they were happening in real time. *If he says no,* she wondered, *what then? And if he says yes…* she could feel her heart racing every time she thought about them being anything other than 'the friends' they had been for more than half her life. *What if one day, we break up? Or do I even - love him, like that?* She knew she loved him but was not convinced it was the same type of love needed for what Misha meant. Only then, she laughed out loud; thinking of their weekend together, when it rained. "No." She shook her head. He has someone else, so even if I do feel that way, which I do not, he still has to get 'her' out of his head. And with that, she stilled her beating heart and carried on making calls. First to arrange an interview with the local radio station designed to promote her practice, and then with the local paper. Everything seemed to be happening at once.

Sarah's wedding would be that weekend, but there was still so much for Elizabeth to do. She would be staying with Elizabeth in Knockholt while they finalized the plans for the reception. But first, she was on her way to get her from the airport.

At the airport to welcome the sister of her late friend, who at that same airport five years ago, she said goodbye to, she swallowed as she felt a small lump forming. She looked around eagerly, she did not want to miss Sarah when she came through customs. Realising, 'self-employed' could sometimes mean working even when remote and mobile, it crossed her mind to quickly check in at the office, but she soon found out the Wi-Fi connection was poor. She moved away from the entrance to Sarah's exit, and that was when she saw him. She had to blink a few times, but she knew him all too well. "Come-on," she chided herself. "Surely, if there's anyone I should recognize even from miles away, it's him. Two months a part does not change someone so much that you can't recognize them in a very busy airport as crazy as this was, she continued on her path of self-rebuke. As she peered across shoulders and between luggage, she knew. Still, she told herself, she could not be sure or maybe she didn't want to believe it. Fear of being disappointed, she admitted secretly. Then quickly looked around, hoping no one could read her thoughts.

The third time round, it was his eyes looking into hers that convinced her Mathew Roberts was truly in the building. Transfixed, her feet were as obstinate as they could be as her body took on a mind of its own. Motionless, breathless even. He made his way towards her but what to do, how to react, what would she say to this person who up until a year ago, she thought she knew so well. She attempted to shake her head, but that too seemed disconnected. *Try, at least be present*, she told herself.

Only when he wrapped his eagle wing like arms around her that every inch of her began to work again. Back in manual mode, she willed her somatic nervous system, at least her limbs to respond. Admitting Biology was not one of her favorite subjects, she could however recall doing enough to pass the dreadful subject and as the intricacies of the physiology of the nervous system sprung to mind, she knew she had to recall enough to at least remain standing at this precise moment. Late, she could decide what or who to blame for her earlier embarrassing demeanor.

"I've missed you." He whispered, then continued. "What are you doing here? Are you leaving? Okay, that is a NO - you are at arrivals not departures. Silly question, my bad! Are you here to pick me up? I didn't tell either of you I was coming today." Mathew rambled on, totally oblivious to her being rendered mute.

Unable to speak, she pointed to Sarah who was making her way to them and to whom she now knew she owed immense gratitude for rescuing her from what she kind of felt was a truly awkward moment. This, for her was a new feeling toward him. Until today, she had never had this kind of 'awkward moment' with Mathew, the man who had for years and years, been her best friend. One with whom she had shared so much and had been through so much with. Years of laughter interspersed with periods of melancholy.

She thought she knew him well and acknowledged now that, that was a while back. He was all grown up now; and a part of her wanted to know the 'new Mathew'. *Or did she already know this version of him*? And as quickly as she surrendered, the doubt came in and she wondered if that was at all even a good idea. If Sarah's plan were to rock the building, Elizabeth was certain, that loud scream did.

"You're getting married, when will you grow up, girl!" Elizabeth scolded.

165

"Mathew, you look nice! Wasn't expecting to see you here." Sarah exclaimed, obviously pleased to see him.

"Neither was I expecting to see either of you." He replied.

Elizabeth could see the puzzled look on his face and would have smiled had she been able to think clearly.

"Are you coming with us?" Sarah said, her sly grin still wide.

"I don't know, can I?" He turned to Elizabeth who quickly nodded then hoped this time, Sarah would keep talking.

Anything to buy her time to find that little organ called, the tongue. If Misha could see her now, she mused inside, wonder how 'impressed' she would be?

The ride home was laced with glances at each other and business talk, anxiety, and unanswered questions. It was only after he was safely deposited at his Penthouse, that she gave herself permission to relax. Left alone to make the one-hour journey home, only then she allowed her thoughts free reign to scour the fields of her heart and her mind, with a sleeping Sarah nicely tucked away in the rear seat. She put the music on and drifted back to how handsome he looked. He had kissed her on the cheek again as he left the vehicle and she was happy he was back and perked up thinking, it would be lovely to have him around for Sarah's wedding.

The remaining few days were very eventful. Her project wedding with Sarah had consumed her and soon she barely had time to think of Mathew, excluding the nights when all was still with the exception of Sarah's voice on the phone to every other person in America beaming up from the kitchen.

On Friday, she was out for one last celebration with some other friends who could not make it to her 'exit day' party. She was leaving the bar when he walked in with someone looking remarkably like Cara. Immediately he saw her, he took his companion to meet her and hugged her in a way she thought was simply cordial. He explained how he had just finished a meeting catching up with the management team overseeing the purchase of the last remaining two offices on that block and laughed out loud when he mentioned the new name he had assigned to the block, "The Elizabethan Row".

On another day or at another time, she knew she would have been somewhat flattered, but not now. Not when he had Cara's twin looking intently at her and she was desperately trying to understand how who she saw in front of her related to the throbbing in her chest or the sudden queasiness she knew did not come from any of the mild alcoholic beverages she had consumed that evening.

"Are you okay?" For a minute, he could see she looked pale.

"Yes, I am fine, I must have had too much to drink." She lied.

"We were about to have dinner, you could join us, and I could take you home afterwards, or I could just get you a cab, perhaps."

She was even more confused just then. Why would he think she would want to sit with him and his 'type', just to make her feel worse than she did for thinking what she had allowed herself to think, after all these years. Then she admitted it. *I knew it, I knew 'this' would spoil everything. There's no going back now.* "I am on my way home." She said bluntly, "See you when I see you. Take care." She realised then that he did not bother to introduce them and told herself she didn't care that he didn't. Afterall, they were just friends and he did not need to explain.

He wasn't sure how much she had had to drink, but from her many facial expressions, he knew he would not be able to forgive himself if she left there on her own and something happened, like, someone taking advantage of her. He said something to his Cara look-a-like, and she knew he spoke, but as loudly as he had spoken, the ache from her head spoke louder and had drowned it all out. Most of her friends had already left and the few she said goodbye to at the bar were either waiting on their partners or had decided to hang out a while longer; but Elizabeth was ready to go and nothing could get her to, 'hang around' a minute longer. She was nearly out the door when he accosted her and clearly outside, away from view when he decided to confront her. Almost forcefully, he searched her eyes, he wanted to know what was going on. He knew better than to buy her 'had too much to drink', story. Elizabeth only drank at home or when they were out together as the triplet. He knew her well. "As you have had, 'too much to drink,' I am taking you home." He insisted. Intent on playing whatever game he knew she was playing.

"Oh, and what about Cara, dumped her already?" She chuckled.

"Cara, what's she got to do with anything?" For a minute there he was confused.

"Well if she's not her, she sure does look a lot like her."

He hurried to keep pace with her, both unaware they were heading in the opposite direction to his car. The last thing she wanted was a lift from him. If there was anything left of their friendship, she knew it could only be salvaged through distance. Starting now. They got to the end of the promenade and looked around. Instantly, he knew they had come the wrong way. It crossed his mind to continue around the bend but he wondered, *what if she had indeed had too much to drink. What if she had changed during the time he had been away and he simply hadn't noticed? What if she was ill?* Guiding her by the elbow he told her he was parked in the opposite direction and insisted he was taking her home.

She declined, insisting on an uber but he refused to relent. "You're stuck with me, I'm afraid." Had he not known better, he would think she is deliberately avoiding him, *but why*? He was between confused and lucid, *was she ill or was she well? Sober, or inebriated?* He had never felt this way with her before and it bothered him. The last person he wanted to hurt or lose was her. He had been there before. He still remembered how he felt when she told him she was engaged, and he wondered sometimes if he would ever get over that recondite fear. He knew his sister had some knowledge of what he was feeling and maybe Marcus but no one could fathom the depth he sank to when he flew to St. Bart's and although he figured out how to prevent a repeat of that, he wondered how to get her mind past friendship. *How could he get her to see him, the man?*

The entire journey home was deafeningly quiet. She thought about him going back to his dinner date after he dropped her off and what their friendship would look like after tonight. He thought she looked even more beautiful every time he saw her and how he could not go back to being 'friends', after tonight. He was out ready to walk her to her door, but she had found her stride and was already inserting the key when he eventually caught up with her. Without so much as looking at him, she whispered what he heard as an incredibly sad goodnight and he knew he could not leave. She did not invite him in something he figured was deliberate; but he would not let her close him out. He had to know what was wrong. Entering the restaurant, he saw her immediately. And she was happy, or so he concluded... and now, between there and her house he had hazard a thousand guesses as to what could have happened to change that so suddenly. Nothing seemed to make sense, not in their context of friendship. She told him she was tired and that she had a busy morning ahead with Sarah's wedding and all; but he had had enough of more and more of her excuses and was beginning to think she lied about having too much to drink and if she lied about that then what else was she hiding.

"Look, I know you are your own person and free to do whatever it is you want. So, as you are home now and clearly not drunk or ill, I guess I can wait until you are ready to talk. Then, you know here to find me." He turned to leave then stopped at the door, willing her to say something and when she didn't, he felt the words coming up and he couldn't hold them back, not that he couldn't- more like the sound of his sister's voice in his head telling him he shouldn't. "I am in love with you, Elizabeth." He had not planned on what response he could expect, given how well he thought he knew her, but he expected something. He waited. When she didn't reply, he repeated it; but this time he was looking at her and it was a few decibels louder. Sarah who was initially out of sight, was now in full view, standing at the top of the stairs; but somehow his eyes wouldn't dare venture past the centre of his focus. So, he didn't see her and Elizabeth had long forgotten she had a house guest who was staying with her in preparation for her wedding.

Less than twenty four hours before the wedding and she still had to accompany Sarah to get her hair and makeup done first thing in the morning and she knew she would have to spend half the night applying some intense eye care intervention to hide the large bags that she knew without a doubt were already forming in parallel with her tears. *So, when, I did not get a silly text or weird emoji or some form of communication from Mathew, and I missed it, was this the reason? And those mood swings that followed, that empty feeling* ... Her mind stopped, came to a grinding halt, just when she felt his arms around her. He saw her tears and remembered how she cried when Izzy died and again later when her mum died, and he did not want her to cry anymore.

"What's wrong, Lizzy?" He pleaded, "Tell me." He was losing his mind guessing.

Suddenly, she felt completely foolish and although she hugged him just as tightly as he did her, she could not bring herself to say it, not yet. "I'll tell you tomorrow." And for the first time, she silenced them both, with a kiss.

Mathew had been spotted in Knockholt a few times that day but had refused to say his reason for the visit and she could only assume either he was seeing Pastor Lammy or repairing the old house and with only a few hours before Sarah said 'I do' she plucked up the courage to ask him to be her 'plus one'.

"Very bad timing, don't you think...I've been here for the past six hours and with only a measly two to go, how obvious an afterthought I am?"

"I am so sorry, I've been so busy; and besides, I didn't want to bother you."

He consented with an hour to go, and when he met them at the church, she had another 'wow' moment. Forcing herself to look away, she thought, *whatever happened in Dubai, I would love to have some of it.* Like a school girl, she could hardly sleep the night before, and opted for half of one of the sleeping pills she got from the doctor after her mother's burial. Since opening her eyes that morning, between the coffee and the amazing sunshine, she could not get Mathew out of her head. And looking at him now, she knew she never would. He had that cheeky grin on his face which puzzled her, *how he could be so boyish and mature, all at the same time?* He kissed her briefly in full view of everyone just outside the church which made her smile nervously. It all merged so seamlessly or so she thought, thinking of them how they have merged from pure friendship to, this. She had not named it yet and as she made her way up the aisle to join the other members of the bridal party, she muttered to herself, "Soon."

The wedding was even more beautiful than she had imagined, and she was teary eyed for Sarah who suddenly, seemed so mature and loved up with Maya's dad being just as stary-eyed. Mathew threw up cute Maya in the air as soon as he saw her at the reception and the little girl never wanted to be anywhere else but with "Uncle Mathew". After telling Elizabeth how stunning she looked in her role as bridesmaid, he insisted by text, that she came to sit next to him. He was adamant and scolded her, stating how disappointed he was and that it was not fair for her to have invited him only to keep her seat in the bridal party while he sat there all alone.

"Surely, your duty is over now, isn't it!"

From her seat at the head table, she searched for him. When their eyes met, like the day at her mum's funeral, this time he smiled back. It was not long, and she was making her way to him. As she did, he met her, and they danced and forgot everyone else in the room until Sarah's voice came across the room in all her high pitched beautiful looking self.

"Finally!" She almost shouted from the microphone.

"Finally!" Everyone applauded whether they knew what Sarah's shouts really meant or not and for a moment Elizabeth's heart raced ahead of her as she found herself wondering if he would possibly do what Paul had done to his sister those many years ago at their graduation ceremony. He kissed her again on the cheek and then she knew. It really didn't matter how it was done, all that mattered was that now somethings had been made clear so much clearer that they could not go back to the way it used to be, no more 'just like old times'. They would have to create, new old times and again she wondered what that would truly look like. But for now, she was happy and held her breath as they danced and had the most amazing time with the girl, she had found a friend in after losing her best friend, her sister, so cruelly.

On the way to hers from the wedding, he all but demanded an explanation her mood last night and this time, it was easy to say. "I guess I am in love with you, Mr. Mathew William Roberts."

"You mean, you were jealous? Are you telling me you saw Ilyanna and you were jealous? She does not speak a word of English. In fact, she is visiting from Germany. We worked on some projects together in Dubai and she is here to seal the deal with some other investors. I took her to After-Eight, to meet her English translator." He was laughing all the time as he spoke. Relieved. Hoping he had arrived at the right conclusion. In fact, he was quite sure he had. He was beginning to find her demeanour quite endearing; and when they got to hers, he kissed her goodnight and had never been happier as he headed to his old place with his newfound peace. "Elizabeth is in love with me, after all." He whispered, as he fell asleep in his father's old wooden kings sized bed.

It was a national holiday the following day and although tempted, Elizabeth was adamant she would not have Mathew stay over and if he suspected her resolve, he said nothing while she breathed a sigh of relief at him not imposing last night as he left her outside her front door. Something had changed. If not in him, she knew she had and she needed time to get used to it... to him, to their new context. It was almost like going from naivety or innocence to suddenly being enlightened, she told Sarah who was at the airport leaving for her honeymoon.

Elizabeth had opted to help at the community church. Later, she had a coffee with Pastor Lammy where they had an unbelievably detailed chat. She placed everything in the open, on the table as up for discussion. For the first time, she shared with him about Mathew's support at the hospital, how he refused to leave after flying half-way around the world to be with her the day before her mother died. He told her that people who are in love generally feel a powerful sense of empathy toward their beloved, feeling the other person's pain as their own and being willing to sacrifice anything for the other person. And for the first time, he asked her pointedly, "Do you think by any chance he could be, you know, possibly having feelings for you beyond friendship?"

She was happy to share her and Mathew's story with Pastor Lammy as she asked for his blessing; and he was happy for both too and said as much to both them at their individual counselling session.

"Like you, I am glad he is not still in that self-preservation mode, you know, after Claire. I presume you are aware of that non-existent relationship and the toll it took on their family. It is widely documented that for boys, it is primarily in older years that they demonstrate psychological issues related to a mother's abandonment, and this speaks to either literal physical abandonment or emotional abandonment."

Elizabeth was blown over by the implications and decided to be grateful they had come this far. What happened next, she would take this in turn one day at a time after all, he maybe traipsing off to Dubai again and a long-distance relationship was neve something she had dreamed of. Time spent with Pastor Lammy was always time well spent and today was no exception. From what she heard, Pastor Lammy had a clear insight into Mathew's world, and it made a difference to be able to speak to someone other than Susan on that level.

Later that evening, she wanted so much to call him, just to talk and smiled when he called her first, just after she stepped out of the bath. Mathew had been thinking, they had late lunches and Sunday brunches and met up and stayed up late, but they had never been on a real date and he wanted that. He wanted that for them. When he told her, he wanted to take her out, on their first official date, she still could not believe it was actually happening. Quickly she shoved all other thoughts aside and for the first time, paid keen attention to the details as she got dressed, and even surprised herself. She was ready when her doorbell chimed.

Although they had no challenges sharing and rediscovering each other, she constantly searched for and asked the questions he seemed to have been expecting and he explained what she always thought. The Claire effect had kept them apart although Pastor Lammy accredited it to God having his perfect plan and Him knowing what was best for each of us and she wanted to accept that. She thought of her dad, her mum and her best friend and knew she had to. He confessed to Pastor Lammy, helping him to work on freeing himself from Claire through him trying to exercise forgiveness and he admitted to being on that continuum. Exactly what point he was at, was not yet clear but he knew he wasn't afraid anymore and that was why he came back. She was happy when he added "…and for our friendship."

"I am genuinely happy to hear that. Glad to have you back. I missed you so much."

They smiled at each other as they spoke and chatted through the night, trying to fill in the gaps since he left. It was early in the morning when he took her home and she was happy he would be staying in Knockholt, at his old house and not making the one-hour journey back into town at that time of the morning. She knew she would worry and be tempted to have him stay over. Again, she was not ready. She was not sure anymore, what it would be like just the two of them under the same roof, all night. That is their past, as she now called it, her 'age of innocence' and she wanted to protect her heart too.

She was back at work in her own practice, first thing on Monday and all though her place of work was literally her back yard, she was careful to dress the part. She had been not too long seated at her desk, when Misha called. Checking up on her, in her first month as self-employed. Once again, Misha expressed her pure joy at Elizabeth's 'legacy'. Both women were over the moon to see what stakeholder engagement project had produced, and when she confessed to Misha of her seemingly 'prophetic gift bearing fruit', her now really good friend laughed as she confessed to seeing that coming. "The only one who was in denial, was you. And I get that. Although friendship first is the better route to a successful relationship, you two were on a whole other level. I think he has been in love with you forever, Elizabeth…and you too with him. Maybe subconsciously, neither of you had the faith in your bond to know, it was not going to go wrong and then you lose the relationship and ultimately the friendship."

Elizabeth had to agree with her wise 'older-younger' owl – younger version of Pastor Lammy she had come to realise-but definitely far less holy, friend. She laughed out loud as visions of Misha's wrath on display in the Board room, suddenly came alive in her mind's eye. They chatted for a while longer and again, Misha voiced her disappointment at having lost who the older woman now called her bright light around the office; but admitted she had to follow her heart. They had long since had to abandon their plans of monthly meeting and thought it could be reinstated 'one day' but for now too many things were happening along each of their journey's which had made that impossible.

"You'll do great, Elizabeth." Misha reassured her. She was happy for her mature friend's vote of confidence and knew she would never forget her.

Business was slow to begin with, but she was happy nonetheless. A few months further into being her own boss, and Ben, her ex-colleague had sent her a client. A man who had moved to the country from the Caribbean and was finding it difficult to complete an ongoing three-year divorce proceeding. From the paperwork, his wife had allegedly bribed friends of her father who was a government official in the Bahamas. Elizabeth knew it would be a difficult one, but she wasn't in a position to turn anything down and besides, the man desperately wanted to see his children. She knew only too well what that must mean to him. She had her assistant get on to it immediately, and by the end of the week she knew she had to take a trip to the island for at least a few days.

It was at the end of the day that she looked back at the accompaniment to the referral which was accompanied by a large bouquet of red roses and a card asking if they could at least have lunch together. She declined. The following day, she opened an email from Ben. "Who do you think you are" was his salutation. Aghast, she very quickly closed her mail and at first wanted to close the new client's file too. The last thing she wanted was a rude misogynist pretending to have a crush on her disrupting her newfound tranquility. After a deep breath and a quick exhale, she recalled her goal which was to help others and quickly concluded: Mike she could help, Ben she would stay away from. No longer did she care that she had offended him by turning down his advances, she just wanted Mike to be sorted out as quickly as she could manage it. She owed Ben nothing- a lesson she learnt from Misha and smiled as she saved the message in a folder marked – Bad Men - 1. Ben. Another thing Misha taught her. "Save everything. You will never know how or when it may be used.

Remember, it could come back to haunt, or you may need to use it." They had laughed out loud with each other at the time and she smiled again now as she thought about it. She still missed her time with Misha.

Over the months, as word got around, she could hardly make ends meet as she took on a number of pro bono cases which Mathew suspected but wouldn't dare interfere. She no longer expected Susan to visit, neither of them wanted her to travel unnecessarily and earlier that month she was admitted for a weekend as she needed to have sutures put in "the babies are bearing down", she told her. They were so happy that she was having triplets and although they refused to know the genders they were just praying and hoping that they would be three healthy babies.

Everyone was happy when just before Christmas, and at just under seven months, two little boys and the cutest little girl made their appearance and after just a month on remaining in the neonatal unit… they were ready to go home with their parents and a nanny. Paul had already adjusted at work and Mathew had moved in with them temporarily. He was desperately looking forward to being an uncle and was incredibly happy to be with his sister. They all knew that it also meant being closer geographically, to Elizabeth an advantage he took and without fail. He visited her every day.

She had completely forgotten about bad Ben when he took his arrogant self around, for an unannounced visit. This time, to personally refer a client. Prior to his rude email, Elizabeth didn't mind having his referrals as they were always paying clients and she was slowly able to pay her assistant from the practice as opposed to making the payments from her savings, but she was less than impressed with him coming over unannounced and definitely displeased with his last email.

"Thirty minutes-drive and you may not have seen me."

"Took my chances. I know you well, Elizabeth. I was certain you would be busy working." He grinned. Obviously pleased to see her. He handed her a large brown envelope which she thought she would look at in detail later, some other time but she had a date with Mathew and she was not about to abort it for Ben's show of arrogance. A quick look at the summary and she would need to come up to speed with the most current information on employment law. She would be forever happy for her five years at Stevens and Stephenson's and could not be happier to have had the experience she had, but she knew this was where she belonged. In defiance and as an attempt to show him out, she walked around her desk, but he quickly grabbed her hand and only a valiant fight on her part prevented his kiss. Struggling to regain composure, she aimed her right hand at his face, but he was quick to pull away.

She had been extremely happy to see Mathew in the past, but nothing compared to that moment when he entered her office. "I can see you are done here sir, please leave."

Elizabeth had never seen him so enraged other than after he had met Claire that last weekend, and wondered if he would have hit Ben. He was there to take her to lunch, and she was happy he was on time. She was beginning to wonder if Ben would have walked away that easily had he not come in. Ben looked at Mathew with fire in his eyes and Elizabeth could see they are as evil as his intentions.

He had been away again only once since they confessed to being more than self-adopted siblings and over the months since he had been back, they were never apart except when at work. It was still a puzzle to her, just how he managed to make her laugh every time he called. Today, he was being rather mysterious. She had mentioned taking on an apprentice and that they would be finishing a little later than planned. So, they decided to meet outside her office, but now she was happy he had made his way in. It was anyone's guess what Ben could have done to her, and she shuddered at the thought.

They drove silently at first but later, they were back to chatting amicably. He turned in the direction of his apartment but then changed into another direction she thought she recognised. It only became clear after she arrived at the somewhat familiar gate. He stopped outside one of the properties and as they alighted, she enquired about his friend and what he was like. Mathew went into monosyllables with primarily "okay" responses which she found extremely frustrating but thought better to wait. "All will be revealed," he told her, in the longest sentence he'd said since they arrived. Together, they carefully made their way up the beautiful front steps towards the Mahogany large heavy-set door.

"Wait, put this on. No, I will put it on for you." Her heart raced but she managed to remain calm. He applied the blind fold and shortly after, she could hear keys and the creak of the door implying it had opened. She held onto his hand tightly and followed his lead until she heard the repeated creak followed by a firm close and the dangling of keys again. She was certain she could hear music in the background and a bigger smile spread across her face.

"I cannot dance, Mathew let alone to dance blind folded."

"Who said anything about dancing, well not yet anyway." He retorted.

"Okay."

"Well, as I wasn't around, to share with you on your birthday, for the first time since we have known each other… I thought it would be nice if I used today to make it a special belated birthday present to you." She could smell his cologne as he came closer and she reached out to touch him as he kissed her cheeks.

He stepped back and instructed her to walk forward in a straight line and collect the boxes in her path. By the time she picked up the first, she began to protest and rebelliously removed her blind fold to reveal a path of mixed rose petals and a number of other boxes in her path. She screamed as she opened the first box she had picked up and revealed the tiniest Chanel purse she had ever laid eyes on; a brand he knew she was very fond of. Shaking, she went forward and almost missed a tiny red velvet box which she shook before ripping the paper off. It was a necklace with two little hearts made of diamonds and she brought her hands to cover her mouth as she looked at him just standing there grinning back at her. The song in the background changed then and he beckoned her to continue along the wide entrance with the biggest chandelier above her head and the broad winding staircase just ahead. The third box was huge matching the pair of wellies he got her and when she enquired, he told her, "Well, you may never know where our first holiday as a couple will be," and he winked at her as she felt her heart skip a beat. There were another two boxes which beckoned at her, but she was beginning to feel quite hot from the surge of adrenaline and overwhelmed by all the emotions. *Pause, wait, inhale-exhale*, were all the things her mind warned her to do but Mathew's voice kept her heart going. He tried to sing along to the song that was playing in the background which cracked her up and surprisingly made her legs quite impetuous to take the last step to the fourth box. A medium sized box with so many layers, she thought it was a trick. Until a bracelet emerged from all the rubble. "Forever, my love." She read in her softest pitch, surprising herself but Mathew even more.

Mathew, the environment, together they did things to her head and her heart; but her tongue, untamed was quick to scold. "Mathew, did you even stop to think about the environment?" He recognised the mischief in her voice and knew she was as or even more surprised than he had anticipated. She loved each gift, and he loved her. He made his way to the end.

Directly opposite, he created a carpet-like path of petals, throwing the leftovers at her as she laughed and attempted to throw some back, but the wind simply scattered what little she managed to collect on her way to the final task. To her left was a simple gown, no bow, or strappings just a beautiful valentine gown hanging to the left of the large mirror. He instructed her to get in as he turned his back and waited for her to get dressed. It fitted her perfectly and the navy blue caused her skin to glow. Very slowly, she smoothed the sides of it down, then pushed her hair back. Anxiously, she glanced at the half mirror on the entrance hallway and gasped as she saw how beautiful she had to admit she looked. It was too much to take in. From Ben's attack to being in one of Mathew's 'show houses' amongst a sea of rubbish lying on a bed of roses. It was too much to take in all at once, but she willed herself to be in the moment. She knew it was one she would remember forever. A million ways to say thank you went through her head and having decided on a version, she turned around in time to find him down on one knee. He cradled a single large diamond platinum band between his thumb and index finger. She knew her heart had stopped and she felt her eyes welling up. She knew her lips moved and something vaguely audible escaped her – something sounding like 'yes', but was there a question, she couldn't quite be sure but she was hoping he heard the many times she said yes because she knew too that finally she was depleted of all residual oxygen and nearing collapse. He caught her and like a well-trained coast guard, gave her the kiss of life.

Eventually, he drove her home. There was no point going back to her office. It would have been impossible to get anything done after all that had happened that day. Without looking back, she made her way inside, desperately trying to still the butterflies which were quickly multiplying in her stomach. Shutting the front door firmly behind her, she could not resist calling the only person other than Mathew, whom she could think of at that precise moment.

"Susan, your brother is acting rather strange." She teased.

"Is he? I think my brother is in love." Susan replied, drily. "And has been since he was, about sixteen!"

"What! You knew?"

"I've known from the first day he followed you to the library, just so he could take a picture of you on the phone you supposedly did or didn't knock out of his hand; the details of which I can't seem to recall at this precise moment."

"But why didn't he…?" Elizabeth was startled.

"Why did he not … come out?" Susan asked.

"Why didn't he or you or someone – anyone, tell me?" Elizabeth was trying to decide whether to laugh or cry. She was so happy, until this conversation commenced.

"Elizabeth, he was afraid." Susan confessed.

"Afraid of what, Susan? That's crazy." Puzzled even, she enquired frustratingly.

"Afraid you would leave, maybe - like mum, perhaps." She paused. "He loved her. She left, and in his earlier years, before you came to Champion, he felt it was his fault. For a long time, he internalised that; but thankfully he listened to you and got counselling! Have you noticed he does not 'shop' so much anymore? He invests meaningfully, I supposed in preparation for the family he is counting on having one day. With you." Susan teased. "So, tell your soon to be sister-in-law exactly how you feel, Lizzy."

Elizabeth deliberately engaged a long pause.

Susan texted a big HELLO, accompanied by approximately ten open eyed emojis. Elizabeth was not surprised by the text; she knew her friend could be persistent.

"I think I should tell him how I feel before I tell you, isn't it?" Elizabeth teased. "One more question. Why did he watch Richard and I and not say anything?"

It was Susan's turn to pause. "You mean not tell you how it almost killed him? I guess time to find oneself and what one truly wants are important to one being ultimately, happy. It was not enough for him to choose you, that had to be reciprocated..." Elizabeth was grateful for her honesty.

"...and he needed to be sure he could handle the possibility of my rejection – so counselling..."

"I did worry about your ability to pick up on non-verbal cues, but I suspect that after recent events, you have now mastered the art." She knew her sister-in-law was wondering how she missed the signs but decided against engaging with her at that precise moment. Not via WhatsApp.

Elizabeth hung up from her friend, believing Mathew had to be prepared for this, for her. He needed to deal with his feelings for Claire and she had to find herself. And after all she had been through, she was now thankful it was out there, and that Mathew was now free – no longer burdened with the weight of his mother's actions. She sighed deeply and chuckled as she exhaled.

Just before she went to bed that night, she prayed and as she put out the light, she texted Susan. "It's pretty clear now, why you hated Richard." And was surprised when her friend replied – "I did no such thing, but, if it is any consolation, this morning Matt texted me to wish him luck. I told him I will do better than that, I would say a prayer for him. And I did."

First thing in the morning, Elizabeth looked outside her mum's old bedroom window and there he was, sitting in his car on her driveway where she left him the evening before. She knew he had left; she had watched him go but was totally oblivious to his arrival that morning. Things had changed. He no longer used his key, although he kept it. And she was happy for that. She ran downstairs to him.

He saw her and came out to meet her and before either of them knew it, they were in each other's arms. Then a car pulled up, blocking him in. They were both startled when Susan alighted. She too joined in the hugs then insisted they went inside, to celebrate.

She handed him a brown envelope, a letter she said she found during the renovation work a few years ago.

"It had slipped beneath Dad's desk drawer, and when I pulled it free it ripped but here, it's addressed to you." Her vague expression made Elizabeth's heart race.

The two-page letter was obviously written while he was on his dying bed in the hospital or when he was newly diagnosed, Mathew could not say precisely when but his father's words were remarkably chilling in parts and liberating in others. He implored him to try and find it in his heart to forgive his mother, and later, after a long pause which led Susan to withhold Elizabeth from going over to him.

He continued "…and marry Elizabeth. Son, that's the only time you will be genuinely happy." He laughed as he welled up and looked from Elizabeth to his sister. "Why, didn't you say anything?"

"You were meant to find it, find her. Without me, and definitely without dad dictating from heaven."

CHAPTER SIXTEEN
The Epilogue

"Two weeks, like who gets married in two weeks?" She exclaimed. She was enjoying being engaged but also, she wanted it to be the day she always dreamt it would be. Besides, she wanted Pastor Lammy to conduct the ceremony and he was already away on a six month's mission to Uganda...but exactly two months later, they exchanged vows. And the day was just as she had envisaged it. The last of the autumn weather had been kind to them. It was lit with the sun and some occasional fresh breeze. Mathew could not believe how beautiful she looked and smiled as she slowly made her way up the aisle accompanied by Paul, her makeshift give-away-father. No longer terrified of roses, firmly she stepped on each one lying in her path creating a beautiful décor along the path all the way to the alter. Mathew had requested every colour to be included and in his vows, he promised to love honour and protect her, his orchid, amid the sea of roses and this time when she remembered her mum instead of shedding a tear, she squeezed Mathew's hand.

With three children running around she was happy Mathew had gone ahead and bought the Farnborough house he had shown her years ago on the detour. What looked like a show house then she has made into a home and was surprised to see how easily they had fit in everything they had between them, and everyone, and today she was playing host to her family; Susan and Paul with their three year old boys and daughter. They had invited Pastor Lammy too. Evelyn and the rest of the ladies from the 'pack' had continued with the morning run and although she was too far away to join in, they had remained good friends and any minute now, she was expecting them.

"See, we needed the twelve rooms after all." He said with another of his boyish grins and mimicking her tone he added, "Two weeks? Who plans a wedding, in two weeks!"

Quickly she joined him in the pool for a last splash just before the nanny brought the children down and her guests started pouring in. She kissed him and, in the distance, could see Susan approaching. Her life has been pricked by some roses but equally it has been blessed with some amazing orchids. Her mother's words rang truer in her heart today, than they ever had before, as she felt more alive than ever and suddenly, she realised, she is just like the orchid Hazel described.

Printed in Great Britain
by Amazon